FLESHED OUT

ROB ULITSKI

Thank you so much!
Rob Ulitski

PASTEL WASTELAND

Fleshed Out

E-book Edition ISBN: 978-1-7390802-0-4

Print Edition ISBN: 978-1-7390802-1-1

Published by Pastel Wasteland

First Edition: October 2022

This is a work of fiction. Names, characters, businesses, places, events, locales and incidents are either the products of the author's imagination or used in a fictitious manner. Any resemblance to actual persons, living or dead, or actual events is purely coincidental.

Cover art by: Jorge Fernando Lucena Barros

Interior Illustrations by: Meg Barker (@megmayoillustrations), Adetya Isnurprasetyaji, Mishan Mondal

Sign up to the *Deadly Dispatch* newsletter and keep up to date with Rob's latest work at:

www.robwriteshorror.com

Follow Rob:

@robwriteshorror (Instagram)

@robulitski (Twitter, TikTok)

ACKNOWLEDGEMENTS

It takes a team to bring a project like this to fruition. Firstly, I want to thank Alex Davis, who has helped me develop my writing skills and shape my initial ideas into the collection you're about to read, as well as happily provide answers to all manner of questions along the way. I couldn't have done it without him.

I also want to thank my sister Bekah, for casting a keen eye over each of the stories, and offering up suggestions to tighten and trim the content and enrich the narrative.

I also owe a huge thanks to Joseph, Andrew, my Mum, Meg, Jorge, Adetya, Mishan and my wider family and friends for all of their support with this project in various ways - they've all been integral in creating this piece of work.

Thank you all more than I can possibly put into words.

I'm vacuum-wrapped in a seamless flesh,
an earthly form in a fragile mesh.

A bundle of cells which interweave,
with blood and bone in a meaty sleeve.

INTRODUCTION

The human body terrifies me.

For all of the beauty and wonder contained in our worldly forms, my brain often drifts to the fragility of the shells that protect us. We rely on an incomprehensible tapestry of processes and functions just to survive each day, and in a world full of danger, disease and death, it's a miracle that we get through a single day intact, let alone an entire lifetime (if all goes to plan).

Of course, to think of life in such a way would be completely pessimistic. We owe a huge amount of gratitude to our bodies, which allow us to experience a full spectrum of life experiences, and give a physical form to the imperceptible. They show up for us day in and day out, and though many of us don't treat them as well as we should, the human body is a robust and adaptable feat of human nature.

It's common advice to write what you know, and when it comes to body horror, I have an overflowing well of fears and nightmares that are born from this very subject. The dichotomy of life vs death, fragility vs robusticity and human vs inhuman are brought to gruesome life in the following thirteen stories, which I hope will excite and haunt you in equal measure, and take you on a thrilling journey through an amalgam of different subgenres and narratives.

Storytelling for me is the combination of complex characters and conflict, and in the first story, *Hair,* I approach themes of motherhood and trauma through the lens of a serial killer. Troubled pasts are a recurring theme in the stories, such as with *Carnage* and *Doug,* where relationship issues are brought into grisly focus, and *Fused,* where familial relationships are the root cause of the conflict. Societal issues were also on my mind when writing, especially with the government and their treatment of the National Health Service, and these anxieties spill into *Crystalline* and *Vending Machine.*

Overall, however, my biggest inspiration was the human body itself, and the myriad of ways it can help or hinder us as we move through our lives.

The human body fascinates me - and I hope this book evokes all of the above emotions in you too.

HAIR

Natalia was soaked through with blood, fresh tangles of hair dangling from her puckered lips.

Her date for that night, Pearl, was slumped on the tiled floor of the modest kitchen, her scalp removed with careless abandon. The meaty part of her head was slopped on the black marble counter, and Natalia tugged follicles from it in greedy handfuls, slurping them from hand to mouth. Like delicate stir-fry noodles, she gulped them quickly and efficiently, a satisfied grin following every bite.

The fibrous chunks tickled the inside of her cheeks as she slapped her tongue around, forming small, bite-sized balls that were ready to swallow. As each one slid down her throat, she felt the abyss in her stomach shrink, finally feeling satiated for the first time that week.

The metaphorical void inside of her had been a permanent fixture for as long as she could remember, and after years of experimenting with everything from dust to chalk to pieces of glass, she had found something which made her feel whole. There was something about another woman's hair that felt so taboo yet gratifying. She didn't get the same buzz from plucking her own hair, nor artificial wigs—Lord knows she had tried—so she had to procure it in different ways.

Pearl's eyes glared at Natalia in disgust, unblinking and unwavering, as if she had known what was coming as her last breath slipped away. Natalia continued to chomp, cleaning the edges of her lips with her darting tongue. She snatched the flesh from the counter, and tore out gristly lumps with her jagged, yellow teeth. This ritual wasn't about feeling famished, this was something deeper, more primal.

There was a sudden commotion at the front door—Natalia's cue to leave. She unzipped her worn backpack, pulled out an oversized blue jumper and slid into it. She stuffed the remainders of Pearl's scalp into the main compartment, and carefully slipped her rusty hunting knife in there too.

After double checking there were no more fibers on the floor or counter—she had to make sure that she had collected all the tasty goods on offer—she quietly left through the back door, walking into the dark, humid air of nighttime Barsville.

Located in the Midlands, Barsville was known for its piercing cold winters and dreary way of life. Grey for as far as the eye could see, there was very little nature left, having been replaced by brutalist structures and fast food restaurants. Crime and corruption underpinned the city, and a blind eye was often shown to anything except the most serious of transgressions.

Pearl's murder would be investigated, of course, but with local government funding cut to within an inch of its life, none of the CCTV would be working, and if it were, the poor lighting would make the footage unusable, so it didn't concern Natalia. In several moments, there would be a high pitched shriek as Pearl's roommate discovered her limp, scalpless body, and she'd inevitably call the police. They'd arrive a few hours later, take some photos, put out a few calls and wait for any leads. None would come, of course, because no-one would have seen Natalia exit the house. It was far too cold for anyone to voluntarily expose themselves to this winter, and the high-rise flats that loomed over that part of the city were all abandoned, the buildings too expensive to upkeep.

So, Natalia slipped into the night, savouring the leftover strands of Pearl's hair between her teeth, and made her way home.

* * *

Home. Home for Natalia had always been in Barsville, but she had moved around more than any other resident, she was almost certain of it.

She started in her parent's house, and was swiftly dropped off to live with her uncle when she was nine years old, after her parents lost their jobs and descended into deep poverty. Natalia then fell in with the wrong crowd, and moved from place to place ever since. In her mid-30s now, Natalia still didn't have an official place of her own. She didn't have anything official as it happened—not a bank account, birth certificate, or up to date medical record—and that was just the way she liked it… Living in the shadows without a trace, able to do whatever she wanted.

The last few months had seen her stalk from house to house, living in whatever space she could find, whether it be a shed, a locked room, or in her present case: an attic.

It wouldn't be this way forever, of course, as Natalia had dreams of being a mother. Nothing else came close to the anticipation of giving birth someday, and though she didn't have a partner to give her a child, she had another plan in mind.

Wendy's loft was cosy and cluttered, the perfect match for someone who wanted to stay hidden but comfortable. She had broken into the modest detached house a couple of weeks ago, on the run from the police for a petty crime, and had squatted there ever since. It wasn't the most accessible nor the easiest place to use as a base, but it was fine for now.

Wendy was around the same age as Natalia, had short ginger hair cut into a bob hairstyle, and was a single mother to little Abraham, who was around three years old (though didn't young mums all speak in months instead of years? That would make him thirty-six months old; Natalia had to keep up with the lingo if she was going to be the best mother she could be).

Natalia peered through a small crack in the flooring, observing them both as she settled back into the space. Abraham was running around his playroom, whilst Wendy hung out on the landing, talking to someone on the phone.

"I never leave him alone, why would you say that to the judge? I want to make this as easy as possible, but... well you're his dad, of course I want you to speak to him!"

A tinny, unintelligible voice erupted from the phone. Wendy bit right back.

"I will do *anything* it takes to protect my son. If you keep threatening us, I will make sure you never see him again. He is safe here, with me. End of story."

She hung up the phone, and embraced Abraham.

Her voice was pitchy and exhausted. Natalia could tell she was trying to hide her emotions from Abraham, and it seemed as though it was working at the moment. But those emotions would permeate his little brain, Natalia knew it all too well from her own experience. She could still recall her uncle scolding her for the tiniest of transgressions, not eating her food, staying in the bathroom too long, oversleeping by a couple of minutes.

But she was letting her brain get ahead of itself. Wendy was a great mum, from what Natalia had seen. In fact, she was constantly getting inspiration and tips for when she finally had a little one of her own.

All in good time...

Keeping quiet, Natalia trod gently over to her makeshift bed, which was constructed from gathered cushions and left-over clothes in the attic space. There was an existing electric point installed for a small overhead light, so Natalia used this to charge her smartphone, which she had stolen a few weeks earlier. She laid down carefully, avoiding a small toolbox tucked just underneath where her feet would rest.

Swiping through dating apps was her favourite pastime.

Tonight, she was looking to start up another conversation with a local hottie, preferably with a thick, full mane and a cute, innocent smile. Police sirens echoed around the desolate town, whilst images of Pearl's lifeless body flickered in Natalia's mind. She was gobbling the leftovers of their little encounter straight from her backpack, and was already anticipating the next date and the next tasty snack.

There were plenty of girls on the app, and as Natalia quickly swiped several profiles away, the adrenaline rush grew stronger and stronger. A menagerie of different faces, eyes, noses, hairstyles... and she could only choose one.

A few swipes later, and she had matched with Daisy.

DAISY459 (29)

Young fun-lover, looking for someone to share my life and hobbies with. Freak in both the sheets and the streets, I'm not afraid to ask for what I want.

Distance: 6.2 Miles away

From her profile image, Natalia admired her smooth skin, piercings, and a gorgeous, voluptuous head of curly black hair.

Without wasting a moment more, she launched a chat window and fired off a message.

Hey Daisy, great profile. How you doing?

She'd check for an answer in the morning. She laid her phone down by the side of the bed, and checked through the crack for one last snapshot of the family life downstairs. Abraham was asleep on a beanbag, and Wendy was stroking his forehead whilst sipping on a cup of tea. Everything was calm again. It would have made the perfect family photo.

* * *

The front door slammed shut, and Natalia shot awake. It was 7.30am, and whilst there wasn't a clock in the attic, Wendy's schedule ran like clockwork. It was time to take Abraham to nursery.

Natalia had slept in the bloody white t-shirt and jumper, and the stain had seeped through, forming a crimson patch on the knitwear. She slipped out of both items and unzipped her jeans, stripping down to her underwear. Before doing anything else, she checked her phone.

1 Message

She clicked quickly, her finger darting to the notification.

Hey Natalia. I like your profile. What are you looking for?

Daisy had a green circle by her avatar, suggesting she was still online, so Natalia cobbled another message together.

To be honest, I'd like to get out and have a coffee with another human, I've done nothing but work from home all week!

There was a slight pause, before the reply…

How about tonight? Or is that too forward.

No— tonight is great. I know the perfect place.

* * *

Natalia manoeuvred a section of a clothes rail out of the attic, the metal dangling in mid-air above the landing. A few seconds later, she smacked the wall with it three times, crumbling away some of the neat plasterwork.

She stopped in her tracks, listening for the slightest hint of a sound or presence in the house. There was nothing but the cyclical buzz of the fridge and an intermittent squeak from the fire alarm, which begged for a new battery.

No-one was home. She unfurled the metal ladders out of

the hatch and carefully manoeuvered onto the steps. A few rungs later, she sprang onto the carpeted landing.

Natalia walked into the bathroom, and cranked the valve to start a hot shower. Wendy's hairbrush was placed on the tiled windowsill, and had built up a small collection of loose hairs from her twice-daily routine brushing. Natalia snatched it up and untangled the hairs, teasing them into her mouth. She swished and swirled before swallowing hard a few times, forcing the strands down her throat and past the tonsils.

Just before stepping into the steaming hot shower, an ungodly sound rumbled from Natalia's stomach. Doubled over in pain, she gagged and stumbled over to the sink.

"No," she whispered, and shot back upright, covering her mouth and rubbing her stomach, which seemed to distend from her frame. After several wet gulps and swallows, the feeling had passed. A few strands of hair had escaped her lips, but she forcefully jammed her fingers down her throat and compressed them back into her gullet.

Natalia stepped into the shower and began to work away the week of dirt, grime, and murder that stained her skin. Several lacerations were scattered around her facial area—souvenirs from her deathly encounter with Pearl—and as she massaged the wounds, clots of blood fell onto the PVC floor in crimson globules.

Her hands worked their way down from her neck to her breasts and then to her stomach, which was grossly misshapen and lumpy. She caressed the bulging pockets of flesh as tears of joy seeped from her eyes.

* * *

Natalia heaved the ladders up behind her, and slid them back into their locked position. Reaching out of the attic, she curled her toes around a beam to make sure she didn't fall out, and pulled the trap door shut in a swift motion. She'd had enough practice by now to get it to stick first time, but only after a few dozen dodgy attempts, which nearly ended with her falling to her death.

Whilst downstairs, she had collected a jumble of random makeup from the bathroom and Wendy's bedroom. Bright red lipstick, a half-used tub of moisturiser, an unbranded, neon eyeshadow palette, and a highlight stick for pale skin. It was a random variety of products, but she would do what she could to make it work.

Just behind the makeshift bed, a shattered antique mirror leaned against a wall. A beautiful patterned frame enveloped a few large daggers of reflective glass, which Natalia used to guide her application of the makeup.

A light covering of moisturiser to quench her thirsty dry skin, a dusting of blue eyeshadow on her tired lids, a bold red lip and enough highlighter to upstage a drag queen.

She slipped on a light blue vest, fishnet top and jeans—from Wendy's wardrobe of course—and took a final cursory glance at herself before reaching for her phone.

Natalia opened a chat window, and found Daisy in her recent messages.

Just leaving now, see you soon.

* * *

Every service station in the UK had a similar aesthetic, and the Barsville complex was no different. A gargantuan car park adjoined a large concrete structure, which housed a variety of food establishments, shops, and washroom facilities.

The building was a thirty-minute bus journey away from Wendy's house, with the addition of a rather hazardous trek

Portsmouth has a well-known literary history, with writers including Charles Dickens, Sir Arthur Conan Doyle and Graham Hurley all having Pompey connections. But did you know there is an active community of writers taking inspiration from the city, today? The **Portsmouth Authors Collective** is a group of small and independently published writers from the local area, offering the full range of literature including poetry, short stories, all genres of fiction, memoir, travel writing and local history.

If you enjoy reading our books, please help spread the word by writing a review and posting it to **GoodReads.com**, **Amazon**, or social media platforms. Reviews are a tremendous source of encouragement.

Find out more about the **Portsmouth Authors Collective** by checking out our Facebook page or our website: PortsmouthAuthors.wordpress.com

We can also be contacted by writing to PortsmouthAuthorsCollective@gmail.com

Thank you for your support!

The Terminal Velocity of Cats
Carol Westron
Night Mare
a bowl of Atoms
Poems by a Pompey girl
AND MANDARINS
PETE ADAMS
THE BANDAGE
The SONGS You've NEVER Heard
Dream Train
HOME SWEET HOME
ALAN ELLIOTT
Don't Step on the Cracks
A Victorian Murder Mystery
Strangers and Angels
CAROL WESTRON
ADI AND THE OLD TRAIN
WRITTEN BY CAROL WESTRON
ILLUSTRATED BY ADAM HALSALL
On the Shoulders of Lions
WALKING PORTSMOUTH
Beachcombing
A VICTORIAN PORTRAYAL
CHARLES DICKENS
HELEN SALSBURY
Sometimes When I sleep
Just a Smile
Dene Woods
CRIME SCENE - DO NOT CROSS
About the Children
Carol Westron
EMERGENCY DRILL
CHRIS BLACKWATER
SHOCKING TALES
PAUL NEWELL
JW Metcalfe
PANTHERA: Death Song
A MORE PERFECT HUMAN
C J POWELL
Missing Words
WE ARE THE LIZARDS
Margaret Jennings
Carol Westron
KARMA and the SINGING FROGS
Connecting Doors
Locked Room Murder Mystery
Onia Fox
PETE ADAMS
RITE JUDGEMENT
SHOCKING TALES
EDWARDIAN PORTSMOUTH
PAUL NEWELL
Girl Pompey
OUT AMONG THE ICE BEACONS
GARETH HOWELLS
Single to Sirkeci
Permanent Verb
Poems by Gareth Howells
Andy Hanlon
THE TRUE PICTURE
ALISON HABENS
Should I Wear Floral?
HAWK
PETE ADAMS
BLACK ROSE
Payback
Christine Lawrence
Mount Alexa
LENA CHERE
This Game of Ghosts
CAROL WESTRON
MORSELY MANOR AND THE MAGIC MIRROR
R J WEBB
PETE ADAMS
ROAD KILL
Silver Manes
Lena Chere
GHOST AND RAGMAN ROLL
PETE ADAMS
Grandma's Poetry Book
Enemy Closer
suspense thriller
Onia Fox
JW Metcalfe
PANTHERA: Death Spiral
Girl Pompey
LISTLESS in TURKEY
Onia Fox
Adi and the Ghost Train
CAUSE AND EFFECT
PETE ADAMS
A BARROW BOY'S CADENZA
PETE ADAMS
STEVE SHEPPARD
SHOCKING TALES
VOLUME II
PAUL NEWELL
THE WEDDING DRESS
A Victorian Portrayal of GHOSTS and the UNEXPLAINED
The Essential Visual HMS Victory
AJ Noon
CRIME SCENE - DO NOT CROSS
The Fragility of Poppies
PETE ADAMS
Bored to Death in the Baltics
IRONY IN THE SOUL
VICTORIAN PORTSMOUTH

down a country road and across a motorway bridge. The venue wasn't built for customers arriving on foot, but it was the perfect location to keep out of sight of any locals.

Aside from the obvious chain restaurants, the Barsville services housed a new milkshake spot, which served ice-cream shakes, American-style bar food, and a specialist fusion menu. It was expensive of course, but it would be the perfect backdrop for date number one—plus Natalia couldn't eat a huge amount of solid food anymore, so a shake would do the trick. She'd rounded up the change she found on Wendy's nightstand, and swapped it for a ten pound note on the journey in. She made a mental note to pay it back as soon as she could, because she didn't want little Abraham going without.

Waiting in a shadowy smoking area outside, Natalia kept refreshing her dating app, anxiously counting down Daisy's distance away from her. She was about five minutes away by her estimation, so she quickly sparked a cigarette in anticipation of her arrival.

Natalia had lifted a pack of Kingsway Blue Menthol from Pearl, and was planning on finishing the last few tonight, before throwing away the last piece of evidence which linked her to the scene. If Daisy smoked, she would offer her one to share at the end of the date, a perfect way to wind down phase one of the evening, and get them more acquainted before the real action got underway. If she was lucky, the smoke would stain her hair with the rich musk of tobacco, which would send Natalia's attraction over the edge.

After a few drags of the minty-tinged stick, a violent growl erupted from her stomach. Doubled over again, she took a few deep breaths, setting down the cigarette and wiping tears from her eyes. Her protruding stomach rumbled in a deathly fashion, the vibration rattling her entire body.

Strands of hair began to regurgitate from her throat into her mouth, and for the second time that day, she had to force them back down, gagging in the process. Not a moment after the sensation passed, Daisy arrived right by her side, dressed in a cute floral dress and minimal makeup, her curly locks perfectly teased.

"You must be Natalia."

* * *

The neon red lighting of *Shakey Jakes* was pretty full-on, and more reminiscent of a sports bar than a casual dining place on the motorway. That said, the room was full of ambiance, and the table the young waiter had allocated the pair had a great view of the room, perfect for people-watching.

The spotty teen fumbled over a notepad, doing his best to act professional, before blurting out his introductory sentence.

"Welcome to Shakey Jakes, I'm Tom and I'll be your server today. Should we start with drinks?"

Natalia grinned, and nodded to Daisy, inviting her to order first.

"Erm, I think I'll have the… Uh.. What about, no… Sorry."

"Two Frosty Petes and two waters please." Natalia took the lead, and aside from an awkward smile, Daisy didn't seem to mind. This wasn't the no-holds-barred Daisy the app promised, but it was no problem; taking the lead came naturally to Natalia.

The waiter darted to the bar area, leaving the pair to acquaint themselves.

"So, how long have you been in Barsville?" Natalia questioned.

"Well, officially two years. But I used to come visit

friends, uh, for maybe one year before that. What about you?"

"My whole life," Natalia replied. "Unfortunately..."

Daisy giggled awkwardly.

"You're looking pretty cute today."

"Oh... Thanks." Daisy said. "You too. I like the eyeshadow."

"Thanks, I'm trying something new."

"It's a good look," Daisy replied.

A long moment of silence followed several more awkward exchanges, and Natalia drifted from listening to the music intently (some pop song from the early 2000s) to sifting through the crowd, observing the miscellany of characters eating at the restaurant (the guy in seat 2A was faaaaar too pushy with his date). Then she bounced back to icebreaker questions. She was almost out.

"What's your favourite body part on a woman?"

Not a moment after blurting it out of her mouth, Natalia shook her head, embarrassed.

"Sorry, that was random—"

"No, uh. Well. I guess the smile? It's the first thing I notice on someone," Daisy revealed.

Natalia had a very particular smile, tight-lipped and subtle, so as not to show too much teeth or gum. She hadn't visited a dentist in almost twenty years, so her dental hygiene was a constant source of stress. After years of training herself to hide these features, her mouth opened only very slightly when she spoke,

"Yeah smiles are cool..." Natalia was struggling, and had to steal a moment to think. "I'm going to the toilet-"

"Sure, sure!"

Daisy seemed super pleased to get some respite from the conversation, so Natalia stumbled out back, bursting through the unisex toilet door.

In the mirror, she could see her eyeshadow had started to run, and her blemished skin was revealing itself through the layer of moisturiser. Sweat was beading on her brow, and her face in general seemed better suited to a hardcore drug addict.

She took a sip of water from the tap, and patted her face gently with her wet hands.

* * *

Natalia would win Daisy over, she was sure of it.

So with a more confident stride and renewed attitude, she marched back to the table, her head full of interesting conversation points and compliments—

But Daisy was gone.

Natalia scanned the room.

The overweight guy in 2A was still clinging onto the uninterested older woman, grabbing her arms and leaning in for a kiss, his grubby face just inches away from hers.

An older couple sat happily at the booth in the corner, exchanging pleasantries and compliments on the lashings of food they were enjoying. Natalia thought that maybe they could be her parents. She had no recollection of what they looked like, so this often passed through her mind when she saw the elderly.

Finally, at a table in the corner, a young mother breastfed her baby, looking lovingly at its chubby cheeks and needy eyes. Natalia latched on to the scene for a moment, before turning back to the door just in time to see it swing shut, Daisy pacing away from the building nervously.

Natalia followed, throwing her crumpled paper money onto the table on the way past.

"Was it something I said?" Natalia remarked.

Daisy span on her feet and froze, sliding her hands into her pockets.

"I'm sorry, this was a bad idea. I've just broke up with a guy, and I thought—"

"A guy?"

"Yeah, Jacob. Uh, you didn't need to know his name I guess. Sorry, I'm just all messed up right now."

Natalia reached forward, aiming to place her hand on Daisy's shoulder, but Daisy shrugged away from the gesture.

"Sorry, it's not you, I—"

"I know another place we can go" Natalia said. "It's a bit more low-key, no-one will even know we were there."

"That's not it, I'm sorry, I... I'm sorry."

Daisy turned away, and headed towards a small blue car. Natalia didn't follow her, but paused for a moment, locked in thought. She snatched one of the last cigarettes from the packet and walked towards the motorway, readying herself for the long trek back.

As she walked towards the silent city, her frame shrunken and deflated, she noticed the mother and baby in the window again. She was playing with his tiny arms, as if he was dancing on the table, and they were both laughing. Not fake laughing, but a real, roaring fit of laughter.

Determined, Natalia turned back to Daisy, and started to pick up pace.

"Daisy, wait!"

Daisy broke into a jog, and then a sprint to get away from Natalia. She opened her car remotely, and slipped into the driver's seat.

"Why are you running? Daisy come back here!"

Natalia's words hissed around the air ferociously, chasing Daisy down like angry wasps.

Inside the car—darkness.

Daisy was alone, but couldn't see her date anywhere. She was just in pursuit, so she couldn't be far.

She slowly turned her head to the right, looking out of her window.

Nothing.

And then to the left, to the passenger window. She paused, but no-one was there either.

She could hear her breath and heartbeat in her chest, each pulsating manically in unison.

Where was Natalia? And what did she want so badly?

The engine was off.

The keys slid into the ignition easily enough, but the rattle of her teddy bear keyring seemed too loud, too intrusive in this tense moment.

She went to turn, instinctively looking into her rearview mirror—

—and Natalia was in the backseat, lunging forward before she could even finish the thought.

A phone charging cable slipped over Daisy's neck, pinning her back to the headrest. Retching for air, the skin of her neck bulged either side of the plastic, her throat caving slightly from the pressure.

It wasn't working quickly enough, so Natalia began to tug the cable in a rapid see-saw motion, the frayed, exposed metal scraping away layers of skin with each pass.

Daisy jolted forwards, but it wasn't enough.

She tried to press the horn, but it didn't make a sound.

To both of their amazement, the cable snapped, and without a second thought, Natalia grabbed a chunk of Daisy's beautiful curly locks…

… and the entirety of her hair slid off in her hand.

It was a wig.

Natalia was frozen in shock. The audacity. The lies. She

had only been slightly angry before, but this had been a huge waste of her time.

Whilst Natalia pondered these thoughts, Daisy slammed her body against the door, pulling the slightly sticky handle, and it flew open with a huge creak.

Natalia slid out the back, and in the same moment, Daisy's phone slipped out of her pocket, dropping onto the concrete surface of the car park.

Her delicate hand reached down to collect it, but just as her skin made contact, her entire arm quickly jolted up with a distorted *snap.*

With all of her strength, Natalia crushed the door against Daisy's arm, cracking her forearm with the first hit. With repetitive strikes, she mauled her arm between the cold metal, bone and muscle interweaving in a pulpy mash. The screams were guttural and panicked, and attracted some unwanted attention.

"Hey you!" a random stranger shrieked, sprinting out of the service station and towards the pair.

Natalia had fucked up, her emotions overtaking her common sense. She had been so careful up until now, but Daisy's trickery had pushed her over the edge.

Why was it whenever Natalia wanted something, she had to fight for it? Things never went smoothly, everyone either used her or abandoned her. She wasn't going to let it stand any more. The tides were turning, she could feel it, and soon enough she would get exactly what she wanted.

Before leaving the scene, she picked up Daisy's phone, placed it between the door and the car frame, and smashed it shut. The forceful hit shattered the plastic device and mangled Daisy's arm—which was still caught between the metal—in the process.

Natalia discarded the broken mobile, and ran into the night.

Daisy slipped out of the car door barely conscious, instinctively placing her arm out to support her weight. Instead, it snapped back towards her body. Her forearm held on by frayed ligaments, blood gushing out of the horrific wound.

* * *

The motorway was dimly lit—another casualty of the funding cuts—but a handful of cars intermittently trailed by.

As luck would have it, a silver people-carrier was heading towards the city, and Natalia decided it would make the perfect ride.

She ran into the road, placing her life in the hands of the oncoming driver, and with a loud squeal of tyres against tarmac, the car came to a halt.

"What the fuck are you doing lady? Is that blood on you?"

"Please help me!"

Natalia put on her best damsel in distress act, encouraging the driver to step out of the vehicle. He was a short, portly gentleman, definitely middle-aged, though a lifetime of smoking had weathered his skin, hiding his true age. His bald head glistened under the tungsten glow of the streetlamps.

"Let me call the police."

He turned back towards the car, reaching for the phone in his pocket at the same time, and without missing a beat, Natalia grabbed his shoulders and tossed him to the side.

The keys were still in the ignition, so all she had to do was jump in, close the door, put her foot down and escape into the darkness.

* * *

She cruised through the city, clambering through residential streets, studying every-passer by with a hawk-like stare. Though it was pushing ten at night, a variety of people were still out, and Natalia was on the hunt. She was starved, broken and addicted, and needed her next fix.

There was a young ginger guy with flowing locks, but in the short moment she had to investigate him, she noticed he was balding, and probably thinning in the scalp area.

A woman was waiting on the next street corner, most likely a prostitute, but her hair was shaven close to the skin. No good.

The next person she saw made her slam on her brakes. An older woman, probably mid to late 50s, with a grey perm. Natalia opened her backpack, quickly armed herself with her rusty hunting knife, and jumped out of the passenger side of the vehicle.

The woman started screaming before she even got close, probably startled by Natalia's sudden presence and the feral look in her eyes. She grabbed the woman by the back of her head, clumping the hair between her first, and quickly sliced off chunks with her knife, with jagged slicing motions. She kicked the woman to the street, and started to immediately devour the bouncy strands.

The woman stretched her hands out, her fingertips grinding against the wet tarmac. Natalia devoured the tresses of grey perm, and felt ready to go in for a second portion. Her body had another idea entirely.

A shooting pain ripped through her stomach, crippling her to the floor. The woman took her chance and escaped, as Natalia flailed in the foetal position, clutching onto her waist. Tangles of hair erupted from her mouth, and her distended stomach started to growl angrily.

"Not yet! It's not time!" she screamed to herself.

Choking on the fibers, she forced her hand away from

her midsection, and wedged the damp strands back down her gullet.

Just a little while longer, please.

* * *

Natalia struggled out of the car, and back onto the street. Wendy's house was just around the corner, but she didn't want to arouse any suspicion. She could already hear the sound of police sirens whirring in the air, echoing across the desolate city, and it was only a matter of time until her misgivings caught up with her.

Before today, she hadn't paid much mind to getting arrested or even being caught—she had been careful, not obsessive about cleanup or hiding her tracks, but careful enough. But with the last few interactions, she had been messy.

The piercing cold air raised goosebumps on Natalia's arms. The fresh smell of home-baked pies emanated from the house she was currently hidden in front of, and though she didn't really crave food any more, her mouth began to salivate. She imagined a family inside that house, enjoying each other's company whilst the mother cut the pie, serving it with custard and a sprinkle of delight.

Snap the fuck out of it.

Natalia came back to Earth, and started to stalk around the street, making her way to the rear of Wendy's house.

She still had a fistful of hair entangled in her fingers, half-eaten strands pasted to her palm with mud and grit. It would probably be the last bit she needed, so she kept it safe and close.

With an almost subconscious movement, she hopped onto the wall, placing her feet into the indentations, and awkwardly scaled the brick exterior. An agonising pain ruptured through her entire body again, encouraging her to let go and fall backwards, but she wasn't going to give in. Not this close to the end.

The loft was especially cold tonight. The insulation was wearing thin, and a crack was beginning to form in the roof, allowing the sub-zero chill to circulate around the small space.

Natalia collapsed to the floor the moment she entered the room. Her head was moist with sweat, eyes glazed over, numb to the horrific scenes she had created that evening. Through the decaying wooden floorboard, she saw Wendy and Abraham, entwined in a long hug. The child's eyes were red raw, and Wendy was on the phone again. Though the sound was dampened, she could just about make out the conversation.

"I swear to you my bathroom has been *used* and my things have gone missing! Someone has been in my house! I'm begging you, please come and take a look for me. Abraham is scared and so am I."

No no no. This wasn't meant to happen.

Natalia pressed her teeth against her bottom lip, drawing blood, whilst her head span in circles. She had no ill will towards Wendy, she admired how much of a good mum she was, and was even learning from her each night as she observed her and little Abraham. This wasn't right, she wanted to be a better person and she'd fucked it up once again.

Right on cue, her stomach started to vibrate, with squelchy flesh starting to pulsate and gurn. She wrapped herself back up into the foetal position, trying to compress the pain, fighting the urge to scream out loud and call for help.

The wailing of sirens was creeping up on the house, increasing in volume at a slow but steady pace. Natalia pulled herself across the floorboards, inching closer to her bed, reaching out for something.

Phlegm-covered strands of hair began to force themselves out of her pursed lips, chunky, congealed wraps of multi-coloured follicles. Natalia choked as she continued to slide herself across the floor, her stomach rotund and ready to burst.

Her hand finally happened upon the small toolbox that lived at the end of her bed. The police sirens were close now, no more than a mile away, and Natalia knew what she had to do.

She hauled the rest of her body onto the bed, and unlatched the small vintage tin.

Inside, a selection of surgical tools—both used and brand new—waited to be used. Scalpels of different lengths and widths. Tweezers. A syringe of clear liquid. One of her very first kills had been a nurse at the local hospital, and she had been saving this selection of tools for a special occasion.

Natalia grabbed the syringe, and quickly ripped the safety cap off with her teeth. She span it in her hand, and drove it down into her abdomen.

She couldn't help it this time, she let out a small screech, thrashing up and down on the makeshift bed as she penetrated deeper. The mirror at the end of it fell with a gargantuan crash, shattering the last pieces of glass that remained in its frame.

"Shit!"

Natalia froze in silence for a moment, before she heard the sound she had been praying would never come.

"Hello?"

Wendy. Sweet Wendy.

There wasn't time to panic. She returned to the tin.

Her midsection started to go numb, the flesh around her inflated belly tingling with tiny pricks of static. Sweat expelled from every single follicle in her body, and though she was in absolute agony, Natalia had the biggest smile smothered across her face. She thought of her family, and how they would regret not being there for this special moment. Even her uncle, the nastiest man she knew, would have been proud of her in this moment. They would all finally see her for the person she was, and regret making her life hell.

After rifling through a few different scalpels, she decided on the sharpest, with the finest tip. The stainless steel glistened under the overhead light, and with a slight hesitation, Natalia brought the tip of the scalpel down to touch her skin. Her breath grew heavier, as footsteps paraded towards the house. The steel nib poked through the first thin layers of her skin, unleashing a stream of dark red blood through the tiny depression. Natalia growled in pain, letting a pained shriek free from her lungs.

In a swift action, she started to slice her abdomen in a vertical fashion, drawing a line from her waist to her diaphragm.

Dark, watery juice started to ooze from the slit, bubbling with viscous gore.

The front door shook with exaggerated vigour, as several police officers congregated at the property.

Natalia could hear Wendy pacing towards the door. She opened it and greeted the officers. Her voice was panicked, uncertain, her safe space penetrated by darkness. It all seemed like a dream, Natalia's drug was kicking in, and it was an out-of-body experience like no other.

The ripped flesh started to dry out in the bitter air, yet the walls of her stomach were still fresh and slimy. She drove the scalpel back into them, deeper and harder. Blood spurted in different directions, mixing with black, inky slime as it spattered onto the wall and floor.

The crowd of police started up the stairs, their footsteps in unison as they charged through the hallway and onto the landing.

Natalia dropped the scalpel, her eyes flickering, trying to battle the immense pain of the DIY surgery. Yet on a subconscious level, she couldn't feel anything. The drugs were far too strong, and her will to finish the process correctly was unmatched.

She pried the fleshy walls of her stomach open, finishing off the wound with a single tear. Stomach acid and chunky gunk spilled from the opening, as she placed her hand on a large, congealed mass of black fibre.

Her eyes teared up as she rubbed her hand over the fuzzy clump.

The trap door of the attic shook intensely, the small silver lock unscrewing with each hit.

With clawed hands, she pulled intently, her fingers interlocking behind the mass, slimy ooze squelching through the gaps in her fingers.

The trap door crashed open, falling from its hinges, as three police officers forced themselves up through the cavity.

Natalia pulled harder now, and with a final, torturous tear, the delivery was over. The black mound of consumed hair had formed to the shape of her abdomen, a solid, fibrous imprint of her internal organs. She cried out with joy and pain, her stomach spilling out its contents still, as she wrapped her arms around the object.

She started to kiss it, tiny kisses around each of its rotund curves.

"My baby! My little miracle!"

"Put it down!"

The police were metres away, tasers at the ready.

She wrapped it tight in her arms, unwilling to let go.

Wendy climbed to the top of the ladder, her curiosity

getting the better of her. Her eyes locked with Natalia's, and in a single expression Natalie saw everything click in her mind. A woman in her attic. A makeshift bed. The makeup that had gone missing. The space she was too scared to visit, because of the possibility of a burglar, her ex-husband, or a ghost. The safety of both her and her child, all artificial.

Natalia reached out to her, a desperate struggle, a gesture for help.

"Please look after my baby. You're such a good mother, I've been watching!"

She still had the mass in one arm, wrapped tight to her body.

"Put it down and put your hands behind your head, NOW!"

Natalia looked straight through the officers, trying her best to connect with Wendy. She caressed the dense bundle with soft strokes as she spoke.

"Look after her, please. Wendy. Like you do little Abraham!"

Wendy doubled over, placing her hands on the floorboards, trying her best not to vomit.

"I SAID PUT IT DOWN!" the office roared, readying the taser.

Natalia was red hot with rage, her faux maternal instincts kicking in at just the right moment.

"GET THAT THING AWAY FROM MY FUCKING CHILD!" she spat back.

The smell was noxious, and the police were all gagging, trying their best to remain professional. Their eyes were wide with fear and confusion, trying to ascertain what had been going on in the moments before they arrived.

Before she knew it, a police officer ripped the black mound from Natalia's arms, and threw it to the side in a cruel act of spite. He violently slammed his foot down into it, breaking down the hair particles in a gooey rage.

Natalia was screaming, crying, engulfed in her own rage and pain. She had lost too much blood, and everything felt artificial. The room. The space. Her body.

She simply started to drag herself backwards, her entrails clinging onto the interior of her stomach the best they could.

"My BABY!"

A taser shot into her chest, but the electrical tingle did nothing to her. She was too far gone.

She simply collapsed, her head flopping awkwardly on a pile of miscellaneous items.

Her acidic stomach contents started to strip the stain from the flooring, as she let out her last breath, expelling a foul-smelling spew of liquids from her mouth and abdomen.

In her final moments, Natalia celebrated motherhood and the joy it had brought her, even if only temporarily. Her family would have been so proud of her.

CARNAGE

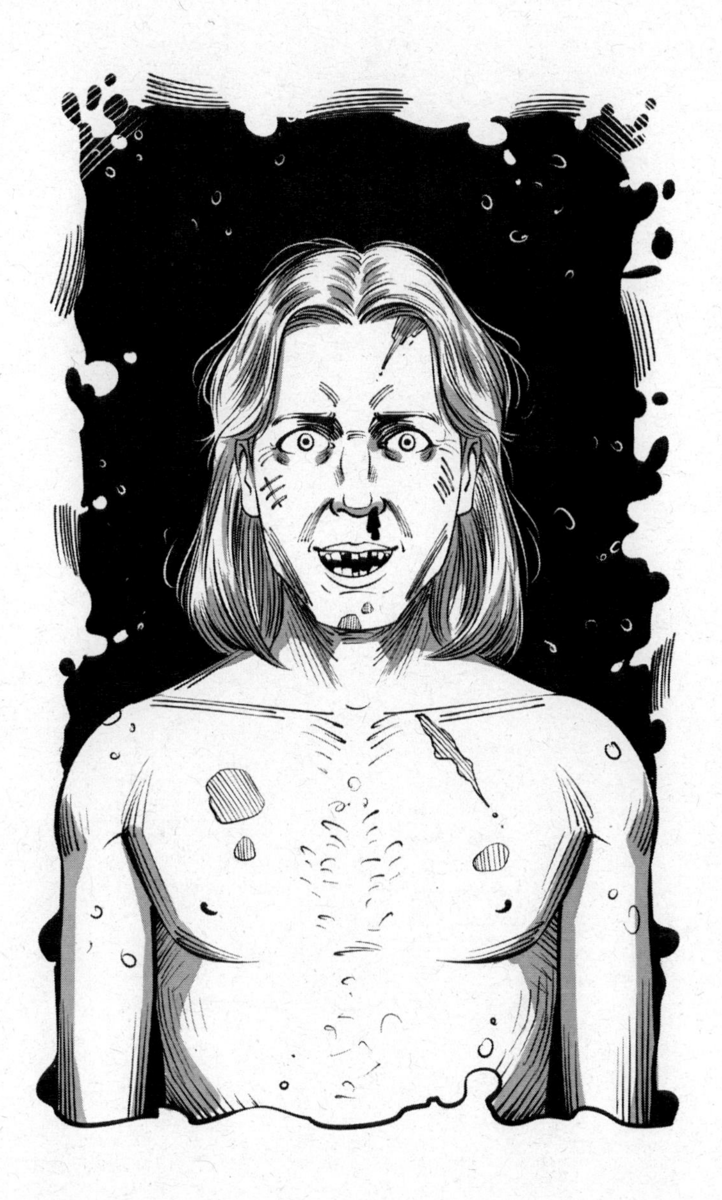

Morgan was driving at well over the speed limit, darting through residential streets without a care in the world. He was incandescent with rage, and was taking it out on the streets of suburbia.

His vehicle was beaten up and on its last legs, paint stripped from its bodywork, faded band stickers plastered haphazardly to cover various cracks and chips. The engine rattled beneath the hood, straining to keep up with the frantic gear shifts and speed changes, not to mention the speed bumps around every corner.

The driver's side window was wound all the way down, and Morgan's long greasy hair danced in the breeze. Vintage heavy metal blasted out of the tinny speakers, adding to the cacophony of mechanical vibrations in the car.

Through the windscreen, the world was a messy blur of street signs and concrete, occasionally peppered with angry pedestrians and cyclists who were inches away from being splattered. Morgan gritted his teeth, tears dripping from his eyes.

It was all Jessica's fucking fault. That cheating bitch.

A large pothole caused the vehicle to judder up and down violently, but Morgan shifted gears and compressed the accelerator even harder. He had no idea where he was or where he was going, but he did know one thing... He didn't want to be here anymore, and he was going to go out in a whirlwind of violence and carnage.

* * *

The suburban maze of roads led to a motorway, where hundreds of commuters were on their way to work. It was 8:45am, and the lanes were packed with stationary cars.

The final road in Egglemore led to an overpass, which circled onto a slip road and then onto the main highway right below. It took barely five seconds for Morgan to get onto the bridge.

Up at a higher vantage point, he had a brilliant idea...

The never-ending queues of traffic below looked like toy cars, patiently waiting in line for someone to come and play with them. Many of the commuters were sat staring into the distance, mindlessly listening to the radio, eating their breakfast to-go or smoking a cigarette.

Morgan headed to the slip road, gaining speed recklessly. His entire body wanted to tear itself apart with rage after what that fucking she-devil told him that morning. A red mist coated his vision, heart palpating out of his chest.

The bridge was full of potholes, and each time Morgan span his wheel to avoid one his car brushed the safety barriers with a metallic screech. The vehicle shook hard, the force of the movement vibrating through his seat.

He ignored all of this, instead focusing on the road and the images playing on repeat in his mind.

Jessica. She finally fucking admitted it. With Cory of all people, that cheating bitch. My own brother.

Morgan had flipped out. He couldn't stand the secrets... The deceit... He and Cory were brothers, how could have have done something so spiteful?

Of course, he wasn't going to let any of it go. Morgan had lost it as soon as he found out, reached into the boot of his car, taken out a wrench, and smacked that bitch full on in the face with it—with a lead-up and a jump to ensure she really felt it. Cory happened to be there at the time, and he got a face full of metal too. That strike had done some real damage, but he managed to run away like the little coward he was.

Oh, and Jessica? He pushed that lying sack of shit into the boot, slammed it down, and that's where she was right now, trying to kick through the passenger seats.

Morgan's phone started to vibrate against the plastic cup holder it was sitting in. Without taking his eyes off of the road, he could already guess who would be calling. As soon as the call rang out, they dialed right back, leaving barely a second between tries.

SCREEEEEECH.

Morgan drifted towards the barriers again, but after correcting his path, his mind settled back on the images from that morning.

There was so much blood. Before starting his rampage, he had opened the boot carefully to check she was still alive. She managed to claw at his chest a little bit, but the fact she was conscious was good. He had a plan...

She'd never be with anyone else. It was kind of romantic, in a way. No matter where she wanted to go, she could never leave him, and he'd make sure there was a finality to this whole thing. Like Romeo and Juliet, their souls would be intertwined forever.

The phone started to vibrate again. Morgan was getting pissed off.

He snatched the device from the cup holder and swiped to answer.

"What?" he screamed, swerving away from the barrier.

Through a tinny speaker, he could hear a voice pleading with him from the other end of the line.

"Morgan, please. Your car's gone. Where are you taking her?"

"Nice to talk to you too, bro!"

The car hit another pothole, jerking the car to the side, the tyre rubber screeching against the tarmac.

"You need to stop! We need to talk!"

"No, actually we don't need to fucking talk Cody!" Morgan laughed.

Jennifer started squealing again from the boot, her high-pitched voice sounding comically over the top.

"Shut the fuck up you cunt!" Morgan screamed.

"Please, don't do anything stupid—"

Those were the last words he heard before catapulting the device onto the concrete outside.

SCREEEEECH.

Fuck this. Morgan was bored of the anticipation. God was obviously leading him to something, he could feel it in his bones.

So, with a swift turn of the wheel, he hurtled across the lane, smashed through the metal safety barriers, and careered off of the concrete, nose-diving towards the road below.

In slow motion, he received a rush of stimuli from the world around him...

The jarring screams of Jessica in the trunk... A cascade of police cars right below, escorting what looked to be some kind of tanker, plastered in yellow hazard signs and warnings... The frozen stares of onlookers getting a jolt of adrenaline to break up their deathly boring routines...

The vehicle was heading directly for the tanker, and it was too late to swerve away.

SMASSSSH.

The car mashed into the side of the tanker, the matte aluminium exterior caving on impact. Morgan could just about make out a slogan on the signage: *'Making a Better Tomorrow, Today.'*

Glass shattered at every angle, giant shards driving through the engine and tearing it into several pieces. Oil sputtered out in a burning stream, blistering Morgan's forearm upon impact. The framework of the car crumpled in on itself, the back of the vehicle forcefully thrusting to the front.

Jessica's body hurtled into the dashboard, smashing

through the passenger seats and pummeling through the gap of the two front seats. Her face erupted onto the hard plastic, and the explosion of the airbag sent fleshy mounds of skin and shattered teeth across the remnants of the windscreen, and into orbit around Morgan's head.

The vehicle obliterated the chamber of the tanker, spewing a cascading torrent of viscous orange liquid onto the road outside.

The tanker lost its bearings, and charged into a pile of commuter vehicles, totally demolishing several of the first ones it hit in a bloody annihilation of metal and flesh. The mangled frame of Morgan's car rammed into the tarmac, ejecting him and Jessica onto the open road.

Exposed body parts flew about the scene, a severed wrist here, a dismembered leg there. Gushes of crimson splattered in all directions, as crumpled bodies careened across the road, like human bowling skittles.

* * *

Morgan awoke to a scene that should have haunted him, but instead filled him with excitement. *He* had made this happen. A chain reaction, all from one tiny gesture. All of this was Jessica's fault, and that bitch was folded in half somewhere behind him.

In front of him, a large slice of metal bodywork had completely obliterated some old woman, vivisecting her body into two mutilated halves.

Another guy, barely eighteen, had been crushed by an airborne motorbike, with track marks that had removed his facial features. The sloppy goo from his eyeball was crusting on the side of his face, and his teeth were sprinkled around his person.

The metal tanker lay on its side, spilling out a fuck-tonne

of viscous orange slop, liquid enough to splash and splatter but thick enough to envelop anything that came into contact with it.

Within minutes, the entire road and its contents were covered in this slime. Morgan was bent into a savagely contorted position, his spine cracked and exposed through his back, his neck at an unusual angle. How he was still alive was beyond him, but as he slowly moved his eyes around, he noticed the strangest thing…

Everyone on that road was alive. The crushed guy with no face… The two halves of the elderly woman… Even some hot blonde girl—who was quite literally in three chunks—was breathing.

How the fuck?

Morgan could feel some kind of buzzing on his skin. His flesh was slowly… melting? Was that the right word? The liquid was engulfing his flesh, symbiotically binding with his cells and slowly disintegrating into this pool of communal slime.

He could feel himself floating closer to the centre of the crash, the liquid somehow pulling everyone towards a middle-ground. The slime had grown exponentially, the people and vehicles—and everything in the immediate area—had been scooped into this grotesque blob of mucus.

People were screaming, confused, helpless, scared. But Morgan was loving it. He had no idea what was happening or why, but the suffering made him feel good.

A few crows flew overhead, and one of them was stupid enough to land right by him. Its claws immediately liquefied upon landing. It fluttered its wings frightfully, but it was too late. Before long, its form had melted into a distorted, sludgy black pile of feathers, its eyes still blinking, beak still snapping at the air. For some reason, the slime had quickly digested this animal, but everyone else was assimilating at a much slower pace.

Morgan couldn't explain it if he tried, but he could feel the crow's emotion as it came to rest with the others. The panic and helplessness made way to an acceptance... And then an enjoyment. There were a million emotions in this pool of slime, and it was almost like they were interconnected.

* * *

The terror and panic continued. There were several others like Morgan who had entered a blissful state of acceptance. Acceptance of their death. Acceptance of their own mutilated bodies. Acceptance of this communal experience. But there were far more who were completely losing their minds, trying to lift their deformed limbs from the floor, only to find them melted like mozzarella cheese on a pizza.

Curiously, several more birds landed on the slime, and after a while, Morgan realised they were doing it intentionally. They weren't trying to avoid the slime—they were coming towards it.

Across the highway, a man jumped from a bridge, tumbling to a presumably bloody death—but even though he imploded on impact, his fleshy vessel started to amalgamate with the rest of them.

A car radio on the overpass was blaring an emergency station, and Morgan listened intently.

... there has been a serious incident on the Egglemore overpass going into Junction 5 of the motorway this morning... residents are encouraged to stay indoors and drivers... towards the site should turn away right now. Repeat, do not enter the vicinity... victims families' are slowly being informed... police have expressed that recording of the scene is strictly forbidden...

Morgan was *elated.* He had made the news... The national news..

My God.

With a rough snap, Morgan managed to jolt his neck back into position. How he wasn't dead yet was beyond him; this liquid was some crazy science shit. He half-wondered what had been in that tanker, and whether it had been God's will to lead him to that place at that precise time, to experience this whole thing unfolding.

The dead weren't dead anymore, and though that likely included Jessica right now, he still thought it was pretty exciting to get some more time to explore this new life... As part of a communal vessel.

In his body, he could feel every synapse, every shared nerve of each participant in this gloopy mess. Everyone's emotions were sloshing together, a bittersweet cacophony of pain, laughter, horniness, helplessness. It was like a brilliant, undiscovered fetish, and he was ready to ride this wave to the very end.

Morgan's clothes had all but melted away. His skin was absolutely mutilated, lumpy like porridge, and various bones had started to puncture through his flesh. But nothing hurt... There was no real pain, on an individual level. It was dulled by the absolute cacophony of emotions that radiated in this mess.

A drone flew overhead, followed by a news helicopter.

NEWS247 was painted on the side of the copter. It was quite a distance away, but Morgan could make out the reporter leaning haphazardly out of the side of the vehicle, reporting on the scene below.

He was jolted out of his trance by a teenage boy, who was screaming right next to him, incessantly crying out for his parents. The guy was at least fifteen or sixteen; why was he being such a little bitch?

A sly smile grew across Morgan's face as the teen looked right past him to something else.

"Oh my God, Mum?"

The guy had clocked his mother a dozen or so metres away, slowly dissolving into the communal pool. He started to drag himself in her direction, his gooey flesh shredding from the bones in his legs.

"I'm coming, Mum!"

Morgan started to shuffle, the bones in his neck loose and creaky, causing his head to gyrate in an awkward pattern.

He was within metres of the boy now, and without warning, he grabbed a fistful of his hair and forced his head downwards, planting his face into the slime. The teen shrieked uncontrollably, his pain matched only by his mother's guttural wails.

After a few moments, the slime moulded with his face, and he was unable to pull away. Morgan climbed atop him, forcing his weight upon his shoulders, half anchored by the slime yet able to wriggle freely. Within minutes, the boy's body was disgustingly contorted, but it had proven something to Morgan.

He wanted to test out the life-preserving properties of the gloop. And the fact the boy hadn't suffocated in the liquid proved that death wasn't possible. This was some next-level shit.

* * *

Darkness fell, and sirens echoed around the eerily quiet motorway. A perimeter had been drawn a few hundred metres around the widest points of the accident, and only emergency services were allowed in and out.

Helicopters still roared above, of course, the only chance for the ravenous news stations to get their latest headlines.

A few people from the group had started to sing in unison, a community singalong of sorts. Backdropped by a squealing chorus of pain, it certainly was a surreal scenario.

The singing was the kind of pastime you'd expect at a vigil, yet it was strangely comforting. Joyous renditions of *Hallelujah* and similar Christian music echoed around the highway, and though he wasn't a religious man, Morgan enjoyed the relative novelty of the moment.

Jessica was only a few metres away. He had caught a glimpse of her just before nightfall, but had lost sight when sunset passed. The streetlights hadn't come on yet—Morgan presumed they had either been kept off to discourage the press, or maybe to protect the mental health of the hundred or so people who were part of the slimy mess. But as soon as the light was back? Oh boy, would he have some fun…

A hodgepodge of animals and manmade items had started to liquefy in the sludge, turning it a weird, dirty brown—like when you mix too many colours of plasticine together. Morgan wondered how long it would take before they were all just unconscious gloop, or indeed if they would live that long. The slime had started to accelerate its effects, as if it knew that a foreign body had come into contact with it. He hoped that he still had his senses intact to reach Jessica before it was too late, so he could see the fear in her eyes as she realised she wouldn't be able to escape.

That's what happens when you fuck with me.

His fantasy was interrupted by screams on a loudspeaker. He couldn't place the direction of the sound, but there was panic in the air, and a low rumbling vibration. Sirens began to blurt at full volume, and the sudden flashing of the emergency lighting illuminated a horrifying sight.

On the motorway bridge, several dozen people were running in a wild congregation, jumping from the concrete and diving into the sludge. Like a shit version of the Olympic diving competition, they fell head first into the slop, and though their bones shattered on impact, the jelly kept them alive, just like it had the other residents. Morgan could feel the power of the community growing. And he could feel the magnetism the decaying slurry was emitting. It was drawing people in... Not just people, but cats, dogs, horses, cows... Any living organism with the ability to move itself was heading for the road, and it was only a matter of time before this would start to spill out into suburbia.

The cordons were already being stepped back, the battle lines redrawn as the organic matter grew and grew. At this rate, he'd be pulled away from Jessica with no way of talking to her, and he wanted to ensure that he got the last of his rage out before they all melted in the dark abyss.

* * *

A white hot light knocked Morgan out of his trancelike mindset. Roaring flames erupted from a large flamethrower tied to a helicopter, hovering just above the mass. People cried out in searing pain, the gloop bubbling and deforming, before resetting in its original shape. The fire was charring the organic matter left on human bones, but it did nothing to the ooze. If anything, it helped rejuvenate the liquified form of the slime, which then reset and grew further out onto the road. The idea was quickly abandoned, and the singing from earlier had turned into a riotous cacophony of rage.

Moments later, a torrent of bullets fired into the crowd. The government were obviously at their wit's end, trying to force the hand of this organic enemy, but firepower wasn't going to work either. The bullets ricocheted off the concrete and metal fragments, and just slid neatly into the slime, losing all momentum the moment they made impact. This idea was, once again, abandoned.

* * *

The sun rose slowly, and the brown gloop was starting to smell like rotten egg. The putrefied sludge was murky and slushy, enveloping the warped tapestry of human body parts contained within. All organic matter had a weird sheen to it, like wet silicone, and Morgan became aware that his limbs were melting into the pool, his bones starting to jellify into the sticky mass.

Several bodies were connected to him by fleshy strands, and he guessed it would only be a matter of time until larger parts of them began to interconnect.

Willing his maimed body to spin, Morgan finally set his eyes upon Jessica.

He had lost his individual fingers and toes now, but his arms still had a bit of muscle left inside. Just enough to slowly drag himself through the slime. Jessica seemed in a much worse state—her arms had been forcibly dislocated behind her back in the crash, and her mangled body was writhing and putrid.

Inch by inch, Morgan started to drag his body through the slime, severing the sludge connections he had made to people nearby. Bloody layers stripped from his flesh as he did so, but there was no pain in the sludge.

Jessica clocked his presence, her one working eye drooping to the side, open wide with fear. She tried to move, bless her heart, but she was a grotesque, breathing statue at this point. She wasn't going anywhere.

"Oh Jessie, baby!" Morgan taunted, twisting his mangled face into a grimaced kiss.

She emanated a panicked shriek, and though her body was unmoving, he imagined she was shaking life a leaf on the inside. Morgan smiled, continuing his cumbersome crawl towards her.

A voice suddenly sparked up on a loudspeaker. Morgan just about managed to twist his head in the direction of the sound, and saw a man addressing the crowd, his back turned away from the tempting sludge.

"Residents of Egglemore, this is your Mayor. I must thank you for your patience and understanding whilst we worked hard to identify and overcome this situation. We are afraid to say we have reached a roadblock with our investigation, and are having to move to a stage three quarantine."

Morgan chuckled, buzzing with excitement and pride.

Look at what he had done. Look at what he had caused.

Morgan turned back and continued to drag his contorted body closer to Jessica, who was trying her best to slide away.

"I have been informed by our very best scientists that the organic matter in the spillage was a relatively new experimental drug on its way to human trials. An accidental collision ruptured the payload, and has caused the disaster we have on our hands now. For the safety of our fellow residents and country-people, we must contain this matter right now."

Various members of the sludge community started to scream and shout, writhing in frustration, trying to escape this mess, the reality of their situation finally setting in.

Morgan was within arm's reach now, and he slid his wet arm stump across Jessica's cool stomach, which was exposed and bloodied. He smiled, licking his lips.

"A series of controlled explosions will be carried out in two minutes, around the perimeter of the infection. The ground will be disrupted, and we aim to implode the road to the soil a few metres down, effectively quarantining you underground. This will allow us to create a series of systems to enter and exit the infection area, and slowly bring you back to higher ground one by one."

Bullshit, Morgan thought. He knew what this government was like. This wasn't a rescue mission. It was a containment one.

With all the might left in his body, he slid his deformed frame on top of Jessica, mirroring her position as if they were making out, ready to fuck (in missionary, of course, her favourite style). He was face to face with her, and his exposed skin was already starting to slowly melt and amalgamate with hers. A small whisper escaped her broken throat, croaky and helpless.

"Ssssh baby. We're going down together, you stupid slut. You're only gonna feel me from now on. Forever and ever."

"MORGAN!"

What the fuck?

Just past the containment area, Morgan could see a figure jumping up and down, trying to fight the emergency services to let him through.

No. It couldn't be.

Jessica's eyes widened when she heard the voice, and she tried her utmost to spin her neck in the direction of the commotion.

Well fuck me...

It's him.

His brother Cory was flailing his arms, trying to break through the containment area. Morgan could only just make out his features, given the distance and his failing eyesight, but this gave him a huge jolt of excitement.

"MORGAN! GET OFF OF HER! BABY, I'M COMING!"

Jessica started to squeal softly again, and Morgan just erupted into a fit of laughter. He had no idea how in the hell Cory had tracked them down, but this was just *too* perfect.

"YOU FUCKING BASTARD!"

Cory was forced to the ground by a police officer, but continued to scream a torrent of profanity at him.

Morgan flopped out his tongue and started to lick Jessica's face, smiling and giggling as he slopped his putrid saliva over her mangled features. He gyrated as he did so, enjoying the vibration of their grotesque frames rubbing up against each other.

"Thank you all for your complicity and extraordinary resolve. Goodbye," the Mayor finished.

The cacophony of screams were immediately drowned out by the loudest, heart-stopping roar of explosions. A parade of lights set off around them, and the concrete immediately gave out, crumbling in huge chunks underneath the sludge.

The mass slid through the emerging hole, falling a dozen metres into a grave of soil. Bodies shifted and toppled on top of each other, mutilated piles of flesh and grime. Piled high, they were like sardines in a tin of dirt, and it was only moments until the Mayor broke his promise.

Through a crack in the mass of carnage, Morgan—who had miraculously stayed glued to Jessica, right where he wanted to be—could see several trucks pull up on the overpass above the scene and start to funnel wet concrete right on top of them.

The liquid seeped through every crack, every air hole. They were slowly suffocated, turned into a foundation for a new highway. And in his last moments, as he felt Jessica convulse in tormented pain, he couldn't help but feel like this was the perfect end to his story.

The communal mass stopped writhing. Set into the concrete, every body, every piece of flesh was permanently contorted, ready for several lifetimes of conscious, apathetic agony. Morgan was intertwined with Jessica, her flesh blended with his, one form and one body.

* * *

From that moment on, that stretch of motorway was known as the singing highway. If you were unlucky enough to have a break down at any point of that one-hundred foot stretch, you'd start to hear a weird song emanating from below the ground. Renditions of Hallelujah and various other songs. It would be enough to drive you mad, and you'd jump onto the floor to try and dig under the concrete, to try and join the chorus of singing. And within a matter of moments, you'd be obliterated by oncoming traffic.

CRYSTALLINE

Helena couldn't go on living as she was.

Her small, two-bedroom flat— illuminated by dim floor lamps and several glitchy LED fixtures in her ceiling—was falling apart at the seams. A whirring static from the television fought against the hiss of a white noise machine, creating a cacophony of frustrating sound that she had long become acquainted with. The sound helped settle James' migraines, but had the opposite effect on Helena. She very much looked forward to the day that she could live in peace again, and mull over the minutiae of life in a calm silence...

James was her younger brother, and currently inhabited the larger of the two bedrooms. His space consisted of a bed, some medical equipment, and a few books, but no kind of decoration or flair. The floors were covered in mismatched, thick rugs in the event of a fall, and any sharp items had been removed in anticipation of potential anger outbursts.

The twenty-four year old man had suffered a multitude of issues since downing a toxic cocktail of drugs at a house party a couple of years prior, and his barely-older sister had taken on the role of his carer.

The traditional care system had long become null and void, thanks to continuous spending cuts and the abolishment of the National Health Service, and the pair barely made ends meet. Helena had a part-time side hustle as a cam girl, and a couple of clients gave her enough resources to cover the house and the bills, with a little to spare on a skimpy new dress every month or so. Even the sugar daddies were penny pinching in these times, but she was thankful for what she could get.

James was settled in bed, having just eaten a slurry of chicken dinner, blitzed into a gloopy, unappetising soup. His eyes were heavy, flickering open and shut, so after wiping away the sweat from his forehead Helena switched off the overhead light and crept into the hallway. The rhythmic beep of the medical machines faded away softly as she shut the door and made her way into the kitchen.

The claustrophobic space was marred by peeling wallpaper, swollen patches of black damp, and crumbling brickwork, but she had tried her best to hide the rot with an ill-assorted combination of second-hand canvas prints and cheap pastel paint.

On the kitchen table, a flurry of letters were strewn from one side to the other. She collected them into a rough pile and slid them to the back end of the surface, next to the window. An old laptop sat idle right next to them, with a cheap webcam clipped to the screen. Her technical setup was as dated as the structure around her, but it did its job.

She double clicked the trackpad, patiently waiting for it to spark to life, but it didn't. After a few more clicks and a tap of the keyboard, it slowly crawled into a standby position, and then onto her home screen. A notification popped up in the toolbar, and a rudimentary app opened up in full-screen.

The camera started to transmit a live video, and Helena shook her hair over her shoulders. She undid the first two buttons on her blouse, plumped her cleavage into prime position, and grew a shy smile on her face.

Another video joined her on screen. The square box showed a video feed of Tommy, a fifty-something year old Londoner with rough yet traditionally handsome features. He smiled, showing off a set of sparkly veneers.

"Long time love, how you keeping?"

Helena chuckled.

"Well, well, well. I wasn't expecting you back so soon."

Tommy grinned.

"If memory serves, you went off with that girl… Madison. I take it it didn't last?" Helena teased.

"Nah, you know me babe, I'm just too kinky! She weren't into the feet stuff or the bondage so I had to get rid of her."

"Shame. But at least I've got you back now. I've learned some new tricks since we last spoke." Helena teased.

Helena reached down and undid another button on her blouse. Tommy watched in anticipation, but she was going slow, taking her time. He was her only booking that night, so it was in her best interest to make it last. In an ideal world, she would have been at Tommy's house, performing in person for a much bigger sum. Unfortunately, the waiting list for external carers was gargantuan, and without one of those, she couldn't leave James' side. Helena was effectively on house arrest, so her only real social time was on these calls.

Leaning back on her chair, Helena crumpled herself into a ball, showing off her dirty white socks and stroking the webcam with her toes. Her body was awkwardly positioned, as to avoid the floor lamp behind her, which immersed her frame in a warm orange glow. It was one of her better lamps, so she didn't want to accidentally knock it over.

"You like what you see Tommy boy?"

Helena undid the final button on her blouse, and sensually slipped it off of her shoulders, discarding it on the floor.

A low groan emitted from his mouth, and Helena continued to caress the small lens with her foot. Outside, the wind seemed to pick up, rattling the decrepit window frames against the crumbling exterior walls. Tommy was touching himself off-screen; Helena could tell by his relaxed facial expression. This only made her want to perform better, so she started to groan softly in collaboration.

The sound of cracking metal debris echoed outdoors, but Helena was too focused on her performance to notice. She was obsessed with how she looked on camera, how excited Tommy was to experience her in this intimate moment.

Tommy's moaning became more regular, and that was her cue to take it up a notch.

With a practiced twist, she undid the back of her bra, and let the straps slip past the top of her shoulders. As the material slid down her pale arms, an ominous screech emerged from her garden. She broke character for a moment, staring towards her back door, listening to the sound get louder and closer.

Before she could utter a word, the doorframe imploded and a wave of shattered glass sprayed across the kitchen. Helena dove from her chair, avoiding the rain of shards, and landed hard on the tiled floor. The laptop followed suit, clambering to the surface with a thud.

A scent of rotten ammonia filled the air, and a sickly heat radiated from the unidentified black mass that had crashed into her kitchen. Helena covered her mouth with her hand, gasping to avoid the toxic smoke that engulfed the object.

From the cracked laptop, she could hear Tommy's voice rhythmically calling her name, checking to see if she was okay. For some reason, her eyes started to weep salty tears, and her head felt dizzy and confused. She squeezed her eyes shut, slumped onto the floor, and fell unconscious.

* * *

Helena woke to a smoke-filled kitchen, shattered tiles, and a slew of melted appliances. It was the crack of dawn, and the orange light from outside was masked by a dusty haze.

The culprit was a gritty black rock, around the size of a large pumpkin. The mass had indented the corner of the kitchen floor, cracked several tiles, and splintered a cupboard on its journey.

Her laptop had run out of juice, so Tommy's voice was no

longer ringing through the tinny speakers. She shoved some debris to the side and climbed to her feet, brushing off the dust from the fall. With bruised hands, she re-did the clip on her bra, and grabbed her blouse from the floor.

Just as she leaned in to study the rock, a brash alarm echoed from inside the house, snapping Helena into alert mode. She sped through the hallway and directly to James' room. Splayed over the bed and onto the floor, his limbs were awkwardly entangled from a fall.

"Shit, shit, sorry—"

Helena grabbed underneath his armpits, and with an almighty heave, she lifted him back onto the bed, untangling his limbs. He had soiled his underwear. With a deep sigh, she grabbed a fresh pair from a small basket. The smell of faeces battled with the pungent scent in the kitchen, and Helena made a mental note to run around with some air freshener at her earliest convenience.

* * *

The broom kicked up plenty of dust as it weaved through the debris. Helena swept the broken fragments of her kitchen into a neat pile at the side of the room, whilst she held her mobile phone between her ear and her shoulder, on hold with the police.

"How can I help?"

"Hi, I just explained to the other guy that something flew through my window late last night?"

"We don't deal with animals, that would be the RSPCA ma'am."

"What? No. Not a bird!" Helena explained.

"Please be more specific ma'am."

Helena was quickly losing her patience.

"A big rock smashed my window and has *destroyed* my kitchen. My insurance won't cover it, and I just need to know what my next steps are."

There was a pause at the end of the line.

"Erm, well. It doesn't seem like a police matter, ma'am. Let me check and call you back."

The call handler hung up the phone. Helena shook her head frustratedly and walked over to the mass. With the bottom of the broom and the splintered leg of one of her kitchen chairs, she rolled the rock over to the back door, and threw it outside into the garden.

Right on cue, there was a thunderous knock on her front door.

"Fuck me!" she muttered, sauntering down the hall and to the front of the house. Her hand gripped the handle, as she bent down to squint through the peephole. James was shouting too, expressing himself in the only way he knew how, but the sound was muffled enough to ignore for a moment.

Two men were standing outside of the house, dressed in official uniforms, with name tags blazoned on their jackets.

"We are here to collect an outstanding charge for rent arrears," one of them shouted through the door, detecting her presence.

Fucking bailiffs.

"Now's not a good time!" Helena called back, but they weren't having any of it.

The less patient of the two men slammed his fist on the door again, cloaking his impatience in a rhythmic knock.

"It never is, I'm afraid. Please open the door."

"Look, I'm gonna call you guys! I promise. I just really need to sort something out right now!" Helena said.

"We need to talk today, not tomorrow, not the next day. We will enter by force."

Helena clenched her teeth together, fantasising about a violent outburst, but ultimately keeping her anger reigned in.

"I'll consider a payment plan! I'll look at what I can offer, come back next week. I have to go!" Helena shouted, before walking away from the front door.

On her journey back to the kitchen, a wet drip tumbled from the ceiling above. A large area of the plaster had become damp and grey, and the moisture was dripping from it in tiny beads. Helena shook her head, and continued... Then she remembered James, who was shrieking a slew of nonsensical words.

* * *

Helena felt flushed... exhausted, in fact. Her skin emanated a strange heat, the type you experience in the beginning stages of sunburn, but she hadn't been outside the house in days. Her forehead felt particularly sore, but she didn't have time to sort it yet.

Instead, she was tending to James, who was having a full-blown anxiety attack because a spider had landed on his sheets. With the edge of a newspaper, she flicked the tiny insect into a used Tupperware container, and threw it out of the window, knocking the plastic against the frame to confirm that it had indeed left the building.

James was soaked through with sweat, but after a few reassuring words and a sweep of the room, he settled back into a nap.

The door closed with a gentle creak, and Helena could finally exhale. A neon yellow 'final warning' notice dangled from the letterbox, which meant she had bought herself some time.

Helena's bedroom was painted a pale pastel pink, with sky blue curtains and carpet. Before James had moved in with her, it was the first room she had decorated, in anticipation of selling her house and going travelling. She had been twenty-four years old at the time, and only a couple of months away from flying to Bali to work as a digital nomad —then James had his accident. The fantasy of walking out of her front door with a laptop and a small travel bag whipped around her mind on a daily basis, but she distracted herself from the thought. She had to focus on the present moment to avoid spiraling out of control.

In her cupboard, she had a rotating choice of outfits, mainly dresses or t-shirt and jean combos. In one drawer, she kept all of her most prized possessions—including jewellery from her late parents—and a few collectable items she thought would be worth something someday.

Scanning over the items in the cupboard, Helena carefully calculated how much she thought each of the possessions was worth. Her gold jewellery would probably fetch the most, followed by a sovereign ring and silver necklace. The debt was piling up, and she knew that even a token payment could keep the bailiffs at bay long enough for her to try and sort James' disability payments out.

Helena loved her brother. She really did. But she also despised him, and as toxic as that thought was, it was something she felt in the deepest depths of her bones. James hadn't experienced responsibility. He went from alcoholic teen to drug-fuelled adult without as much as a weekend job, burning through a small inheritance, and it was always up to Helena to clean up his mess. Quite literally, now…

She pulled out some of the jewellery and tossed it into a pile on her bed, ready to pack up and contact the bailiffs first thing.

* * *

It was only midday, but Helena was ready for bed. She squeezed a packet of frozen peas against her forehead whilst tinkering with the laptop, attempting to reboot it.

A deep crack segmented the screen into two distinctive, diagonal quadrants, but she could just about make out the desktop page when it finally loaded. Beneath the frozen veg on her head, a curious crawling sensation flowed through her skin. It was enough to make her remove the package and squish the newly-formed lump between her fingers, feeling for any trapped debris or pus.

Helena set down the laptop, and ambled into the bathroom.

Her face was red, alright. Just beneath her hairline, a small bump had formed, topped with a pus-coloured head that was just begging to be popped.

It didn't have the usual texture of a zit though—the contours of the lump were ever so slightly jagged, as if a minuscule piece of brick was stuck right underneath. Not able to resist, she slipped her fingers to opposing sides of the bump, and squeezed with gentle force.

There was an initial resistance, but it didn't last long. Within seconds, the spot erupted, smearing a snotty globule across the mirror, coloured deep yellow with streaks of bright red blood. There was a slight clatter in the sink below as the pus ejaculated over the porcelain.

Helena slammed her hand into the bowl, to catch whatever had fallen before it escaped into the drain. After sifting around for a short while, she was taken aback to see a tiny diamond, traced with blood and pus. She held it up to her head inquisitively, comparing the size of the rock to the bleeding crater in her face… It fit the fleshy crevice perfectly.

* * *

Helena was back on the laptop, catching up with Tommy. She showed him the rock, rolling it between her fingers.

"And you're saying to me, that came out of ya face?"

Helena smirked in disbelief.

"Yeah, I mean it came right out of this hole."

She leaned towards the camera to show the crater on her forehead, which had already started to crust over in a curiously short space of time. Tommy recoiled.

"Look, darling, I love seeing ya hole but this ain't the kind I mean, if you know what I mean!"

They both giggled for a moment.

"I'm sorry about last night by the way. Something smashed through my window..."

"Babe I was worried! You just disappeared, I held on for a couple of minutes but didn't wanna get charged too much. I'd rather save that for the action shots."

He winked, and Helena grinned.

"I bet you do... So, uh, do you think it's real?" Helena remarked, drawing attention back to the rock.

"I mean... In the pawn shop, we get wedding rings and sovereigns. It's hard to tell." Tommy answered. "But send it over and I'll have a look. If it's worth anything, I'll split it with ya 80/20" he continued.

"90/10." Helena teased. "Final offer".

Tommy grinned and nodded.

"Alright. But no charge for this little chat then... And next time, I get full tits within two minutes."

"Deal," Helena chirped.

And with that, she repositioned the camera, slipped her legs above the table, and prepared to rub her dirty, two-day ripe socks all over the lens again. Tommy grinned, already starting to moan under his breath.

* * *

There was vomit everywhere. James hung out of the bed, thrashing violently, completely overwhelming Helena's slender frame. She was doing her best to keep him stable, whilst also holding a phone between her ear and shoulder.

"It's getting worse. I told Doctor Lane two weeks ago I needed some support," she barked, flustered. "And I... what do you mean no-one is available? I pay through the roof for insurance, and...well I've only missed one payment and I'm paying that next week—"

The phone slipped and smashed onto the floor, cracking the screen. Helena cursed, trying to wrestle with James as he flopped about, all whilst crouching down to retrieve the device. She squatted, as low as she could go, but it was no use. After a few moments, she pushed him onto the bed forcefully, just in time to hear the line go dead.

"Fuck!" she screamed, taking a moment to calm down. James had returned to an almost catatonic state, his eyes locked onto the ceiling above.

Helena leaned over to grab a Tupperware of ready-made soup—a blitzed chicken stock puree, James' favourite (well, as far as she knew—he didn't really react or give any social cues at all nowadays, but he didn't spit it out, so she considered that a sign of his acceptance).

As she turned to pour some into his bowl, his eyes trained on her instead, and the most violent roar exploded from his mouth. His face was red, and he seemed to be in the midst of some kind of manic episode. With a clenched fist, he thumped Helena around the jaw, thrashing up and down again, vomiting over his bare chest and stained duvet.

Helena lay on the floor, bleeding from her mouth. Tears began to stream from her eyes, and she didn't help James this time. Instead, she jumped up and exited the room, slamming the door shut. His wailing didn't dissipate for another five minutes, but Helena was long gone by then.

In the garden, she stared up at the sky, the salty tears drying on her skin. Her phone began to vibrate in her pocket, and she quickly swiped the screen and held it up to her ear.

"You better not charge me for these calls." It was Tommy, being his usual upbeat, cheeky self.

"Well that all depends on the information you have for me."

"I have good news I suppose."

"And that is?" Helena pried.

"The diamond. It's real. And worth a pretty penny too. You got any more where that came from?"

Helena laughed in disbelief.

"No kidding?"

She traced her finger over her forehead, and to her amazement, the wound had already closed right up.

"That's great news actually. I needed some good news," she sighed.

"Having a hard time love?" he asked inquisitively.

The tears started to well up again, and Helena tried her best to keep things professional.

"Oh you know how it is Tommy. Living day to day like everyone else."

He grunted in agreement.

"Keep your head up hun. I'm here to chat if you need me."

* * *

The warm water streamed over Helena's naked body, the caked blood washing away in a murky jet of crimson. She gently massaged her neck as she cleaned her hair and moved to her face.

The shower was the one place in the house that Helena

felt safe. Away from the panicked cries of her fading brother. Away from the threatening calls of the bailiffs who hounded her for debt payments she had no way of paying. Away from inconsiderate doctors and the crippling expectation of a world that had gone to shit. All she needed was a moment of pause, to gather her thoughts and strength, before heading back out to the war zone reality.

She continued to clean herself, wiping away frothy passion fruit-scented bubbles, but her fingers stopped in their tracks, as she rubbed an unusual lump on her right temple.

It was tender, and she couldn't apply much pressure. As she followed the contour of her face, she noticed a similar lump at the bottom of her cheek. She had presumed it was inflamed from the almighty punch in the face earlier, but it creaked ominously, as if something was broken… or rattling. She prodded at it, examining every slight movement, trying to work out exactly what was happening.

Helena twisted the tap to stop the water and snatched her towel from across the screen. She wiped her feet on the rug, and stepped towards the mirror.

In the reflection, she noticed her face was slightly dried out and scaly, with cracks starting to appear in a very delicate formation. As she trained her gaze on the lump, she noticed that it had actually formed under the skin, on the inside of her cheek, right by her gums.

She slid her finger into her agape mouth, and traced the juicy lump, before steadily applying more pressure. Her gum compressed slightly, further and further with each increase in pressure. The shape of whatever was broken inside the flesh was becoming clearer as she pushed, and with one last nudge, the skin broke, unleashing a torrent of blood and stinky yellow pus.

Helena gagged, hanging her head over the sink, allowing the bodily juices to flow right out of her lips. A spiral of gunk formed in the bowl, but the foreign object was still lodged inside. Impatiently, she reached inside and tugged at her back teeth, steadily rocking back and forth with her fingernails to remove the object. The pain was immense, and her open mouth allowed her foul breath to escape right into her nose, increasing her urge to gag.

Finally, with a small snap and a broken piece of tooth clattering out of her mouth, she had removed the object. She ran it under the cold tap, and stood for a few moments, admiring its crystalline quality. It was otherworldly... ethereal. Like nothing she had ever seen.

Cleaning herself up, she was ready to get back to the real world, before she remembered the lump by her temple. She started to squeeze hard, begging for the clammy release.

* * *

"How much Tommy?"

Helena had a hoody slumped on her tender frame. The hood hid her face, and only the cracked, inflamed skin of her hands was exposed to the sunlight outside. She held the phone up to her head, shaking in pain.

"I reckon we can get a few grand. Five easily."

"I have more. This week I've pulled out fifteen. That will get us to about thirty right?" Helena said.

It had been two weeks since the initial event, and the crystals had continued to grow and erupt. Some were tiny, some were marble-sized. They began to spread like acne, tiny diamond-filled pustules clustered across her chin and cheeks. The inflamed skin had taken over her entire body, but only her face offered the bountiful stones.

"When can I see you again? I'd love to talk over cam, I have plenty of cash now," Tommy asked.

"Soon," Helena responded, before hanging up.

She stumbled into the house, tripping over her own feet, trying to find her balance.

Inside James' room, the dirty washing had started to pile up. She was feeding him tinned tuna and beans, but had lost the strength to create anything from scratch.

James was calm but unwashed, sweat and dirt caking his face and body, with food stains covering most of his bedclothes.

Helena carefully slid the hood down over her head, and picked up a yellow-tinged rag. She moistened it in a bowl of stale water, and began to rub it over James' gaunt features. After wiping away the majority of the visible stains, she wrung out the cloth, and used it on her own face.

A strange mixture of bloody phlegm came off with each swipe. She was carefully patting the rag around a jagged rock which took up the majority of her left cheek. It had broken the skin with extreme pressure, and protruded at least four inches from her cheekbone. The deep red gem had a crystallised structure, rough and ready with a slightly reflective surface.

Her head bowed slightly from the sheer weight of the rock, and the skin around the wound was crusty and infected. She intermittently tugged gently on the object, seeing if it would budge, but its structure wasn't limited to the visible piece. Like an iceberg, it was growing beneath her face, and the pressure gave her a headache like she had never imagined.

Her phone started to vibrate, and she slowly put the rag down, before retrieving the device from her pocket.

"Hello?" she croaked.

"Hello, Ms Jacobs. This is Doctor Lane. Apologies for my late reply. The receptionist notified me that your premium has been paid, so I can finally talk to you!"

"You were waiting for money?" Helena enquired.

"Well, you know that we aren't a charity, Ms Jacobs! We have to prioritise those who support our business, we've always been very patient with your payment plans. I must admit, when we saw the balance had been paid in full, we all gave a small hurrah!"

"My brother is dying. You should have called earlier."

"Well that's why I'm calling now, Ms Jacobs. There is an experimental treatment in France. Very promising, but also very expensive. I'm not sure of your financial position, but it seems to have turned around, so I—"

"How much?" Helena barked.

"We're looking at an estimate of one-hundred thousand, plus travel and fees."

"Okay. Give me a couple of weeks," she muttered.

After hanging up, Helena continued to rub the rag across her face, breaking the skin and letting the pus trickle down her neck.

* * *

"Can we come in and discuss the payment plan? There were a few notes we wanted to hash out."

The pair of bailiffs were standing outside of Helena's front door, emanating a much calmer aura this time around. She had sorted a payment plan—a mix of a cash and possessions—and they had come to collect the first installment.

Helena ignored their words, shuddering as their loud, cocky voices rang through her head. Instead, she swung open the front window, grabbed her jewellery and cash in clumps, and threw them out into the street. Watching them scatter and flail for paper notes and small items was a small pleasure, and just as quickly as she had opened the window, she slammed it shut to continue with her day.

Later that night, Helena fumbled on the trackpad, her fingers trying to remember the placement of the keys. She had never been the most technologically-minded, but at the same time had never expected to forget the layout of a keyboard.

She was tired, of course. In the three weeks since the event, she had dealt with countless near-misses with James. Her vision was severely impaired by the perpetually growing rock, and she had forgotten to check up on him for two days straight. By the time she woke up from an extended slumber, he was lying in a menagerie of shit and piss, and had projectile vomited all over his body. The stench was rotten, she was sure. But in all honesty, her senses had dulled to a near nonexistent level. The only one that had survived this mutation was her sense of touch.

She double-clicked the trackpad… and again…

Finally, the laptop sparked to life. The webcam app was already loaded from last time, and Tommy quickly joined the call.

"My God," he exclaimed, choking on the last word as if to snatch the sentence right back into his mouth.

"I've made up my mind," Helena stuttered.

The crystal was now taking up the majority of the middle of her face. It tingled with agony. The infected skin was red raw, shimmering with bloody gore. The muscle had deformed around the rock, like a tree growing around an object that had been left on it over a matter of years.

Her neck veins were protruding out of her skin, struggling to balance the extreme weight of the object. Her left eye had been mostly gouged out and displaced over a painstaking couple of days, and her other one was permanently disfigured by the burning red glow of the prism.

She could hardly make out the screen, but followed Tommy's tinny voice, and attempted to keep her composure.

"I can reach ninety thousand comfortably. But I spoke to my partner, and we will get the hundred. But are you sure there's no other way love?" Tommy begged.

"No. We have to do it and I trust you, but I have to be sure this goes to James."

"Of course. Anything for you love," Tommy responded.

"Hey, Tommy," Helena croaked, her entire body shaking in excruciating pain.

Without waiting for a response, she ripped open her blouse, and showed him her bulging breasts. Tommy chuckled, and Helena tried her best to do so too.

* * *

The warm water streamed over Helena's naked body, the caked blood on her face washing away in a murky jet of crimson.

Her head was balanced on the tiled wall, her frame twisted awkwardly, the remnants of her beautiful face staring directly up at the shower head. The water pooled onto her jagged features, and washed over the rock, before splattering onto the floor.

When she was finished, she wrapped a towel around her body, and stepped out of the room.

* * *

With the same rag she had been using for a week, Helena washed down James. She couldn't see him, but held his hand with her free hand. She intermittently checked his pulse to ensure he was still alive, and silently prayed that he would make it, and live a better life than the nightmare he currently endured. The doctors had a new term for his illness—*'mora corporis syndrome'*, or quite literally 'body on pause', and that was a phrase that summed up this whole experience.

It was such a stupid mistake, one that plenty of young men had made. Mixing recreational drugs on a hazy night out, celebrating one of his best friend's birthdays. He had fallen into a coma later that night, and to this day, Helena couldn't shake her last words to him.

One day, you'll have to take some responsibility and look after yourself.

She hoped that this statement would become true, that he could indeed look after himself one day. When she was long gone, after the treatment, maybe he would regain at least a semblance of his normal life back.

After finishing up stroking his body with the rag, she gently backed out of the room for the last time.

Helena sat in her kitchen, struggling to breathe. Propped up on a stool in the middle of the room, her head raced with nightmarish thoughts.

What if she died and Tommy didn't keep up his end of the bargain? What if he left with the diamond and the money and left James to die in his own filth?

What if he was caught and imprisoned for murdering her? Would James be dragged into the care system, ripped away from the chance of the treatment?

She tried to calm her mind, though her increasingly hazy thoughts suggested she didn't have much time left. The rock was growing backwards as well as forwards, and she was sure it was slowly encroaching onto her brain stem.

With perfect timing, the front door squeaked open, and Tommy announced his arrival.

"Helena, babe?"

After a slight pause, she responded, and Tommy slowly entered the room.

"I'm so sorry love. God I wish I could help. Are you sure we can't get you to the docs?"

"No." Helena snapped. "This needs to be private, and I need you to stick to the plan. Please."

Tommy nodded in agreement.

"Do you have the paper?" Helena ordered.

Tommy withdrew a contract from his backpack. Though it would hold no kind of real legal weight, it made Helena slightly happier to be signing an official agreement. It was the best she could ask for, given the circumstances.

"I wrote it exactly as you asked," Tommy explained. He grabbed a pen, and tucked it between Helena's fingers, presenting the page to her on the back of a phone book, so she could sign.

She scribbled her name on the dotted line, aided by Tommy's direction, and he slipped it right back into the bag.

"And love, you're a hundred percent sure? I've never done anything like this."

"You're my only option Tommy," she answered. "You're the only one I trust."

Tommy smiled.

"From webcam wanks to this, who could have imagined?"

Helena returned the smile, her lips distorted by the imposing, jagged rock.

Tommy slipped a syringe from his backpack onto the floor, and took off the protective lid.

"I managed to get my sister to sneak this out for me. I don't know if it will work, but worth a try."

He plunged the needle into her neck, and her face grimaced slightly.

She immediately felt a wave of euphoria, a transcendent feeling of calm which washed over her and dampened the pain she had felt for the best part of a month. The burning tingling faded away, and she slumped back on the stool.

Tommy helped lower her to the floor, and rested her head on a pillow from the living room. The intermittent beeps from James' room slowly dissolved into the atmosphere, and Helena's mind was finally at rest. She could still feel, but none of it was real any more.

Moments later, after checking her responses with small scratches to her neck, Tommy began to slice the outline of the rock with a razor-sharp scalpel. Blood and pus erupted from her chalky skin, and the rock began to slowly loosen.

Helena felt the warm waves of blood on her face, but the pain was so distant, it was like she was out of her body, experiencing the entire thing from a different perspective.

Tommy started to dig at the skin around the crystal, and applied pressure to jiggle it slowly out of position.

Like having a tooth pulled under anaesthetic, Helena could feel the blunt tugging motion, as her skull started to give up the rock, her brain being bashed around in its place.

It wasn't loose enough yet. Tommy started to carve the muscle away, grimacing at the sight of his friend's mutilated face, frothing with blood as he ripped away chunks of wet flesh.

Finally, the incision was deep enough, and the object was ready to be taken.

"I'm sorry love. Rest easy."

Helena was most of the way gone now, experiencing only vibrations and light, slowly slipping into the next world, finally at peace.

Without further warning, Tommy tugged with all of his strength. With the sound of crushing bone and tearing meat, the rock slushed out of her skull, leaving a trail of gore and gunk. Tommy gagged, managing to hold his nerve, and slipped the basketball-sized stone into his backpack. He stared at Helena's mangled, crushed head, and knew it was an image that would never leave his mind.

But he would keep his promise. He would sell this rock and pay for her brother's treatment. He'd even help find him somewhere to live in the interim, it's the least he could do.

But he'd be taking an 80/20 split... of course.

HEAL

It was a long way down to the floor... But Leah had already climbed this far, there was no point in backing out now.

Jamie and Todd were way ahead of her, already exploring the dilapidated remains of the Egglemore Hospital reception, their flashlight teasing a whole host of decay. The space had a heavy damp smell, owing to the years of stagnant rainwater sloshing around at ground level.

Leah turned carefully on the broken wall ledge, letting her legs dangle, carefully transferring her body weight downwards. Her blistered fingers gripped the brick, releasing as soon as her frame was perpendicular to the wall.

She fell for a few seconds, before landing in a practiced crouch. Large chunks of crumbled brick followed her, smashing on the floor and disintegrating on impact. She momentarily held her hand over her head for protection, and swiped a torch from her backpack when the danger had passed.

"You good?" Jamie called out.

Leah nodded, dusting herself down, and joined the boys. Her nose had started to trickle with blood, but she quickly swiped it away, not wanting the pair to worry.

The reception had a cracked green and white colour scheme, with a few rows of peeling pleather chairs, a faded wooden desk, and gutted light fixtures. Glass and litter were scattered across the floor, displaced by each shuffle of the explorers' feet.

"What route are we taking?" Todd asked Jamie.

"The notebook says right ahead," Leah remarked, holding said book open and flicking through its dusty, watermarked pages.

"If we go a different way, we could get stuck."

And they didn't want that... This hospital had no cellular service at any level of the interior structure, and unlike most derelict buildings—which came complete with security company, guards, and various safety features—this location had a history of freak accidents and deaths, so wasn't afforded the same protection.

Leah had procured the notebook after searching several used book stores, having discovered a few old scans of its pages on niche blog site Urbexjunkies.

Urbexjunkies.com was a site full of urban explorers from across the globe who offered tips, photo stories of adventures, and a forum, all within a social networking platform. Leah was a pretty recent subscriber to the site, but Jamie and Todd were original members.

The Egglemore Hospital was the holy grail of urban exploration. The trio had driven four hours to get there, and were on a mission to be the first explorers to ever reach the healing garden. Legend had it the garden was full of rare wild plants which had untold healing properties, but was completely entombed in concrete when the complex shut down. Two past members had tried to crawl through the constricted, seemingly makeshift tunnels on past visits, but had both lost their nerve just a few minutes in. They had taken the notebook back with them as a souvenir, but sold it on when they realised it had no real worth... To them, anyway.

Leah slipped the notebook into her backpack, and took the lead. She wasn't go to lose her nerve, and she was pretty damn hopeful Jamie and Todd wouldn't either. Her life depended on it.

* * *

Leah remembered the first time she got sick. Fresh in from work and making a fancy spaghetti bolognese, she noticed a drip of red down her blouse. The recipe called for a copious amount of red wine, so she had presumed she'd been a little vigorous adding it in—before feeling the blood streak down from her nostrils.

Since her diagnosis, doctor after doctor had given her a death sentence, with varying timescales: two years, one year, four months, a week. It was impossible to tell with such a rare disorder, they had explained, but she was a ticking time bomb and would probably fail to see her twenty-fifth birthday.

She had searched the internet far and wide for answers and miraculously happened upon *Urbexjunkies* and the low-res scans of the notebook. The healing garden was a last ditch attempt at saving her life. It was a huge shot in the dark, but she was willing to give it a go.

* * *

Notebook Journal Entry - Wednesday 7th September, 1983 - Doctor James Ray

"The garden is coming together nicely. A variety of wild flora from Egglemore county has been propagated in this facility, and it has taken to the soil well. These plants will soon be extinct in the local area, due to a flurry of new housing developments. My intention is to protect and continue breeding these plants, and experiment with their natural healing properties, which are little known to local residents. With a little luck, we may be able to cure some of the more complex ailments we see at Egglemore, particularly diseases of the mind."

* * *

The trio had entered the hospital from an access point at the rear, scaling a rusty gate, breaking down a thick wooden panel, and shattering the glass of a dusty conservatory.

According to a hand-drawn map in the notebook, they would need to drop down to the basement, bypassing a network of obliterated rooms above them, and resurface through a steep, cramped tunnel. This led straight into the garden, via a drain access plate.

The basement was dark and dingy, as expected, and the rainwater completely engulfed the friends' feet and shins. The rotten damp smell was overwhelming, and the scuttling sound of insects was more than unnerving.

"This place is a wreck. No wonder people don't come here," Todd complained.

"You guys don't have to come any further, I appreciate you helping me get this far," Leah said.

The boys looked at each other and shook their heads.

"Don't be stupid. We're gonna be the ones to get in there. Do you know the bragging rights we'd have?"

Leah smiled.

"Oh, and obviously helping save your life and that too," Todd said.

After five or so minutes traversing the access tunnel, they reached what seemed to be a dead end. A menagerie of different materials had been piled up to create a barrier. Doors, concrete blocks, metal panels, all forced into a Tetris pattern.

"No wonder no-one has ever made it through. How are we going to move this?" Jamie said.

Leah shook her head. Todd joined her.

"I guess bit by bit," Jamie concluded.

It took the trio around three hours to move all of the material, tugging at broken edges, heaving the remarkably heavy blocks, smashing up the wood to create wedges, allowing them to manipulate bigger piles of rubbish out of the way.

When all was said and done, they took huge pride in stepping through the section of tunnel, unexplored for many years. The physical toll of moving all of the furniture had worn them out, so they moved at a slower pace than when they first entered.

They walked another ten minutes or so, and came up to another dead end. However, just above them, there was an opening in the ceiling. A vertical tunnel this time, which would no doubt lead to the garden… finally.

The actual entrance to this tunnel was fairly sizeable, and the remnants of an access ladder clung onto the enclosure. The rusted metal fragments on the floor in front of them had presumably been the top part of the ladder.

"Any takers?" Leah asked.

* * *

Leah was first in the tunnel. At five feet tall and 100 pounds, she was slender and easily slithered through the first segment of the opening. Se scaled the last rungs on the ladder, and called down to the others.

"I'm coming up to the brick. Get ready to catch me if I fall."

With pinched fingers, she dug into the brick, slotting her digits in between the crumbling gaps. After a couple of mighty heaves, the rest of the crevice started to narrow, so much so that she didn't need to grip too hard with her hands. She writhed, forcefully squeezing her hands above her body, so that she was leading with her fingers, and not her head.

Leah dragged her bare elbows against the brickwork, desperately trying to drag herself through the miniature aperture. With outstretched fingers, she tried to claw her way at the same time, but she was well and truly stuck. The cold, brittle masonry was digging into her ribs, and brief inhalations were the only respite from the compression.

"Come on mate! You can do it!" Jamie called from below.

With a small flicker of encouragement, she dug her trainers into the wall, and extended her toes as much as possible. Her body grated against the brickwork, scuffing already-tender elbows, but she shifted a few inches. Using the same technique, she managed to squeeze herself up to the drain door, and she could feel the bare metal on her fingertips.

"Fuck! We're gonna make it!" Todd screamed.

With a final deep breath, Leah kicked against the brickwork, her calves on fire, and shoved against the door. It gave way ever so slightly, a heavy metal creak echoing down the tunnel.

"That's good, do it again Leah!" Jamie said.

Leah didn't hesitate—with one final slam, she lunged against the cover, and it tumbled over on its edge, leaving a circular aperture free to climb through. Before she could celebrate, she lost her footing, grazing her arms as she fell back several inches. Her body had been manipulated into an unusual shape, which had allowed her more space to breathe, and gravity took advantage of this loophole. With lacerated fingers, she crawled back up towards the daylight, and grasped either side of the hole, hauling her body weight up and into the garden.

Sweating and breathless, Leah looked up, and was treated to an absolutely astounding sight. She peeled down to her vest and jeans, discarding her jacket on the floor.

* * *

Notebook Journal Entry - Friday 7th September, 1984 - Doctor James Ray

"It's the one-year anniversary of the garden. The outdoor space has been a hit with patients and visitors alike, who enjoy sitting on

the benches and breathing in the fresh air, looking at the plants. The selection is otherworldly, and we have managed to infuse the soil with a new chemical fertiliser, which has enhanced the saturation of the colour, and transformed the plants into something completely spectacular. No other plants exist like this in the world, we have created a new species which will put the hospital on the map, and hopefully attract extra funding. We've also made steps in extracting chemicals from the plants, and are preparing to use the first of these extracts in a trial in the New Year."

* * *

The whole trio had now surfaced, and were looking at the natural display in front of them, completely awestruck. The vegetation was extraordinary: neon blue petals adorned furry yellow stalks, red bulbous lumps grew atop almost completely transparent leaves. Backdropped by the decaying, frayed structure, and remnants of mid-80s décor, the plants were thriving, the open air room providing just the right amount of light and moisture.

Jamie and Todd took selfies around the garden, ready to brag online about their adventure, and the fact they were the first explorers from UrbexJunkies to get into the complex.

Leah slid down to the floor and ripped open the notebook, flicking through until she reached a page in the middle. A photograph slipped out, which she had been using as a bookmark. The vintage Polaroid was of Doctor Ray himself, standing in front of the garden with a smile on his face. The colours had faded and the photo itself was pretty tatty, but it came with the book, so Leah thought she would keep in intact.

On the page, there were a series of skillfully drawn diagrams of each flower and its various mutation stages. The trio marked each one off with a pencil, spending the best part of an hour matching the images to their real-life counterparts. Then it was time to get down to business.

Leah stood in front of the tangle of flora in front of her, carefully studying the shapes, colours and properties of each individual plant.

"What are you looking for?" Todd asked inquisitively.

"According to these instructions, *villosus circum,* which is like blue and round, with tiny yellow spikes. And this other one."

She showed Todd the notebook, pointing to an unnamed specimen, which was neon green, with yellow, furry leaves.

They spent a few minutes examining the selection, before finally landing upon a bountiful crop of both species. Leah reached out and grabbed the first, grazing the tiny spikes and admiring its bulbous shape.

"Let's get this party started," she said.

* * *

Notebook Journal Entry - Tuesday 15th January, 1985 - Doctor James Ray

"The first trial was an overwhelming success. The concoction below has saved a woman in her mid-30s, who was surely on her way to an early death, in the most curious manner. I will continue to study her progression, before writing out the entire process, but below are the plants I used in her treatment. We are onto something big here, I just know it. This notebook will form the basis of one of the biggest steps in our evolution in recent history."

Instructions

- *2 of the villosus circum plants (rounded body, blue colouring with small yellow spikes)*
- *1 of the currently unnamed stipula viridi species (saturated green colour, yellow, furry leaves)*

1. *Crush the villosis circum, capture the red juices inside and administer through mouth*
2. *Tear the leaves from the viridi species, fold and administer for patient to chew*
3. *The stalk from the latter plant should be squeezed, the juice captured and rubbed on the tongue*

* * *

Leah was already onto the third part of the process, gently rubbing the juice from the stalk across her tongue.

Jamie and Todd stared, half-expecting her to turn into a superhero, half-expecting her to die from poisoning. Luckily for them all, neither of those things happened.

"There," Leah said.

"Feel anything?"

"No. Not yet. Just got a horrible, sour taste in my mouth now."

She plucked another few plants, and threw them into her backpack, just in case she needed different ones later down the line. If she didn't, they'd make great souvenirs.

"Well, that must mean it's lunch time," Todd said enthusiastically, ripping a metal lunchbox from his bag.

"I bought sandwiches, tortilla chips, grapes, and yoghurts."

"What a weird choice," Jamie teased, before grabbing a tin foil-wrapped sandwich. Leah did the same.

"Thank you," she said.

Partway through demolishing their overdue lunch, the three of them froze in their positions. The most ungodly screech emanated from underneath them, similar to the one in the hallway, but much louder… and much closer.

Leah jumped to her feet, dropping the rest of her sandwich, and stalked over to the access panel on the floor. On cue, a second scream blared through the concrete shaft, deep and wet and definitely not human.

"We need to find another way out," she instructed.

"Why are you so rattled?" Todd asked. "It's obviously just an animal."

Leah was already scouting the area, peering around concrete walls and through windows to ascertain the best direction. The garden sat in the middle of the complex, flanked by three hallways, with the fourth side blocked by a dead end. The access tunnel underneath was a no-go, due to the creepy animal, so they'd have to choose a different direction.

"Fuck," Todd moaned, holding his bleeding hand tight. He had touched one of the sharper-looking plants, and paid the price for his curiosity. His blood dripped onto the soil, and then onto the paved ground.

"I have a plaster in my backpack, one second." Jamie said.

Leah was just about to announce her decision when a third, deadly scream echoed from below. This one was much deeper, much creepier, and more concerning. It sounded human, in a way. It wasn't an animal at all.

"What the fuck is that?"

Todd dared to poke his head over the access tunnel, which was wide open to whatever was underneath them. He slowly rose and turned his face to the others.

"I think we should go."

* * *

Notebook Journal Entry - Thursday 7th March, 1985 - Doctor James Ray

"I think I was a little too eager with my progression to bigger experiments. The first test subject is radiant, doing very well, and I have administered the same treatment to half a dozen other

patients. The board have even agreed to fund two more years of the experiments. However, I decided to perform an experiment on myself, due to having very few subjects available at the moment.

I ate the skin from one of the currently unnamed plants today, a beetroot-like bulb which grew directly in the soil. I am now vomiting twice an hour, having dizzy spells when I stand, and have blood seeping from my right eye. There may even be a small infection underneath. As a precaution, I plan to destroy this species in the next cycle. If it were to get into the wrong patient's hands, they could do some real harm. I only consumed a small fragment of the peel, a larger dose would surely be fatal."

* * *

Leah smashed the window into one of the adjacent hallways, and the two boys climbed in directly after her. The room contained a clutter of vintage treatment apparatus, a storage facility that had fallen deeper into decay than the rest of the complex.

Todd grabbed an old scalpel from the ground, and span back to the window, raising it towards the shattered glass frame.

"What did you see?" Leah asked. She shuddered directly after asking the question.

"We need to find an exit," he replied, unwilling to give up any other information.

Jamie sprinted to the back of the room, but the door was blocked by a pile of dilapidated equipment.

"This might take a while."

Without either of the boys noticing, Leah propped herself against a table, her body abundant with pain. Her skin felt itchy, too taut, too dry. She loosened her jacket, scratching her stomach through her vest.

An unusual sensation erupted underneath her skin, and

suddenly, a large patch of her chest separated with a juicy squelch. It was only a few millimetres, but a large trickle of blood spat from the laceration. Leah screamed, and Todd turned to face her.

To an observer, it would have looked like a cut or normal laceration. But Leah felt the two sides of her body begin to separate, like opposing ends of a magnet. She screeched in shock, trying to dampen her outburst to avoid drawing attention to the trio, but completely overwhelmed by the sight.

* * *

Notebook Journal Entry - Friday 8th March, 1985 - Doctor James Ray

"I don't feel good. Anger is overwhelming me. The other patients are still doing well, but I believe I have made a big mistake.

One of the patients STOMPED on the plants today. On purpose. I argued and explained to my manager, but he wouldn't tell her off.

So I BIT her right on the face. Took a chunk clean out of her face. What is happening? What is wrong with me? Why do I want to bite people... I want to taste them.

* * *

"Aaaarrrrgh!"

Leah flailed, her skin inflamed and yellow. The separation had torn her from head to midsection, a tear that was slowly fighting its way open. Blood and mucus was seeping from the laceration, and a squelchy mass of flesh had blown through her stomach.

With absolutely awful timing, the mysterious scream erupted again. But this time, each and every one of them saw what it was standing outside the shattered window, stalking the wonderful garden.

And Leah knew exactly who it was.

From the photo…

Doctor James Ray.

James and Todd started to heave the equipment out of the way of the door, and had cleared the way, just in time for Doctor Ray to be halfway through the window, his milky eyes trained on Leah's bloody wound.

The trio bounded through the hallway, whilst Leah forced her skin back together with stiff fingers. The flappy flesh felt unreal, as if a silicone suit had been around her real body the whole time. Agonisingly painful, Leah was trying to control her breathing to keep her calm, and avoid any more of the skin pulling away.

Faded signs adorned the hallway, each suggesting a random destination, but not an exit from this place. All of the windows were boarded up, and the corridors merged into a maze of indistinguishable architecture. Eventually, with a mix of tiredness and fear, Jamie took a sharp left and slammed his mass against a random door. Todd joined him, but Leah couldn't. She slipped onto the wall, half-standing and half-sitting, her skin slipping from her in two halves, her shell flayed. Underneath the stripped flesh, a wet, hairless being was slowly growing.

Leah tried to breath, envisaging getting out of the complex and emerging as a brand new person. She'd had no idea what would happen when she ingested the plant, and though her skin was quite literally falling off, it didn't feel *wrong.*

Beneath the rot and danger of her old vessel, she could feel something emerging. Something fresh, something new. Something unharmed by the world.

But there wasn't time to think about that yet.

* * *

Notebook Journal Entry - Sunday 10th March, 1985 - Doctor James Ray

"Plants and angry Ray seemed a jolly way forwardsss, i ray dont know the bloody stripes on my hands annd jolly ray no jolly, angry. falls off ray, isnt right medicine i need it. i angry forward go——

That was the last entry in the journal. The rest was torn out.

* * *

"What the fuck is this? Is that her?"

Todd and Jamie couldn't believe their eyes.

They had broken into the room, a small treatment centre, funnily enough.

Leah was plopped on the dirtied bedsheets, her skin slipping from her bones, but something even more disturbing was waiting underneath.

Her bag was discarded to the side, the notebook peering out the top of it.

Her shell was separating, but a brand new Leah was emerging. Like a Russian doll, the casing had been stripped away, and a hairless, smooth and wet body was waiting. It's eyes were flickering open, confused, and Leah's former body was already decaying. The new Leah was breaking through, like a butterfly. To her, the old skin was just a suit that she had grown too big for, and she was shedding it away.

And after a few minutes, the new her smiled.

Naked, shiny, and new, Leah had no hair or eyebrows, and glistened with a wet sheen.

* * *

Doctor Ray slammed against the treatment room door, splashing a torrent of chunky bile up the chipped wood. The man existed only in name and vague facial features—his skin was mottled and mutilated with various gashes and cuts.

"FEED!" he screamed, slamming against the door again, before snatching his head down into his forearm, and tearing a chunk of flesh away with cracked teeth. A host of similar bite marks, at various grades of decomposition, lined his arms.

Inside the room, Todd and Jamie were by the door, reinforcing it with a desk chair and small table.

"This isn't going to hold!" Todd screamed.

Leah sat up, her new body glistening under the overhead skylight. She wore her former vessel as a skirt of sorts, the flesh still wrapped around the bottom of her stomach and legs, but fully discarded from her shoulders. Leah examined her new body, the smooth skin, bald head, and eyebrows. But she didn't seem concerned at all... she seemed overjoyed. Perhaps the pain had gone or perhaps she was in some kind of trance, but the very sight of her metamorphosis was too strange, too unexplainable. Jamie switched between staring at her and the door, overwhelmed by the two scenes unfolding at once. Todd was also panicking, but tried to keep his cool, searching for a way out.

"This isn't working!" Jamie wailed.

"Stop screaming," Todd said, notably quieter than Jamie. "The only way we get out of this is by being clever. Can we get through the skylight?"

Leah looked up. The boys followed.

"No," she muttered, staring at the reinforced glass, and making a decision without any real information.

"We're going to die. Oh fuck me!" Jamie wailed.

"Shut up man. We're not going to die. There has to be a way out."

"There's nothing here," Leah groaned, adjusting to her new body, cracking bones and stretching muscles.

"Then I'll go out there," Todd said.

"Don't be stupid. You won't make it," Jamie warned, but before he could even end his sentence, Todd had pulled the chair out of the way, and had the door halfway open. Jamie fell back to the treatment bed, and stared as Todd stalked around the door, disappearing into the darkness.

* * *

Doctor Ray had gone, leaving only the smear of his bodily fluids on the wall. Todd paced quietly, the soles of his trainers gently compressing with each step. The silence was unsettling; no buzz of electricity or cheerful birdsong to listen to, just the awkward emptiness, the total absence of sound.

Another step forward.

Todd's breath felt too loud. He tried to regulate his breathing, squeezing his lips shut and using his nose to inhale.

RAAAAAAAAAARRRR.

From the other end of the hallway.

The sound tore through the silent air, but Doctor Ray was nowhere to be seen.

Todd turned his head left, and right… Circled his position, checking every angle.

Another step forward.

He wasn't there.

The door to the treatment room slid open, a crack of light escaping. Todd could see Jamie's eyes peering from behind the wood. Todd felt exposed in the desolate hallway, and suddenly wished he had grabbed a weapon of some kind.

Another step forward.

He was nearing the middle of the hallway, studying the walls to see if anything stood out, offering any hope to this nightmarish situation. On a small pinboard, a montage of old letters and notices were strewn across the space. Todd meant to pay attention to his surroundings, but was drawn in by a headline.

"Mysterious illness spreads in Egglemore Hospital: what you need to know."

The body of the text was too small to read. He carefully leaned in, his face almost touching the notice, trying hard to read the text.

RAAAAR!

This time, Doctor Ray was right behind him.

With a wet slap, he knocked Todd to the floor, throwing him into the stained wood. The boy's head pounded the surface, his forehead splitting with a cavernous laceration. Todd's arms sprawled out towards the treatment room, where Jamie's eyes were still peering out, petrified, but he couldn't reach them.

He couldn't reach anything.

Doctor Ray grabbed his ankles, and with unwavering strength, lifted him from the floor, and rammed him back into the ground face first. Todd let out a squeal, and the doctor did the same thing again.

Jamie heard Todd's spine shatter with the impact. The treatment room door was now wide open, and Jamie was on the floor reaching out into the hallway. But it was too late.

Doctor Ray heaved him from the floor, with superhuman strength, and dug his teeth right into the boy's neck, severing a chunk of flesh and devouring it whole. The light in Todd's eyes extinguished just as the Doctor grabbed another wet mouthful.

"FEEEED!"

* * *

Jamie grabbed the bag, his heart beating out of his chest, and Leah followed him out into the hallway. Doctor Ray was deep into his feed, and it gave them just enough time to bypass him and sprint in the other direction.

Leah stopped momentarily. Reaching down, she pulled her legs hard against the skin suit, and the rest of her previous body slid right away, folding onto the floor in a wet slush. All that was left now was the new Leah, her naked, glistening body, a picture of perfect health. Jamie quickly stripped off his jacket and wrapped it around her. They quickly stole a glance at the map in the notebook, and formulated a way out, diving back into their run as soon as they saw an exit.

Doctor Ray's terrifying scream echoed through the hallway, suggesting he'd finished with Todd and was looking for his next meal. The pair sprinted hard, passing through treatment rooms, a reception, various hallways, and a dining hall.

Then they reached the exit.

It was completely demolished, the room behind it had caved in, leaving nothing but a landslide of rocks.

They were trapped.

* * *

Doctor Ray was close, Jamie knew it.

They were both hiding in a small storage closet, illuminated by a couple of strips of light which entered through cracks in the ceiling. They consumed the last of the leftover lunch with their bare hands.

"Do you feel better, at least?" Jamie joked.

Leah nodded. Better was an understatement. She was quite literally a new person.

"Are you still... *you.* Do you think?"

Leah took a few second to mull that over. She certainly felt the same. Her memories were intact, she felt the exact same fears, like, dislikes, emotions... But no pain.

She nodded, having come to a decision.

"Yes. I am."

Leah reached into her bag, and took a big bite out of an apple. It was horribly sour, but she took tiny bites and swallowed.

Moments later, she remembered that she hadn't even packed an apple.

This was a plant. It was pinkish, and looked like a bulb of beetroot. Something she had plucked by accident. Little did she know, she had made the exact same mistake that Doctor Ray had all those years ago.

Little did she know that they would be trapped in that storage closet, fearful for their lives, for over twenty-four hours, whilst Doctor Ray stalked outside, waiting for a chance to sink his teeth into them both.

Little did she know that after those twenty-four hours, she would start getting angry.... Getting hungry...

Little did she know that whilst Jamie kept opening the door and getting met with an angry monster, causing himself to spoil his pants and ration the last few tortilla chips and drink his own urine, that she wouldn't feel any of those things. She didn't share those problems.

Little did she know that whilst they both hid from the flesh eating creature outside, another one was transforming right in that storage closet. Right inside her. One combination of plants had saved her, offered her a new life. The other was snatching it right back. Nature knew best, she thought to herself. There was always balance, no matter how much humans fucked with it.

Little did she know that Jamie would taste so juicy... So

succulent… Enough for ten feeding times, all on her own, to the dismay of hungry little Doctor Ray outside.

Once there was no more Jamie, she would start to consume the flesh from her arms.

When she'd had enough of that, she would start on Doctor Ray.

No thoughts rattled around her head now, just a simple instruction…

FEED.

DOUG

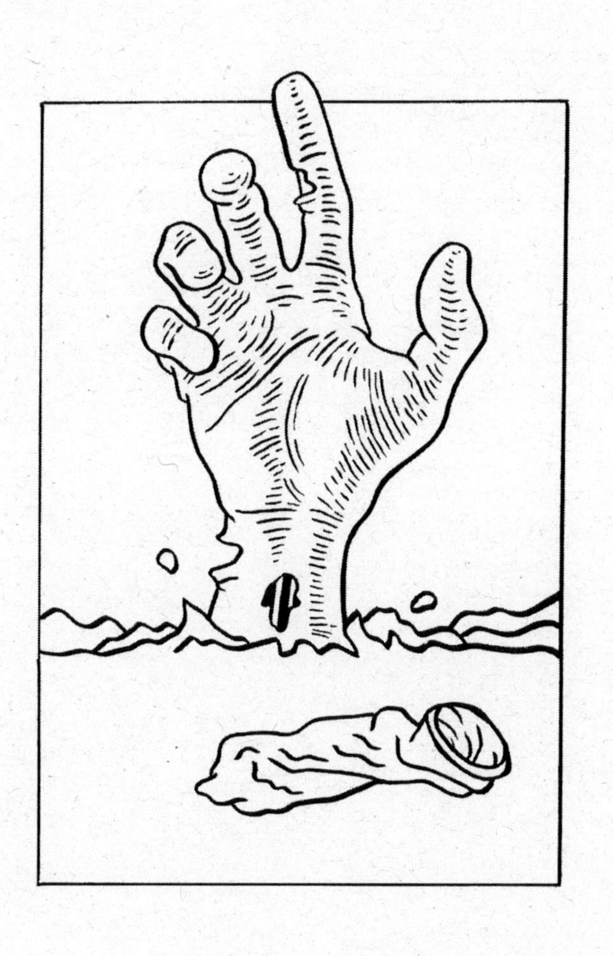

"I should have known you would do this again," Dan spat, dragging his hands through his hair frustratedly. He paced around the living room, bouncing in a different direction each time he met an obstacle, like an old DVD player menu.

Jen stood with tears dripping down her face, although Dan knew these weren't for real. She was trying to make him feel sorry for her.

He stopped moving for a moment, staring at his wife with a mix of confusion and anger. There was an acidic feeling in his chest, his lunch making its way up through his oesophagus, ready to be spewed out. But he held it in. He had too much to say.

"Four years, Jen. Four years, and this is the second time you've cheated. What the fuck is wrong with you?"

She started to fake-wail, the least convincing sadness he had ever seen, an amateurish display of spiteful self-pity. Jen seemed to clock his indifference after just a few moments, so she moved to her backup plan—the offensive.

"How do you think I feel? Having to find intimacy outside of my home? I'm lonely Dan!" she shrieked.

Dan started pacing around the room again, this time extending his maze-like journey in and out of the kitchen, continuing to scratch his head and rub his eyes. He stuttered a few times, and then shook his head.

"And these are just the times I know about. You could be jumping on random men's dicks all day."

"How dare you!" she replied. That obviously hit a nerve.

"We were trying for a baby, Jen. Thank fuck you aren't pregnant, who knows who the Dad would be."

Dan was boiling over, sweat rising above his collar, dampening the creases in his neck. His hands were slimy, nails scratching into his skin. He bit his lip between words, indenting the flesh with his front teeth, ready to peel away the membrane slice by slice.

"Don't be stupid! I used protection!" she whined.

"Oooh thank God for that! It doesn't fucking matter anyway, you're obviously barren!"

That phrase landed like a tonne of lead. A painful silence dampened the room, and without a further word, Dan slid out of the front door, slamming it behind him.

* * *

Dan took a seat towards the edge of the pub, distancing himself from the rowdy table of builders at the bar. He slid open an app on his phone and studied the menu selection, before deciding upon a pint of craft ale.

Whilst he waited, he opened up his phone's messaging app, scrolled to the bottom and entered a hidden menu: *"Deleted Messages".*

There were only three messages in this mailbox, but Dan knew exactly what he was looking for. It was dated almost seven years ago, and contained a very simple body of text:

Shapton Woods, SM38 APB. 3 mins from entrance, turn left, look for the signpost.

The contact hadn't been saved, instead presenting as a string of random numbers. Dan kept reading the text over and over, before clicking on the contact number. It opened with a new message option, and for a moment or two, his finger hovered over his keyboard.

"Beer?"

Dan looked up to find a young waitress leaning over his table, clutching his drink.

"Uh, yeah, thanks."

She placed it on a coaster, smiled, and sauntered back

over to the bar, greeted by wolf-whistles from the young trade crew hanging around the area.

He took a big gulp of the beer and let his phone slip into standby mode.

The pub had a stale yet inviting vibe to it, inhabited mostly by locals and the occasional tourist or out-of-towner. Dan didn't enjoy chain haunts, and most of the town had been refurbished into one or another now, so this was one of the few he felt comfortable in.

It still had a jukebox machine—and not a fancy digital one at that. One with well-worn vinyls which reached as contemporary a period as 1990. An old pop track was blurting from the tinny speakers, and Dan remembered it vaguely as the song which hit number one when he was born. He had found that out in a pub quiz, funnily enough. Probably in that very pub, a few weeks back, joined by Jenny and her friends.

Jenny... Talk of the devil.

A few messages rang up in his notifications at once, lighting up his screen with little green bubbles.

(Jenny): We need to talk. Where are you?

(Jenny): I'm coming to the pub. Message me if you're there.

(Jenny): I'm leaving now. Be 15 mins.

(Jenny): Do you have your phone? Answer me before I waste my time walking. You better be there.

Crap. They were all delayed, owing to the shitty wifi, so he was almost out of time. He wasn't about to have this argument in the middle of the only pub he liked in a five-mile radius, so it was time to drink up.

He gulped the rest, let out a gentle burp, and put his coat on.

* * *

A light mist of rain fell softly from the night sky, backlit by street-lamps, like television static.

Dan instinctively turned right, a practiced routine to start his journey home, before doing a double take. He tapped his left foot, trying decide where to go next. He definitely wasn't ready for another confrontation, but he also didn't want to wander around aimlessly, getting wet for the sake of it.

A sinking feeling hit his stomach—not in a worried or apprehensive way, but more of an excitement. His pulse started to race slightly as he withdrew his phone, and reminded himself of the address on the text.

Shapton Woods.

It was a bit of a walk away, maybe twenty minutes, but he could do with the fresh air.

Decision made, he slipped his phone into his pocket, threw up his hood, and started towards the old bridge, most likely missing Jenny by a mere minute or two.

The lighting on the outskirts of town was much dimmer, owing to a lack of foot traffic at any time of day, let alone late on a Wednesday night. Much of the scenery was unchanged since the last time he took this route, but he did register a name change on one or two road signs, and a much safer footpath than had existed back in the day.

Shapton Woods was about another two minutes north, and consisted of a large blanket of forest and picturesque farmland, popular with photographers and nature lovers alike. The footpath twisted into the entrance of the forest, and he recalled the timings in the text message.

3 mins from entrance, turn left, look for the signpost.

He started a stopwatch on his phone, and used the built-in torch to trace his steps. Pace by pace, he clambered through the slightly damp dirt, whilst a flood of memories forced themselves to the front of his mind.

* * *

He was at the signpost, drawn to the exact right location as if fate itself had pushed him there. The smell of fresh rain and moist nature settled in the air, and the light breeze caused his face to blush ever so slightly.

Using his torch, he scanned the area quietly, not wanting to disturb anything that might be trying to sleep. To an outsider, the place would hold no meaning at all. A random patch of woods, surrounded by nothing but trees and foliage, a nondescript segment of natural land no different to any other.

But to Dan, this is the place that informed his early experimentation. The first time he kissed a guy… The first time he kissed anyone, in fact. It was the place of many firsts, and unfortunately in hindsight, many lasts.

Crack.

A twig snapped close by. Dan immediately fumbled for his phone, and pointed it to the floor whilst he tried to turn off the torch.

Only a few feet away, he could see something moving, silhouetted by the light reflecting off of the floor. He snuck behind a tree, and killed the light, squeezing his eyes shut for a few moments.

When he opened them again, his eyes had adjusted to the dark. And what he saw reignited feelings he hadn't had in the longest time.

A guy, no more than thirty years old, leaned against a tree, shorts around his thighs, being absolutely pummeled by an older man. Mouth agape, Dan couldn't help but watch on, half-hoping that they wouldn't see him—although, would it be the worst thing to be asked to join in?

The pace picked up, erupting into a breathless climax. As it all came to a passionate end, both men clocked Dan, smiling and winking at him. The older guy slipped off his condom, discarding it on the ground, and they both went their separate ways. Dan stood for a few more moments, slowly replaying the scene in his mind.

The distant caw of a crow broke him out of the spell. Dan had only had one drink, but perhaps his mind was playing tricks on him—did that really just happen? He didn't want to alert anyone to where he was, so he decided to trek back towards the pub, then to home, promising himself he'd visit again to investigate in the next few days.

* * *

Dan's lower back was on fire. Crumpled into the front seat of his car, his spine was bent well out of shape, and he was paying for it now. With a grumpy groan, he outstretched his legs, forcing him up out of the chair slightly, and then he slumped right back into it.

He decided against sleeping at home the prior evening, instead parking a few roads away to get some shuteye. Still half-asleep, Dan dragged his right hand across the passenger seat, trying to find a bottle of water, but there was nothing there. His throat was dry and itchy.

The road outside was noisier today, with a steady hum of traffic passing his vehicle. Dan buckled himself into the seat, haphazardly wiped away the sleep from his eyes, and started the engine.

He coasted back around to his house, and drove up onto the driveway. The windows in the bedroom were shut, which meant Jenny had already left for work. Dan felt a pang of relief and relaxed his shoulders, fumbling through his keychain to find the front door key.

It slipped into the lock, and just as he was about to turn and release, he heard a clattering inside the house. He withdrew the key, ear pressed to the door, waiting on another warning sign. There was a voice, talking on a phone.

Jenny's voice.

Fuck.

He must have caught her right between shutting the window and leaving for work. Why hadn't he checked the time? Bad move. Really bad move.

She was talking to someone about him; he could tell by the tone of her voice. Dan was due to be job-searching today, but he didn't have his laptop with him. And there was no way he could get it until she had left.

Withdrawn, he dove back into the car, roared up the engine, and drove in the first direction he could think of. In his rearview mirror, he could see Jenny stepping out of the door, looking over at his car curiously. Did she realise it was him? She must have. He would deal with that later.

Subconsciously, he drove right back to the woods, this time pulling into the car park and sliding right up into a space by the entrance. His eyes were tired and fuzzy still, and he could smell his own musk. It wasn't bad, but if you were close enough you could definitely tell he hadn't showered. He didn't mind too much, he wasn't expecting to meet anyone today.

* * *

Dan retraced the footpath, diverted onto the grass and eventually stumbled back into the same area as last night. There was a distinctive smell of burning, mixed with the pungent odour of fertiliser.

He took another look around, searching for signs of other encounters. Several sets of footprints showed people had been and gone since last night; he could tell by the fresh indentations in the mud.

Dan took a few moments to look around, and then froze, listening to an unusual writhing sound emanating from the ground, right by a discarded condom. With an audible gasp, he took another step closer, completely astonished at what he was witnessing.

The majority of a hand was sticking out of the mud, fingers sprawled and reaching for the condom. The rest of the arm was presumably entombed in the dirt still, but these digits were flailing, yearning for the touch of the used rubber.

Up close, the dirtied hand seemed eerily human. The digits moved independently of one another, and were an expected shape and size. In an act of pure defiance, the index finger had managed to catch the insertive end of the condom, and dragged it close. The old semen from inside was now soaking into the ground right on top of it.

Dan grabbed a stick, and gently tapped on the area around the hand. It didn't seem to notice—or care about—his presence, until he tapped a mere centimetre or two away. Following that intrusion of space, it froze up, and half-buried itself back into the dirt, damp from the various liquids swirling in the mud.

"What the fuck is this?"

Crouching down to get a better look, Dan scanned the area around the scene, but couldn't see any sign of digging.

"Hello? Do you need help?"

How had this person got under the mud?

How was he breathing?

Dan instinctively reached into his pocket for his phone, but he had left it in his car. He prodded the digits again, to make sure they were still alive, and sped back towards his vehicle.

"I'll be back!"

* * *

Dan held his phone up to his ear, his arm trembling slightly.

"I swear to God, that's exactly what I saw."

"We'll send someone out to look at it. It was probably an animal of some kind," the voice on the end of the line stated.

And that was it. Call ended.

Dan couldn't stop thinking about someone being trapped in there. He was ready to go out and take a further look, but maybe the call handler was right. Perhaps it had been an animal, and he was just making things up in his head. It had been a rough couple of days, and being back in the woods was an overload on his emotions.

With the key in the ignition and the engine engaged, he decided he would call for an update later in the day.

* * *

Jenny looked at almost everything in the house, but would not make eye contact with Dan. She feigned interest at boring programs on the TV, the social feeds on her phone, and just about everything else, just to avoid talking to him.

The guilt was eating away at her, Dan could tell, but he wasn't going to make the first move. He'd been forced into that position too many times.

His laptop was open, along with a dozen internet tabs all relating to his job search. But Dan was procrastinating, looking at articles about Shapton Wood, trying to uncover any unusual stories or findings about the area. But aside from a couple of *extremely* vague conspiracy theories, he wasn't any wiser than when he had first started to research.

The mood in the house was too intense. Dan couldn't focus in the middle of this stalemate, with Jenny huffing and puffing her way around the room. He desperately needed to set aside some time for a job hunt, but his mind was too scattered.

Fuck it.

Dan slid up from his chair, closed the lid of his laptop, and grabbed his keys.

"I'm gonna find something for dinner," he said, aiming the words in Jenny's general direction without waiting to see if they landed.

The door slammed closed, and he strolled over to his car. He could feel Jenny's eyes watching him from behind the twitching curtain in the living room, but he paid her no attention.

* * *

Dan pulled in to a gargantuan superstore just off the motorway, ten minutes away from his house. In all honesty, he could probably have found some decent ingredients at the shop around the corner, but he wanted time to get lost and think, wander around a little bit.

The store had an imposing structure, an old brutalist building which had been painted a bright white to match the sterile interior. Inside, rows upon rows of fridges and freezers stocked a vast assortment of groceries.

Dan was halfway through the maze-like arrangement, sifting through fruit and vegetables. As he immersed himself in the simple pleasure of shopping on his own, a rowdy group of teens tore up a shelf of bakery items, discarding the food on the floor.

"Hey you!" one of the group shouted to an elderly shop worker. "Come pick this shit up!"

Dan rolled his eyes privately, continuing to sort through the produce.

"Let's go to the woods and see if the queers are there," one of the teens suggested.

"I don't want to see no old men fucking," another replied.

"Nah but we can steal their stuff and blackmail them to get it back. You know most of them have wives and shit."

The group cackled in unison. Their attitude riled Dan up, even more so due to his earlier discovery. What if that person was still there? What if he needed assistance? These jerks weren't going to help.

Dan placed his basket on an empty shelf and scuttled out of the store, hoping to get a head-start. It was probably pure coincidence—the woods were huge, and there were plenty of spots that people could meet—but Dan had a weird feeling about the whole situation.

* * *

The landscape glistened under the summer sun. The air was silent, carrying the sound of insects buzzing and birds chirping. Dan retraced his steps to the inner section of the woodland, the last patch of dry land before things became too wet and muddy.

There was no sign of the teenage group, thankfully, and it didn't seem like the dog walkers were out yet. Dan strolled through the terrain, taking stock of the luscious scenery. He had never been there on such a picturesque day, and it made him grateful to live in such a green area.

He wasn't paying attention to where he was walking, and it wasn't long until he tripped over a lump in the ground.

"AAAAAAAH!"

He regained his balance, and kicked away a pile of loosely stacked leaves. Underneath them, a face erupted from the earth, along with two hands and forearms, which were stuck in place. The person looked as if they had been buried and left there for a very long time. They were up to their jaw in dirt, with only their extremities exposed to the light.

"Don't fucking trample me again!" it warned.

Dan stared, wide-eyed.

"I'm sorry. I didn't see you."

"No shit!"

Dan was speechless, and wasn't quite sure how to react.

"Walking up in here with your giant troll feet. What the fuck."

He was talking to a man… The *thing* that had been under the mud was a real life person. Dan was dreaming. Or hallucinating. Or something else…

"I-I..."

He shook his head for a moment, hoping to rattle a few helpful thoughts into his brain.

"I was looking for you. I thought I saw a hand earlier."

"I'll be lucky if that hand even works now, thanks a lot."

Dan shook his head again. This was completely bizarre.

"I'm Dan. Who are you?"

"I don't have a name. I heard one guy call someone Doug. I like that name, Doug. Call me that."

"Okay, uh. Doug. Good to meet you. Do you need help?" Dan asked.

"No. I'm not stuck." Doug muttered.

Dan squinted at him, and tilted his head.

"But… you're not, *not,* stuck are you? You've been there a while I think."

Against his better judgement, Dan walked right up to him and grabbed an arm, scraping away some dirt to get better leverage.

"What the fuck?" Doug asked, exasperated. "Stop touching me, I do not consent to this."

"What are you stuck in?" Dan said, doing his best to wiggle and release Doug from the dirt.

"You wanna be a bit more fucking careful?"

It was insane. Doug was literally entombed in the mud, and there was no way of budging him even a millimetre. Dan let go, stepped back, and assessed the situation, like a middle-aged man judging the best way to solve a DIY problem.

Doug was flustered. His head and neck were now fully out of the ground, and his arms were mobile. Aside from that, the large majority of him was still underground.

"What's going on?" Dan enquired.

Doug scoffed at the question.

"I've got some stranger trying to dismember me, that's what's going on."

"I'm not a stranger," Dan quipped. "I already told you my name."

Doug rolled his eyes.

"Well thank God! I can talk to you like a friend then Dan... Don't fucking touch me again or I'll throttle you, you little bitch."

Dan was aghast.

"I need to make a phone call. I'll get help."

Dan felt up his pockets, but his phone wasn't there.

"Fuck. It's in my car. I have to go home and charge it for a bit, I don't have a lead. Will you be okay here?"

Doug stared at him, taken aback by the question. He didn't say another word.

Dan nodded, and turned around to leave.

"Fuuuuuuck dude!" Doug shouted.

"Huh?"

"Can you do that turning around thing again? Your ass jiggling looks so fucking good in those jeans."

"I, uh... What?" Dan asked.

"Fuck man, even better, pull them down and show me in 3D."

Doug licked his lips. They both held eye contact for a moment too long, and Dan left immediately.

"Daddy, don't go! Although I love to watch you leeeeeeave."

The echo of his voice followed Dan all the way back to his car. He shook his head, confused, and headed back home.

* * *

Dan plugged his phone into the outlet in the dining room, and set the table for some dinner. He was ravenous, having not eaten for hours. On the way back home, he jumped into the first shop he could find and rustled together some basic ingredients for a quick pasta dish.

In two bowls, he split the food equally (well, almost, he thought he deserved a little more) and took his place at the table. Jenny joined him, begrudgingly, looking him up and down as she started to eat.

The awkward silence was very much still a thing.

"So… This is what took you three hours to find?"

Jenny could still speak after all…

Dan placed his cutlery into his bowl and looked up at her.

"I had a walk as well. Why, did I forget something?"

"I mean you were out for ages, you could have brought back a feast. Instead there's some tagliatelle and sauce. Where have you *really* been?"

Dan cracked his neck, preparing himself for the oncoming onslaught of words.

"I went for a walk Jenny. If that's okay with you?"

She laughed under her breath, shaking her head as she twisted some pasta into a ball with her spoon and fork.

"And another thing… I don't need to explain myself to you of all people, not with what you've done."

Dan scraped his chair out from under the table, and threw a napkin onto his half-eaten dinner.

"I'm going for a shower."

The bedroom was right at the top of the stairs, small yet comfortable. Dan slipped out of his shirt and trousers, discarding them in a pile on the floor, and slid his boxers and socks off. His feet ached, much like the rest of his body, and it was times like this that reminded him he was no longer a young man. He'd been darting in and out of the woods like a young gazelle, with the body of… well, a slightly older and worn out gazelle.

The shower was scorching hot, just how he liked it. He let the water rain down on his face and body, rubbing a peach-scented scrub across his face and chest, and then into his armpits and groin.

His hands were noticeably dirty, and his fingernails had mud residue trapped underneath them, which he excavated with a nail brush as he washed.

Click.

A metallic sound rang from in the bathroom somewhere.

He waited, but it didn't repeat. So he continued to wash.

As he started to massage his lower body, he couldn't help but think of what he saw last night. The two men in the throes of passion, gyrating as one entity. The wink as they clocked him watching them live out their lustful desires. It gave him a rush he hadn't felt in a long time, if ever. And how he wished he would have invited them to wait a little while and show him the ropes for round two.

Click.

What the fuck was that noise?

He didn't have to wait long to find out. The bathroom door creaked open, and a figure stepped in, feet lightly tapping against the vinyl. The shower screen gently rolled open…

Jenny.

She was wrapped in a towel, and looked peaceful and content. Her eyes met his, and she bit her lip, loosening the fabric covering her body.

"I'm trying to shower, Jenny."

Continuing towards him step by step, her face pulled into a grimace.

"Baby, I'm so sorry how I've acted. You look tense, I just want to help."

Dan was uncomfortable.

"I can tell you want me already," she said, nodding down at his penis. He hadn't realised the thoughts had got him so riled up, but he did know that it had absolutely fuck all to do with her standing in front of him.

"It's just because I've been washing, that's all."

"Oh yeah? Let me help wash you, baby."

Jenny dropped her towel, revealing a trim, maintained figure.

"Jenny get dressed," he said, matter of factly. "This isn't helping."

She laughed, completely blindsided by the comment. Her laughter soon turned into discontent.

"Are you scared of my body, Dan? Don't want this anymore?"

"Please get out of the bathroom, I will be done—" Dan started.

"Fucking forget it!"

The door crashed behind her as she stormed out of the steamy room, leaving her towel on the floor. Dan was just relieved to have her out of the way, so he could go back to washing himself in peace, thinking about the sex he really wanted to have. In the past, he would have felt guilty about this scenario, and somehow brainwashed to go back to her with his tail between his legs, begging for forgiveness.

But he hadn't done anything wrong and wouldn't be apologising this time.

Jenny slept on the sofa that night whilst Dan slept alone, relishing the space and freedom.

* * *

Dan got dressed, putting on a white t-shirt and a pair of faded blue jeans. His thoughts drifted to Doug, and the surreal nature of the situation. He was tempted to call someone official to check up on him, but at the same time, he didn't want to be caught out, and it wasn't like the guy was exactly distressed. A bit messed up in the head, perhaps, but harmless.

Maybe he could take him something to eat, get to know him a bit better, and decide from there.

Dan hopped down to the kitchen, and noticed that Jenny was nowhere to be seen. Thank God.

He opened the fridge and took out some butter and cheese, and quickly prepared two sandwiches, stuffing them into a plastic bag and inside his backpack. Dan slid on his jacket and left the house.

* * *

Having not ventured into the woods for many years—for fear of letting his guard down—he had now been there several times in two days. He was doing his best not to be seen, but had already created a whole excuse in his head for if someone did follow or bump into him down there. Though he suspected if they were in exactly the same place, they'd probably have some explaining to do too…

His phone was freshly recharged, and pleasantly devoid of any new messages. Jenny had never acted out like this before, and he imagined it probably signaled the end of their relationship, though the red flags had been flying high long before the latest rift.

Whilst they'd always managed to get along, the sex had always felt a little bit off, and her mood swings were the stuff of legend. He'd managed to work through their relationship by taking plenty of alone time—including jacking off on his own whenever the chance arose—and that seemed to work up until now.

In the same breath, he had never acted like this before. He was always the one to run back and try to make amends, even if he hadn't done anything wrong. There was a term for that—gaslighting? Stockholm syndrome? He wasn't sure which it was, but that attitude was firmly in the past.

Dan was back at the small patch of land, and to his surprise, more of Doug's body—from his head to just below his diaphragm—was now exposed.

"You still sure you don't need a hand?" Dan invited.

Doug grinned.

"Back so soon?"

Dan smiled. He studied the ground again, trying to assess what this guy was really up to, and then looked back up at him.

"It seems so."

"Tell me..." Doug started. "When does it start getting busy down here?"

Dan shook his head.

"I, uh... Well I'm not really a regular, to be honest. I used to be, a bit more, and back then it was weekends."

"What day is it today?" Doug ordered.

"Thursday."

Doug scowled, letting out a huge sigh.

"I brought snacks, I thought you might be hungry out here," Dan said.

Dan took out one of the sandwiches, and extended it out to Doug, though he didn't make an effort to take it.

"If I give you this, will you tell me what's really happening here?" Dan asked.

Doug shook his head.

"I'm not hungry for sandwiches... I'm hungry for juicy cock."

Dan was stunned. Doug noticed this, and started to cackle.

"I'm sure that tastes great, don't get me wrong. But if you unzip your jeans and let me nosh you off, that's what I really need."

"Jesus, dude."

Dan stepped back, and started eating his own sandwich, looking around the landscape.

"Have you been with a guy before?" Doug enquired.

Dan didn't answer, pretending not to hear.

"Hey? I'm talking to you, Dan the man."

He carried on ignoring him, which really frustrated Doug. So much so that he started making the most over the top, dramatic sex noises Dan had ever heard. The moaning echoed across the woodland at an embarrassing volume.

Dan slowly turned towards him, losing his patience.

"Okay fine. Just shut up man... Yes. Yes I have... But I'm with a girl now."

"Oh." Doug stuttered, recoiling. "Why?"

Dan shook his head.

"I thought I loved her... and vice versa."

"Fuck that. Who needs love when we have fucking. Guy fucking!" Doug screamed.

"You don't let up do you? Do you not have a filter?" Dan said.

"No. But I have a legendary mouth." He winked.

Dan stood up, packing away his sandwich. He didn't want

to get caught down here, and with how unhinged Doug was acting, he needed to be ready to run if anyone came to track down the noise. The whole situation was a total mindfuck, and he didn't know what was real or not at the moment.

"I think I'm gonna go," Dan said.

Doug shook his head.

"No, don't do that. Look, I'll be serious for a moment. Look, when I say I need dick… I actually need it. Look at me."

Dan looked over, but didn't notice anything. Doug gestured him towards him, and pointed down at his body.

Doug's midsection seemed glued to the dirt around him, stitched into a root system, the ground undulating with every movement.

"What kind of costume is this?" Dan asked.

Doug sighed.

"I really don't know how to explain it further. Look man, I come from a seed… And I thrive on man seed."

"What are you even talking about, man? Look, I'm not sure if this is performance art or something, or if you're just completely nutty, but I'm done here."

"I'm telling the truth, dickhead."

"Oh yeah? So *if* what you're saying is true, which I very much doubt, how do you know all this shit? If you're just out here growing?"

Doug was getting flustered now, rolling his eyes like a moody brat.

"You don't ask the trees how they know to grow. Or the bees how they pollinate. It's instinctive. It just *is.*"

Dan stared at him for a moment, and then shook his head.

"I'm calling someone."

"Fuck you! No you're not! If you don't wanna help me you can fuck off and die. Or you can be a darling and help me grow out of this fucking ground."

Dan was too tired to be messing around. His whole body still ached, and he wanted to get a good rest this evening. It was a mistake coming down.

"And what does helping you look like?"

"I'm glad you asked," Doug said. "I know that you saw me, that first night... Grabbing the condom."

Dan was silent for a moment.

"Yeah, and what if I did?"

"There are used condoms around. Bring me as many as you can find. The fuller the better. Don't worry if they're old or anything, I don't taste them... well, unless I want to, but honestly I don't have to... But I do like to sometimes."

"You want me to grab dirty condoms and give them to you?" Dan asked, already over the whole situation.

"Yes."

"Really?"

"Yes."

Dan shook his head.

"Fuck you."

He turned to walk away, and Doug started to reenact a symphony of sex noises again, getting louder and louder with each groan.

"Stop that!" Dan ordered.

Doug listened for a moment, before launching into a full-on, over the top rendition that caused the ground to vibrate.

Dan tried to hush him, but it was no use.

"Right. I'm gonna do this for you, then I'm gonna leave. And maybe call someone. This is super fucking weird."

Dan started to look around the area, searching for the dull yellow-white sheen of dirty rubbers. In all of his wildest fantasies, he'd never thought about touching used condoms, let alone doing anything sexual with them. It was enough to make him gag, honestly, but he still felt like helping out. If only to help him procrastinate a bit longer, to avoid going back to his home issues.

The first one was a long, slim find, half full of semen, and covered in dirt and grass. Dan picked it up with pinched fingers, and threw it over to Doug. It split on impact, and the white juice covered his body.

"Fuck yeah! Bukkake baby!" Doug roared.

Dan carried on searching, slowly collecting a menagerie of deposits. He helped soak the soil around Doug in the liquid, and quickly used some hand sanitiser to wash away the sin straight after.

To his surprise, the ground was slowly loosening up around Doug, and after around half an hour, he had managed to squeeze another inch or so of his body out. It was at this point Dan started to get really curious.

Doug's body up until now had looked like any other guy's. Slim, with a slightly hairy chest, unbroken skin. But the newly-revealed flesh was blistered, and seemed to have roots growing into it, seamlessly attached in a weird plant-human hybrid connection. Around the back, there were several tendrils attaching him to the ground, which seemed to pulsate with blood, keeping him nourished and hydrated. He didn't know exactly what he was looking at, but it surely wasn't the human he had been expecting.

"So do you shoot big juicy loads, stud?" Doug remarked.

He giggled, and Dan started to chuckle too. It wasn't until now that Dan had appreciated how handsome Doug was. He had dark hair, a prominent jawline and bright blue eyes. His cheeky demeanour only made him more appealing, though it did wear thin very quickly.

Suddenly, there was a shuffling in the bush. Dan jumped to his feet, looking over both shoulders, trying to trace the sound.

"I have to go," he whispered to Doug.

"No. Don't leave me, I'm so fucking bored!" Doug begged.

Twigs snapped, echoing through the maze of trees.

"I'll come back."

"What if I die first? I don't have nearly enough semen in me yet."

"Well, maybe it's someone looking to cruise?" Dan said.

"Fuck you, man. You don't wanna help me at all."

Dan was stunned.

"What? I just got you all those rubbers!"

"Fuck off. Go die in a hole somewhere I don't care." Doug spat.

Dan took off. Doug stared at his butt as he walked away, his eyes wide and mouth agape.

"Sexy bastard," Doug whispered to himself.

* * *

The house loomed over him, a reminder of a life he had built on rocky foundations. Dan stared at the front door for a while from the vantage point of his car's front seat. He wasn't sure if Jenny was in or not, but he was hoping she was, so they could reach some kind of resolution, and a decision on what was happening with their lives.

As wildly annoying as she was, Jenny had been the only constant in his life for the past four years. Where others had left or abandoned him for the next best thing, she had been by his side. Aside from the two episodes of cheating, of course, which were big rifts, but maybe not entirely irreparable.

He had let lust get the better of him in this situation, and if he was being honest with himself, maybe he just wanted that chance to go out and experience his old life again. To get close to the edge, without having to jump off into a crazy world of casual sex and uninhibited pleasure.

As he walked towards the door, he started to replay some of the good times in his head. Their wedding day. The day they first met each other's parents.

He turned the key in the lock. On the inside, Jenny was sitting on the sofa, replaying their wedding video on the TV. Fate? Or just pure coincidence?

She was balling, real tears this time, perhaps finally coming to terms with the gravity of the fuckup she made.

"You looked drop-dead gorgeous in that dress," Dan said, a peace offering of sorts.

Jenny flipped round, smiling as she saw his face.

"Baby, I'm so sorry. I don't know where to start. I don't know what's happening to me." She started to cry again, a real, no-holds-barred ugly cry.

Dan stepped forward to comfort her.

"Life's just been so crazy, and I thought you were gonna break up with me. So I made it even worse!" she shrieked.

Dan walked into the kitchen, turned the kettle on, and exhaled.

It was the first time he had felt at home in a while, and being able to rest within the confines of his own house—of his own relationship, in fact—was truly remarkable.

They would need to work hard of course. Marriage counselling. Individual counselling. The whole lot. But he was ready to make this work, to really make it work, if she confessed to her sins, and really committed herself to the marriage.

He didn't understand why he was being so forgiving. Perhaps seeing his true fantasy without rose-coloured glasses had been a shock to the system. Dan wasn't in his twenties anymore, and really wanted a home and a base, not to be out in the woods at all hours, hoping for a sliver of interest from a random hookup, using him for his body and discarding him barely minutes afterwards.

Tea prepared, he settled onto the sofa with Jenny. She put her legs over his knees apprehensively, laying across the couch as they always did. The best day of his life played out on the TV, and he cherished this moment, and the opportunity to relive it all again.

* * *

Dan spat a huge glob of toothpaste into the sink, running his brush under the tap and replacing it in its holder. After sharing a few bottles of wine with Jenny over dinner, he was having trouble seeing his surroundings clearly.

He switched off the bathroom light, and ambled into his bedroom, which was just across the hallway. Jenny was getting undressed, struggling with her balance as she tried to slither out of her socks.

Laughing, Dan went to provide some support as she finished getting changed. In what could only be described as a cheesy rom-com moment, they both looked at each other and collapsed into bed.

Jenny climbed on top of Dan, and it wasn't long until he was naked too. Their bodies interlocked, and with a wet thrust, he was inside of her. Like a bittersweet memory, he became enamoured in the moment, lusting for each push, but his mind wandered to her infidelity. He tried to keep up the rhythm, performing as she expected, being the man she needed him to be. But he found himself losing grip, quite literally.

Then he thought of Doug. It was so wrong, but his brain kept diverting to his image. He imagined what it would be like if he was with him instead. What would Doug's expression look like, if Dan provided the answer to every one of his lustful desires?

He didn't last long after that image. The two sweaty

bodies stayed locked together for a moment, until Jenny pecked him on the cheek and hopped off of his appendage, grabbing a towel and heading to the bathroom.

Dan collapsed back onto the bed, body glistening with sweat, imagining what he would say to Doug when he saw him next. Would he explain how riled up the thought of them two having sex got him? Or would he pretend like nothing happened, a little secret to keep locked in the back of his mind when he needed a boost. He didn't know just yet, but he did start to realise that there was some kind of infatuation growing. Dan had to see him tomorrow.

Eyes closed, he fell into a comfortable slumber almost immediately. He heard Jenny stalk in and turn off the light, take a sip of water, and tuck her arm around him. His final thought of the evening is how he would balance home life with his fantasy life. For the first time ever, he wanted to try and satisfy a double life, where he got exactly what he wanted.

* * *

Dan's morning coffee tasted sweeter today. It had been prepared the same way his entire adult life, but something about the serotonin rushing through his veins heightened his senses in a dreamlike way. The world seemed brighter, warmer, happier... Food tasted better, his coffee was on another level. And his fantasies had only become more insatiable.

Laptop open, he was scrolling down a tedious list of job advertisements, all sharing the same lacklustre salary and benefits. He stood up to stretch his legs, already tiring of the job hunt, and traversed the apartment to look for Jenny. It was getting close to time for her to leave for work, and God knows she didn't have any lunch prepared. If she was in a good mood, he might even offer to make it for her, and get some more spousal brownie points.

He clambered up the stairs quietly, listening as a soft voice emanated from his bedroom. It was Jenny, but she was barely above a whisper. It sounded really awkward and unnatural, so he decided to hang back and see if everything was okay.

Against his gut feeling, he pressed his ear up against the door, and started to compress his breathing slightly, so he'd be able to make out the words she was saying.

"I'm not saying that… He's a really good guy. We even fucked for the first time in forever last night."

Dan grimaced, unsure of the context or the contact on the other end of the phone.

"No baby look. We have a really fun thing going. I'm not staying, I told you… I mean, that's what I want. I think. I can't think right now."

Dan's heart dropped into his stomach. He was tempted to smash through the door and take her phone away, and give her a real talking to. But he maintained his composure. There was probably more to come.

"No-one knows my body like you, Troy. You know that I live for our time together. I just need to work this out with Dan. We've been together a while, I don't want to just drop it all on him… I've already chosen! I choose you. Just… Give me some time."

By the last word of the conversation, Dan was already halfway down the stairs. He closed up his laptop, and slipped it into its soft case. The thought of her naked body burned into his mind. He made a mental note to get an STI check at his earliest convenience. God knows what Troy might have passed onto her, and by means of association, him.

"Dan, baby? Are you out of the bathroom?"

Dan scoffed, absolutely livid. He wasn't in the mood for a

fight though, so he called up to say he was indeed out and needed to get to an interview, and that he would see her later.

* * *

The pub was busier that day. Rowdy, full of locals, but definitely more lively than usual. Dan had a beer in front of him that he had barely touched—it was only 11:00am, after all. Day drinking wasn't his style, but he momentarily considered giving it a go.

But his stomach felt funny, his chest burned with acid reflux from the wine the night before, and he just didn't feel it at all.

So he left half the pint on the table and got out of there in a hurry.

* * *

The forest was thick with fog, which settled above the ground and dispersed across the depth of the landscape. The trail was second nature now, and Dan was content with his ability to reach Doug, whether it was day, night, fog or sun. He could hear some kind of scuttling sound as he neared the area, but he couldn't place which direction it was coming from.

As he stepped further into the zone, a cacophony of screaming and laughter shot through his ears. The scent of damp wood and mildew drifted in the air, and Dan couldn't help but be alarmed by the unusual feeling in his chest.

Through the foggy atmosphere, he could see what looked like three silhouettes dancing… Or perhaps they were fucking, he couldn't tell around this spot.

No…

This looked more violent.

And it was in the exact position where Doug was growing.

Fuck.

He picked up the pace, shoving overhanging branches back in on themselves, battling the maze of thorny bushes and overgrown roots, until the fog cleared.

"What the fuck are you doing?" he screamed, before his brain had even decrypted the sight in front of him.

Two or three teenagers, all dressed in black hoodies, were grappling with Doug, shoving and pulling his body, trying to uproot him from the ground. His face was battered and bruised, his lower body was oozing a yellowish substance, staining the roots and dirt patches around him. Black blood was erupting from the surface, and several of his lower tendrils had been severed.

As Dan got closer, he noticed it was the kids from the supermarket the day before, up to no good again.

"Stop that right now!" Dan ordered.

"Fucking freak!" one of the kids continued, completely disregarding Dan's order.

Dan panicked, had no idea what to do. What were these teens doing in this spot of the woods anyway? It was well out of the way of the road and any main thoroughfare, and the path leading into the zone was crawling with dense foliage and stinging nettles.

"I said fucking stop!" Dan screamed, stomping his foot in the grass as if it would compel them to take note.

Instead, the same mouthy kid spat in his direction, turned around and slammed a heavy stick into Doug's base. Doug wailed in pain, flailing and trying to get them to stop. Dan had had enough.

He crouched down to the ground, fumbling for something he could use to get rid of the group. His fingers happened upon a large chunk of concrete, presumably a piece of an old fence structure.

"Hey!" Dan warned.

In a split second, he drew his arm back and sprung forward, launching the rock at the loudmouth kid. In slow motion, he saw it crack him on the temple, a gush of blood exploding from his brow. He plummeted to the ground heavily, his limbs thrashing in a panicked dance.

The other kids quickly grabbed onto his sleeves and dragged him towards the road, screaming at the top of their lungs with a pubescent croak.

"Doug?!"

Dan had absolutely no regrets about what he did—he would have done the same for any stranger in need. He rushed to Doug's side, quickly assessing the damage, and tried to determine the correct way to move forward.

The wounds were unlike anything he had ever seen. Doug himself was an uncanny amalgam of human and plant, and as such, there was no precedent for such a situation. If any doubts had remained in Dan's mind about the origins of this creature, they were very much put to rest now. As much as he couldn't explain what he saw in front of him, it was obvious he was something special. Something unexplainable by current scientific standards, and most certainly not just a man stuck in a hole.

Doug was breathing heavily, in a frantic panic and wrought with anxiety. Dan put his hand on his chest, softly caressing the area.

"Calm down. Breathe in and out slowly."

Doug tried to do so.

"Does this usually work?" he begged.

"On humans, yes. And you aren't… *too* far away from that definition, so it can't do any harm."

Dan slipped off his jacket, and tore several fabric strips

from its structure. He folded them each three times, and used them to soak up the putrid mixture of blood and bile that was pouring from several lesions.

He didn't mean to, but the smell overtook his senses, hitting him like a punch to the gag reflex. In an embarrassing display of weakness, Dan spewed across the grass in front of him.

"Oh, fucking wonderful." Doug said.

"I'm sorry," Dan spat through vomit-drenched lips.

Doug started to breathe slower, but his face had turned a weird shade of grey. The colour was completely drained from his entire body, and the rags were now gushing with various bodily juices, too damp to have any effect.

Dan tried to wring them out, intermittently fumbling for his phone to try and call for help.

"What can I do to help?" Dan asked, still searching his person for the device.

Doug shook his head, as Dan came to the haunting realisation he had left it in his car again, a force of habit.

"I'm sorry I hit on you man, that wasn't cool."

Doug sounded despondent, like he was giving up. His wounds were serious, sure, but Dan wasn't ready for him to die.

"What? Don't be stupid. Just tell me, what do I do?"

"I really wasn't being pervy, all the dick talk and that... I actually need to suck dick to survive. I was born from a hodgepodge of random semen, and that's the building block of my body."

Dan shook his head at the incredulous statement.

"You can't be joking like this right now? On your deathbed?"

"Please!" Doug begged.

"There is no way you can know this. I need practical advice!"

"I mean, maybe I'm guessing a little bit, but you saw how I grew with those semen packets!" Doug remarked.

"Condoms, Doug. They're called condoms. Please don't ever call them that again."

They both chuckled over the awkward phrasing.

"Look, I don't have all the answers… But please try..." Doug pleaded.

Dan stood up, plastering what was left of his jacket onto the spurting contusions, finally plugging up the holes.

With his head in his hands, he started to hyperventilate.

"I can't call for help… I don't have time to go back… You're not helping me at all, what the fuck am I meant to do?"

"Dan… Do you want to help me, yes or no?" Doug demanded, his voice increasingly frail.

Dan nodded, a solitary tear falling from his eye.

"There's only one thing I can do… As wild and opportunistic as it sounds."

He stared at Dan's crotch.

"I'm gonna have to suck your dick."

There was an overbearing silence for a few moments. None of this made sense. He had no foundations on which to build a theory with regards to Doug. He had definitely seen this plant-man beg for man-juice. His first sighting of him consisted of a hand reaching out for a used condom. But was it something he needed, or just a weird fetish he had learned from the human inhabitants in the woods? If ever there was a nature versus nurture situation, this would be it.

Dan looked up to the sky, taking a huge gulp of fresh air.

And then a single word…

"Fine."

"Fine?" Doug enquired, almost completely silent.

"Fine. I'll do it. Sure," Dan said.

It was completely mad and unexpected, but he wasn't

going to pretend like he hadn't already been thinking it. In some ways, this was a perfect segue into the sexual conversation, as dark and twisted as that seemed right now.

Dan stepped forward and unzipped his jeans, rearranging his bulge before slipping his dick through the zip.

Doug realigned his body, and stuck out a rigid, dry tongue, his head inching closer and closer to making contact. He was very almost there...

"I fucking knew it!"

A woman's voice. Dan quickly leaned over, compressed his package back into his jeans and turned to find Jenny, standing tall with a confrontational stance.

"You played the victim, saying I was the devil who cheated behind your back, and then you're here in the woods, trying to fuck some kind of…"

She turned to Doug, and scanned him up and down, before continuing her sentence.

"Some kind of diseased gayboy!"

"How- how the fuck… Why are you here?" Dan asked.

"You were acting real strange. Why did you fuck me last night, hmm?"

Doug let out an audible utterance of disgust.

"Getting some in before sneaking out here and fucking this piece of shit, huh?" she squawked.

"Fuck you!" Dan said. "I heard you on the phone this morning to Troy. How he's the best fuck of your life… I was willing to give it a go, but you have burned every bridge now you cunt!"

Dan ripped his wedding ring off of his finger, and hurled it at her face, only just missing her protruding nose.

"What the fuck? You're out of control!" Jenny said, searching the grass for the keepsake.

"We're over Jenny. Get out of my life, you're welcome to

that other guy. Or whoever you want. I'm not doing this, anymore!"

Jenny shook her head.

"No. You're not going to just discard me. Definitely not for *him*!"

She launched over to Doug, grabbed his arm and started to pull him upwards. The rags popped out of their holes, allowing the flow of body juice to stream outwards again. Doug's screams were completely feral this time around, his energy almost completely depleted.

"Leave him alone!" Dan ordered, trudging towards her, trying to move faster than his feet would carry him.

Jenny heaved and pulled, tearing the sinewy strands from the dirt. She turned to Dan, making eye contact as she did so.

"I wanted your baby, you fuck!" she squealed.

Dan was inching closer... Closer. Was it too late?

Doug was completely unresponsive, his eyes fluttering behind his lids.

Closer... Almost there.

The sound of ripping flesh and foliage was isolated in the silent atmosphere.

Dan was finally close enough to reach out and grab Jen.

With a force even he didn't expect, he tore her arms away from Doug. In complete shock, she started to try and hit Dan, but he was stronger than her by orders of magnitude, especially with all of this adrenaline. He squeezed her forearms tight, and with a surprisingly effortless flick of the wrists, he propelled her forwards about two or three metres.

She glided through the air, before falling onto a sharp splintered branch, around four inches in diameter. The wood punctured her left side, splitting the skin and mangling her flesh. The patch of grass around her started to run crimson with thick, gloopy blood.

"Fuck!"

Dan darted towards Jenny, and then stopped.

He turned back towards Doug, started to jog over, and stopped.

Who do I save?

The question rang through his head on repeat. After quickly patching Doug's wounds back up with the wet pieces of fabric, he jogged back over to Jenny, checking over his shoulder for any bystanders.

"Fuck. I'm sorry."

He grabbed her shoulders tightly, and tried to pull her off.

"NO WHAT THE FUCK!?"

She flailed, slapping his hands away, struggling for breath. Dan flipped around to the front of her body, and started to slam his heel on the branch, trying to dislodge it.

Crack.

Crack.

Crack.

After a forceful blow with the heel of his trainer, the branch snapped, leaving a metre-sized stick lodged in her body. Carefully, Dan picked her up and wrapped her opposite arm around his shoulder.

He was walking for them both, as Jenny was quickly losing consciousness.

"You tried to kill me," she stuttered, slurring her words through her limp mouth.

"No. I was trying to save Doug."

"Oh, so you do know his name… I'm going to tell everyone you tried to kill me."

Dan continued walking, gritting his teeth harder with every step. Then he slowed to a standstill.

"If you even threaten that again, I'm going to leave you here to die. Alone. With no-one to help."

He stared at her in the eyes, deadly serious and unwavering.

She gulped, terrified at the prospect of such a death.

They both continued to walk again. Dan dragged her through the woodland, snatched Jenny's phone from her pocket, and quickly called the emergency services.

Dan detailed the location to which he was walking, and the extent of the injury, and made up a simple lie about what had happened.

As soon as they arrived at the edge of the park, he turned Jenny to look at him before letting her go.

"This is it Jenny. You go your way, I'll go mine. I'm going to pack up, and you won't see me again. Go live with Troy, he obviously gives you something I can't, and honestly, I'm ready to start a new chapter."

With nothing more than a nod and a wave towards the ambulance heading towards them, he let go of Jenny, letting her tumble to the floor, and started to jog off back in the other direction.

* * *

A tunnel of trees cascaded towards Dan as he sprinted through the forest, stretching his legs as far in front of him as possible, powering through the various aches and pains he had accumulated the last few days.

His body was soaked with sweat, shoes caked with wet mud, but he was on a mission.

As soon as he returned to the spot, he saw Doug lifeless on the floor.

"Oh God."

He jumped over to him, and started to shake his body, assessing the damage. His body was only about three-quarters of the way out of the dirt still, but the lower quadrant of his torso was heavily lacerated. The body fluid was still leaking out, albeit at a much slower rate.

"Fuck, fuck, fuck fuck!" Dan screamed into the ether.

He span on his heels, looking for help, and realised that he still hadn't gone back to his car for his phone.

In the end, Doug's final words for him started to race through his mind.

Though it was completely crazy, it was the only way it was going to happen.

Dan flopped out his dick, nervously looking at every angle to spot any bystanders, and started to massage in a rhythmic motion. Doug's lifeless eyes started to flicker, and gently open just in time to get a full-face view of the action.

He kept stroking until he sprayed a rejuvenating stream onto Doug, and it started to heal him immediately.

Immediately following the liquid resuscitation, Dan began to pile sticks on top of his body, using leaves and various foliage to try and block the wounds, and hide him from the kids if they tried to come back.

"I need to get some supplies. I need you to hold on," he said to Doug.

Doug was slowly stirring back to life.

"Don't go anywhere," he ordered, half-jokingly.

* * *

The bright overhead lights were almost unbearable. The big box DIY stores had always made Dan uneasy. He wasn't sure if it was due to the overbearing size and liminal qualities of the layout, or just the complete ineffectiveness of the shopping experience.

But none of that mattered right now. He had an objective, a time constraint and a shopping list… And he needed to get going.

Firstly, the outdoor garden centre. He piled a few sacks of soil into his trolley, and wheeled back inside.

As he made his way around the store in a clockwise fashion, he picked up some bamboo sticks, a spade, a two-pack of tarpaulins (on a buy one, get one free offer) and a few other knick knacks.

He headed straight to the self-service checkout after gathering his items, and wondered whether any of the staff would suspect foul play, given his dirtied clothes and questionable shopping list. But no-one seemed to bat an eyelid, so he swiftly purchased the items, and quickly left to load up his car.

* * *

Back at the forest, police sirens stained the environment in pulsating blue and red. Dan managed to cut through a back-road with his car, but it meant the services were scouring the area, and that wasn't good news.

At best, one of the kids might have ratted him out, and that would no doubt take some explaining. It would also give up Doug's identity, and he didn't want to think about what that meant for something as alien as him.

At worst, Jenny might have regained full consciousness and told the police he had attacked her, and that would be a much harder challenge to wriggle out of.

His only option was to avoid them entirely. And that meant working fast and economically, and getting in and out in the least time possible.

Dan began to dig a deep crevice around Doug's base, around ten inches out from his body, and at least two metres deep. He had no idea how far to dig down, but the last thing he wanted to do was cut his underdeveloped legs and feet off before Doug had even had a chance to experience them.

After excavating the man and a huge cross-section of dirt, he dumped him onto a tarp, and dragged him to his car, which he'd managed to park up just a few metres out of the zone.

Dan was sweating profusely, panic overriding his everyday functions. His subconscious had taken over, and every decision was being made without any second-guessing or time for debate. He didn't think anyone had seen him, and that would have to do. As soon as he had gotten Doug into the car, he was turning over a new leaf.

Sirens echoed, and the rumble of engines drew closer and closer.

The crackling of walkie-talkies undulated in the evening air, and Dan could even hear the conversations the officers were having as they explored every inch of the forest, leaving no stone unturned.

Dan was interested in one thing, and one things only; a new life, with a new man, without the pain and heartache of Jenny. He thought he could switch off his emotions, but even the thought of her brought up a slew of conflicting thoughts. For all of the messing around, cheating, arguments and fighting, they had had plenty of good times too. And he had let her get carted off in the ambulance whilst planning to jerk off over another man's body.

He couldn't get his head around the whole concept, but he had made the decisions he had made. Now, he had to get out of this situation without any further disasters.

With a breathless pull, he heaved Doug into the car, manipulating the tarps to drag him into the boot from the passenger seat.

Dan jumped into the driver's seat, locked in his seatbelt, and started to drive. Doug was conscious, and greeted him softly, before settling back into his slumber. He was safe now, and Dan was going to do everything he could to keep it that way.

* * *

4 WEEKS LATER

New house. New life. New job.

Everything was looking up.

Dan had spent a lot of time in his new garden the preceding couple of weeks. He had constructed a spacious greenhouse for Doug to live in (without fear of being found), and was enjoying the company of an intelligent—if not downright cocky—guy.

As he sipped from an ice cold glass of homemade lemonade, he admired Doug's handsome body, which was now exposed right down to the lower thigh. He had grown an astonishing amount in a short timescale - which was even more surprising given his injuries, and the haphazard way he had to deal with them.

Doug met his gaze, and smiled, gesturing at his wrist with his other hand.

It's time.

Dan smirked, got up from his chair, and placed the lemonade on a small side table opposite him.

He walked through the greenhouse entrance and towards Doug slowly, unzipping his jeans.

Doug arched his neck backwards, and extended his tongue towards the ground.

Before they knew it, Dan would be able to pick Doug from the dirt as a fully-grown body, and they could exist as a couple without arising any suspicion of his inner workings or plant background.

But until then, he had a little bit more growing to do.

It was feeding time, and they were both more than happy to comply.

CIRCLES

The infinite space was the brightest white you could imagine. No walls. Nothing in the distance. No-one at all inhabiting the area.

The man lay slumped on the floor, wearing a loose-fitting hospital gown. His eyes fluttered open, and he quickly drew several deep breaths.

He darted up, stumbling on tired legs, before finally regaining his balance. The man reached out in front of him, relying on scarred hands to guide him through the unusually desolate surroundings. The burning light made it hard to keep his eyes open.

The total absence of sound was painful, and his ears rang to make up for the lack of stimuli.

"Hello?"

There was no echo or feedback. His voice came to life and snuffed out almost simultaneously.

In each direction, there was only white. There was no forwards, backwards, or sideways. Each direction was an extension of non-existence, every choice as futile as the next.

* * *

Whurrr.

A near-silent vibration arose from somewhere. The man span on his heels, searching for the sound. Was he imagining it?

Without warning, a gargantuan axe swung towards him like a pendulum, anchored to a thick black rope above. There was no time to move, or to even react.

Swift and sharp, the metal sliced him from genitals to head, right in half. Dissected like a high-school frog, each side of him separated in sticky mounds, falling with a juicy squelch to the floor.

A flicker of black, before—

The man's eyes fluttered open. He quickly drew several deep breaths.

He stumbled up, regaining his balance, before slowly reaching for the front of his gown. He untied the drawstring, and looked down at his naked body, observing a scar which ran from his base through his stomach and chest. He imagined that it carried on and extended right through his head.

What was this?

Instinctively, the man listened out for the vibration. The axe massacre was fresh in his mind, though at this point, he couldn't remember anything about his life. Not his name, where he was from, or any family. He was a blank slate, trying to survive on primal instincts alone.

More importantly—how the hell was he still alive?

There were no vibrations this time. He decided to pick a direction and get as far as he could, starting at a slow walk and building to an awkward shuffle, then a jog, then a sprint.

For a good minute or so, he was successful. But that didn't last long…

Mid-pace, an upside down bear-trap, easily five times the circumference of his body, fell from the sky, and snapped around his waist. Attached to an invisible point above him, the chain was pulled taut, as if carefully measured for this very purpose.

Blood spurted from the man's mouth, as razor sharp metal points punctured him in a circular pattern. Opposite teeth of the trap met in the middle of his organs, and he could feel the pressure as his protruding bones punctured his flesh. The chain loosened, the entire trap lowering to the floor slightly, and the man followed it. His legs were no longer supporting him, his skeleton useless.

Suddenly, the chain retightened, whipping with intense force. The top half of his body slid up his spine like a chicken lollipop, before completely tearing away. He was still fully conscious, hurtling to the floor faster than he could process.

* * *

The man was submerged in a tank, instinctively pushing against the walls surrounding him, trying to escape. The room was different this time. Grimy. Concrete. Dimly lit. Glass walls formed the sides of the coffin-sized structure, whilst a heavy metal grate was laid on top.

The liquid engulfing him was viscous like lube, a dirty yellow slime that covered every inch of his skin. Within the pool, hundreds of little fish were darting around him, sliding their greasy bodies against his scars.

When he stopped thrashing, he noticed a couple of doctors looking over him, writing on notepads.

A thunderous roar followed the hiss of pneumatic pistons, which slowly lifted the grate from atop the structure. The man tried to sit up, his head heavy and ears ringing, but a female doctor pinned him down in the liquid, quickly darting a metal syringe into the side of his neck.

The needle slipped into a small metal socket that had been implanted into his flesh. A matchbox-sized LCD screen had been surgically inserted parallel to it, which displayed a number in hours, minutes, and seconds. Time had almost reached zero, and she seemed intent on making sure it didn't.

A purple liquid spurted through clear plastic tubing, directly into the man's bloodstream. It burned at the entry point in his neck, a sweetly acidic scent emanating from the wound.

Moments later, he was being dragged out of the water by both doctors, his limp body handled like a rag-doll.

They wrapped him in a damp, freshly-washed hospital

gown, and led him out of the room, down a dank hallway and into a cell.

* * *

A few hours passed, and all the man wanted to do was sleep. Or remember something about his life. Right now, the former seemed most likely…

He did finally remember one thing, though. His name—Ben.

Just as his eyes started to close, he was awoken by a rattling metal sound. A slender woman in her mid-forties stood outside the metal gate, striking the bars with a piece of scrap.

"I haven't seen you here before. What's your story, lifer?"

"I, uh—" Ben stuttered. "I wish I knew."

"Ah, you're a tadpole."

"A what?"

"You're actually new new. Under two months. Your memory hasn't caught up yet."

Ben slumped into a seated position.

"You're an inmate too?"

"Yep. Year two."

"And they let you roam around out there?" Ben questioned.

"Yeah. I'm part of the furniture now," she answered. "I'm Robyn, by the way."

"I'm Ben. I remember that, at least."

She smiled, leaning against the bars.

"What's happening here?" Ben asked.

Robyn sniggered.

"At the risk of spoiling all the secrets at once, they're testing out a life-extending drug on us."

Ben rubbed his eyes, half-asleep.

"Which is why we keep being brought back?"

"Yep."

Ben pointed to the small LCD screen.

"And this?"

"It's how long the drug has left before it runs out," she said matter-of-factly.

"What happens then?"

A loud buzzer rang out. Robyn looked back, and turned back slowly to Ben.

"That's the lunch bell. Listen, they're doubling up our scenarios soon, so I'm gonna make sure I get on one with you."

"What does that mean? Why do you want to be with me?"

Robyn grinned at him, leaning in close.

"Because you're gonna help me escape."

Ben sat puzzled as she stood up and nodded.

"Catch you soon neighbour."

* * *

The infinite space was the brightest white you could imagine. No walls. Nothing in the distance. No-one and nothing.

Ben lay slumped on the floor, wearing a loose-fitting hospital gown. His eyes fluttered open, and he quickly drew several deep breaths. As soon as he gained his bearings, he rolled his eyes. His memory was getting better, and he was already over this pattern of events.

He stood up, looking in every direction, checking for bear traps, axes, or any other manner of weaponised torture devices. Right now, the coast was clear.

Step by step, Ben started to look around for any kind of clue as to where he was. If Robyn was right, there was no getting out of the programme, and he couldn't deal with this repetitive chaos much longer.

There were no clues, of course, until he heard a gushing body of water.

To his right-hand side, a tidal wave of steaming hot liquid raced towards him, gaining ground at an impressive speed. He tried his best to dart off in the other direction, but it was futile, as always.

The wave washed upon him, a boiling torrent which instantly stripped skin from his flesh. Blisters popped up on his arms and legs, yellowish wounds seeping wet pus all over his body as he shrieked in agony.

Ben fell to the floor, his boiling skin pooling around his body, his eyes burning with searing heat. Just before he went totally blank, he saw something he couldn't quite believe.

Only a hundred metres or so in the direction of the wave, the water crashed to a stop, sliding up an invisible wall, leaving a transient residue on some kind of screen. A two-way mirror perhaps? It drained off to the sides through some kind of grate.

His eyes turned to jelly, and once again, he was awoken and revived in the chamber.

* * *

Ben was back in his cell, eyes closed and pleasantly solid again.

Metal rattled against the bars. Robyn was back.

"Find anything, tadpole?"

"You know—" Ben started, yawning with a wide mouth. "I did actually."

He told her the whole story, gory details and all, and Robyn was amazed at what he revealed.

"We are on a scenario together next. I got a guard to spill the gossip."

"Do you know what it might be?"

Robyn shook her head.

"No. But we need to think fast."

Ben nodded, totally in agreement.

"I have an idea…" he said.

* * *

The infinite space was the brightest white you could imagine.

The room seemed even more surreal with someone else in it. Robyn looked different in the light, more youthful and human. She held herself really well too. There was no sign of panic or confusion, she had perfected the art of dealing with the scenarios and the fear that came with imminent death.

They were both searching intently, looking for the first signs of this game. Nothing appeared for a few minutes, until a black metal turret snapped up from the floor.

"Here we go!" Robyn called out, readying herself.

With a loud whirring, the turret trained itself on Ben, the direction controlled by his movement. A deafening metallic sound announced the firing of a large rusty spear, which whipped towards him at super speed.

It whizzed past Ben's head, sliced through the air and lost altitude a few hundred metres behind him, rattling to the floor. Both he and Robyn squatted to the ground, shuffling to the side as another spear discharged from the device.

"What do we do?" Ben called out.

The metal whipped past Robyn, missing her body by mere inches.

"Where is the screen?" Robyn questioned.

Two spears fired this time, and one slashed Ben's

shoulder as it flew past. Blood splattered out of the gash, but other than a gasp, Ben kept his head in the game.

"It can't be behind us!" Ben screamed.

"I have an idea! Cover me!"

Ben nodded.

Robyn sidestepped and crouched, keeping low as she ran towards the device. Ben started to flail his arms around, jumping up and down, completely absorbing the turret's attention.

As soon as Robyn was up close, she grabbed hold of the turret, gripped the head and snapped it back in the other direction. The robotics put up a fight, but she managed to force it 180 degrees through pure brute force, her biceps swelling as she did so.

It clunked and spattered, but the emergency stop wasn't quick enough. Three spears darted out of the cannon, discharged through the air, and collided with a massive mirrored screen in the distance.

Metal shards exploded into the white atmosphere, revealing a dirty concrete viewing room. Two scientists were punctured through their throats, the weapons impaling them to the wall with brute force.

Ben and Robyn started to sprint towards the room. Several other scientists scrambled, trying to work out what to do whilst the broken weapon started to smoke and pulsate, spinning around in frenetic circles. One final spear sputtered from the turret, which soared through the air and impaled Robyn's shoulder like a skewer.

She crashed to the floor, fresh blood streaking on the white vinyl. Ben instinctively bent down mid-stride, swooping her up, and dragged her with him.

With her hand around the protruding spear in her shoulder, Robyn dove straight into one of the other scientists, pulling him in and jutting the spike through his throat.

As she pushed his body away from hers, the weapon slid neatly back through the hole in her shoulder, and remained embedded in the scientist's torn-up neck. He fell with a splat, and without a second thought, Robyn dove into an open healing tank.

Wet fish slammed to the cold ground outside the tank as Robyn's sudden immersion forced the liquid over the walls. Ben took care of the final scientist in the room, slicing him with a scalpel and forcing the blade through his eye socket.

The doors were remotely locked, and in perfect unison, a siren started to sound from the loudspeaker. Ben tried his best to snap the locking mechanism as Robyn cleaned her wound in the healing tank, the gungy, exposed flesh already crusting over.

With a final strike, a metal lever bent outwards, and Ben dismantled the lock with force. The heavy door swung open, and he gestured at Robyn to follow him.

"You don't know the way. Get behind me, tadpole," Robyn ordered.

Robyn slipped out of the bath, her clothes wringing wet, and grabbed a hammer from a workstation.

"Gotta be prepared."

She winked at Ben, and began to pace towards the darkness.

* * *

With a violent thrash, the metal hatch from the ventilation tunnel crashed onto the tarmac below. The light of the outside world felt uncomfortably bright, even though the day was overcast and mild.

Robyn dropped first, followed by Ben, who slipped and toppled onto his back. Robyn helped him back up, and they both sprinted towards a large wooded area in the distance, disappearing amongst the flurry of trees and plants that surrounded the prison complex.

* * *

The pair arrived at the main high street; Ben was obviously distraught. A handful of residents moved around at a glacial pace, their skin tattered and infected, their movements glitchy and uncertain. Dead bodies littered the road, with pale flesh and glazed-over, milky eyes.

"What happened here?" Ben asked.

"You don't remember?" Robyn quipped back.

Ben shook his head uncertainly as they both crossed towards a group of buildings.

"A few years back, all the rich bastards moved to a luxury complex about an hour from here. And they took every single resource from the city, every drop of money, and funneled it all over to them."

Robyn grimaced, the memories obviously uncomfortable to revisit.

"Everyone else was left to fend for themselves."

They brushed past a dead woman, no older than thirty, who had obviously jumped from a great height. Her face had imploded, and one of her rotting eyeballs lay ten or so metres from the rest of her body.

"Almost half of the residents killed themselves. There were no doctors to treat us. No therapists to talk us away from the edge. The only emergency treatment is at the jail, and once they know you're ready to die, you basically tick every box for the programme."

"The one we're in?" Ben questioned.

Robyn nodded.

They slipped past another man who had cut his throat, choosing the city hall as his final resting place. Blood had sprayed in a pattern across the wall around his figure as he slid to his death.

"Don't you have family? Friends? Anyone to live for?"

Robyn shook her head, unwilling to divulge any further information.

* * *

The silent world was intermittently interrupted by a petrified scream and the distant crunch of bones. Ben quickly clocked that this wasn't a post-apocalyptic scene—it was very much ongoing.

Some buildings had been completely abandoned, left open to looting and vandalism. Others had one or two solitary workers within, ambling through their days for no real reason at all, other than the comfort of a routine.

Like a modern war-zone, the place was a spectacle of the surreal, void of any hustle and bustle, no traffic or moving vehicles in sight.

On the footpath, Ben spotted a folded newspaper, and grabbed it as he walked. He had hoped to compare the date of publication to the date he was reading it on, but quickly remembered that even that was a mystery.

The headline jumped off the page: *"EASY E EPIDEMIC REACHES TERRIFYING HEIGHTS."*

Ben span to face Robyn, who was looking around with the exact same terror he felt in his bones.

Robyn clocked his confusion at the term.

"Drug dealers started shifting antidepressants at a low cost. Easy Es, we called them. Insanely addictive, made people crazy..."

"And you were hooked on them?"

"Buddy. You were in the same place as me, it's likely we share a few things in common."

For some reason, a memory fizzled into Ben's mind. It was elusive to begin with, but he remembered snatching away a discarded bag of tablets away from a child.

His child.

His stomach immediately dropped, as a flurry of thoughts flooded his mind. First steps. First words. First holiday. Robyn noticed his change in demeanour, and slowed down to match his pace.

"You good?"

Ben nodded. He wanted to be alone with the thoughts for a little while before sharing anything that might dilute the process of remembering.

He had had a child. Where was he now? Was he alive? Did he have a mother?

The memories started to dissipate as he walked, but he willed himself to try and remember more.

* * *

The inmates walked for miles before Robyn suggested they take a break. Surprisingly, a couple of cafés and shops were still open, so they slipped into the first one they found and sat at a rusty metal table. On cue, a woman in a stained apron walked towards them, notepad in hand.

"What can I get you?"

"Two coffees please," Robyn answered.

The waitress looked towards Ben, but he just nodded in agreement. She went back over to the counter and started up the coffee machine.

"You used to come here?" he asked.

"Nope. Just trying to run down the clock."

Robyn turned her head, and Ben noticed the LED screen had under half an hour left on the display.

"You mean... You're going to do it? Today?" Ben questioned.

"I want to be with my girl. I was dragged from the street and revived without any say. This time, I want it done the way I want."

Ben looked at the table, avoiding Robyn's sorrowful eyes. She was trying to be strong, but the emotions were rising to the surface.

"Fuck. She's gone? I'm sorry."

Robyn nodded.

"Thanks."

"What was her name, if you don't mind me asking?"

"Jessie," Robyn said proudly. "She was a pain in my ass, my Jessie. But a wonderful spirit."

Ben smiled politely, mulling over his own situation.

"I had a son," Ben said, interrupting the silence. "I don't remember what happened yet, but that's why I was in the programme. I'm sure of it. I don't think he's alive anymore, and whatever happened, I think I tried to... you know."

Robyn didn't need to ask anything else. It's likely they were in the same boat, and Ben would probably be as uncomfortable talking about his child as she was with hers.

"I'd quite like to see him again."

Robyn nodded, taking his hand.

Ben was locked in his own thoughts for several moments, before turning the side of his head towards Robyn.

"What does mine say?"

Robyn studied Ben's screen, which had sunken slightly between flaps of scar tissue.

"Thirty-two minutes. We're a few minutes different."

Ben nodded in appreciation. They both sat silently for a while, as the waitress brought over their coffees. She slipped back to the counter, and started to clean down the machine.

"Look, I don't want you following me just because we're together out here. If you're not ready—"

"I am." Ben interrupted.

"If you're sure it's what you want, I know a place. It will be painless," Robyn said.

Ben was sure, and after slowly sipping the rest of their muddy coffees, both of their LCD screens clocked in at under twenty minutes.

* * *

Robyn and Ben cut through a park and ended up at a rocky cliff face. Robyn had a brilliant sense of direction, suggesting she was probably a born and bred local, whereas only snippets of geographical memories were coming back to Ben.

Waves crashed upon the cliffs below. The pair stood in awe of the natural world that surrounded them, a complete antithesis to the artifice they had experienced in the days and months prior to this moment.

The drop was considerable, a jagged journey past razor sharp rocks to reach the bitter water below.

Ben and Robyn stood at the top of the landscape, hands intertwined, waiting for their humanity to return, so they could finally put a stop to this life.

The LCD screens were counting down, second by second, the veil of invulnerability dissipating.

Birds sang overhead, fluttering about and having the time of their lives.

They both stood silently until a soft yet noticeable beep emanated from Robyn's head. The LCD screen was flashing at zero. Ben had three minutes ten seconds to go.

Their hands interlocked tighter, as Robyn took a look over the edge.

"You sure about this?" she enquired.

"I am. A hundred percent."

Three minutes turned into two, and then one. The birds continued to sing, the waves continued to crash.

"STOP!"

The birdsong gave way to the roaring propellers of a helicopter. They both looked straight up, and saw the jet black vehicle getting ready to land. Inside the cab, a handful of scientists and a prison guard were waiting, a gun of some type trained on the inmates.

"I'm sorry." Robyn spurted out, breaking her grip with Ben. Without a second thought, she launched her body off of the cliff, tumbling down the jagged rocks as her flesh detached from her bones, her organs splattered over the protruding edges, and an unconscious sack of gore finally slopped into the sea.

Ben had no idea how long was left on his LCD screen but he knew he had no other option. The helicopter was grounded now, the prison guard already on foot and charging towards him. He took a few steps backwards, and his final step hit nothing but the air.

He flew through the atmosphere towards the water, his leg slicing on a sharp rock formation, and head hitting the cliff-edge with blunt force. His body slammed into the water and his corpse started to float alongside Robyn's fresh carcass.

* * *

Darkness. Black.

Was this Heaven? Hell?

The silence was comfortable.

It seemed eternal.

Maybe this was all there was now. A comforting void.

A space between life and something else. A never-ending limbo.

* * *

But it didn't last forever.

The room was the brightest white you could imagine. Every surface was overexposed, owing to the multitude of dazzling lights overhead.

Ben was splayed out, tethered to some kind of restraint on the wall. In front of him, a handful of scientists stared with radiant smiles, their eyes unblinking and minacious.

One of them stepped forward, and addressed Ben directly.

"You will go down in history, Mr Johnson. We couldn't have done this without you."

Ben tried to wriggle out of his restraints, but they were tight and unbreakable.

"Only by allowing the serum to run down to the very last second of effectiveness did you crack the code."

Ben pushed harder and harder, trying to get the restraints to budge even an inch, but there was no getting out of it this time.

"We have managed to develop a perpetual life-extending drug. Of course, we have to do more tests to see how long it will last, but this is the breakthrough we have been waiting for. Your country will remember your name, Mr Johnson."

"Get me out of this!" Ben wailed.

The scientists continued to gawk and smile for a few moments, before excitedly returning to their workstations. The head scientist stepped backwards as two others wheeled in a machine and lined it right up in front of Ben. A phrase was carved into the glossy aluminium exterior: *'Property of Lifelong Corp.'*

The machine was slender, and had a pneumatic arm which moved up and down. The arm was pointed, a razor sharp sword soldered to the end of it, and the workers slid it right up against his body.

The other scientists scattered out of the room, and the head scientist stood forward one last time.

"This is your final test, Mr Johnson… To see how long the serum really lasts. I have lots of shareholders who want to be notified the second things change, so think of this as a continuing experiment. I want to know whether this can really last."

Without another word, he walked out of the room, and Ben was alone with this machine, the pointed weapon digging into his diaphragm.

"HELP ME!" Ben cried, but it was no use. His voice echoed around the room, as if the sound itself was trying to escape the nightmare situation.

A few moments went by, then the machine started to whir.

"Where is Robyn? Did she make it? I need to talk to her!"

Through a loudspeaker, the scientist's voice came through with an analogue rattle.

"Ms Peakes is dead. For real dead. But we don't need her. Only you."

The voice cracked out of range, and Ben was alone again, with only the machine and the silence for company.

Without any warning whatsoever, the weapon punctured him in a swift motion, and dropped down forcefully, slicing through his stomach cavity and bladder. The wound quickly erupted, his intestines and internal organs slopping to the ground below.

* * *

The room was the brightest white you could imagine. Every surface was overexposed, owing to the multitude of dazzling lights overhead.

Without any warning whatsoever, the weapon punctured him in a swift motion, and dropped down forcefully, slicing through his stomach cavity and bladder. The wound quickly erupted, his intestines and internal organs slopping to the ground below.

* * *

The room was the brightest white you could imagine. Every surface was overexposed, owing to the multitude of dazzling lights overhead.

Without any warning whatsoever, the weapon punctured him in a swift motion, and dropped down forcefully, slicing through his stomach cavity and bladder. The wound quickly erupted, his intestines and internal organs slopping to the ground below.

VENDING MACHINE

GO

Murmurs and whispers danced in the air around him, but Marty Michaels couldn't see a single thing. Splayed out on the cold concrete, his muscles were tight and exhausted, his head throbbing to the beat of his pulse. His eyelids flickered, battling with the intense sunlight beaming down from above.

As the world came back into view, a gaggle of blurred shapes arched over his frail body, an ensemble of concerned citizens with their phones drawn.

"We've called an ambulance, don't move!"

Marty jolted up with a burst of energy, springing right into a seated position.

"No, there's no need. I'm fine. Thanks."

Still hazy from the fall, Marty clambered onto all fours, heaving himself up onto his feet. This wasn't the first time he had passed out in public, and it wouldn't be the last.

Marty Michaels was barely forty years old, but he was terminally ill. He didn't have the official diagnosis on paper, or through an app, or however the Hell you were delivered such news nowadays, but he knew it in his bones. What had started as a lump and a dry cough had transformed into jaundiced skin, weird purple rashes on his torso, and blood in his piss.

Every morning at dawn, he hacked up gritty, tobacco-stained phlegm, and he went to bed choking on his own breath. Marty's body was deteriorating at an alarming rate, and his only real joy was being out in the fresh air. There was no way he'd let himself be carted off to a hospice to live out his last days breathing in stale, recycled oxygen, so he planned on avoiding the medical services like the plague they were.

The crowd dissipated, and Marty took off in the same direction he had been walking before the fall. The deserted high-street was crammed with vacant shopfronts, each adorned with faded event posters, a thick crust of grime, and splattered bird droppings. The soulless structures were peppered with a couple of active businesses, namely a coffee shop with an apathetic teen working behind the counter, and a greasy kebab shop with a dried out slab of meat oscillating in the window.

Marty traversed these streets every day, trying his best to keep to some semblance of an exercise routine, and the town seemed to get drearier and more desperate with each visit. He didn't expect he'd be able to do much more now, with scuffed knees and a sore head, but he wanted to get his energy back up before setting off home.

In the sea of grey, a small shopping arcade caught his attention. The white exterior walls were by no means inviting, but the signage was the least derelict of the surrounding bunch, and he couldn't recall ever having stepped foot inside. With a sluggish limp, he staggered over to the entrance, and pushed the creaky glass door open.

* * *

Inside, the shopping complex was washed in modern white decor and fittings, a stark contrast to the diseased structures outside. Though none of the five shopfronts were occupied, they were kept in excellent condition. The glass looked freshly cleaned, the floors dust-free, and a seating area in the middle looked pristine.

There was an ornate marble fountain at the far end of the space, expelling a steady stream of water into its decorative pool, positioned by a high-end vending machine. Black and silver, the machine looked luxurious, the kind of unit you'd find in a first-class lounge at a city airport. The slender curves of the model didn't resemble anything Marty had seen before, but the unit as a whole felt out of place for the local market and, quite frankly, the demographic of the town. That said, its presence captured his attention.

Shiny glass coated a strong aluminium frame, displaying several dozen units of a light brown, cube-shaped product. On closer inspection, they were jelly-like, wrapped in clear packets and factory-formed.

Since his health symptoms first started six months ago, Marty had taken a homeopathic approach to his health. He used several natural medicines and oils, and kept to a mostly clean, unprocessed diet. Superfood shakes and GMO-free smoothies were a staple in his house, and when he did reach for a treat, it usually took the form of a mint or hard candy. But for the sake of getting his energy levels back up—and to avoid circling around the ghost town in search of something healthier—he would settle for one of these snacks.

A variety of slots and holes were incised into the glossy metal panelling, but there didn't seem to be any kind of keypad or coin slot—or, for that matter, a card-reader or anything to take payment.

Instead, a red contoured button poked out from the front-plate. The word 'go' was etched into the plastic, and had evidence of multiple compressions, the only part of the machine which didn't look brand new.

With a gentle prod, Marty watched as one of the small coils unwound, releasing a jelly cube from its grip. The candy dropped into a dark void, hidden behind a brushed chrome flap at the bottom of the machine. A postcard-sized LCD screen sparkled with animated text, instructing Marty to enjoy the treat.

With a delicate touch, Marty retrieved the package from the receptacle. After a quick glance at the lack of branding or pattern on the confectionery, he unwrapped and gorged on the entire treat.

Wow.

It was unlike anything he had ever tasted. Sweet notes of cinnamon and honey intertwined with a smoky, sumptuous base. The texture was gelatinous, but also held its structure, compacting between each bite, moulding to the shape of his teeth as if it were custom-designed for his mouth.

His entire body gently vibrated, the sugar rush dancing in his veins and arteries. His throat and stomach felt warm, a comforting blanket of artificial love. All of the fogginess in his brain had dissipated... he felt more alive than he had done in a long time.

For a few moments, he was frozen in ecstasy, completely enraptured by the experience. His pain and worries faded into his subconscious as he rode the wave of euphoria.

* * *

Marty's apartment had fallen into a state of disrepair. Bought in the early 2010s with his wife, Kate, it was a generously proportioned yet modest space, once fitted-out with the latest appliances and technology. Now, remnants of the life they had shared together were scattered across various surfaces, intermingled with unpaid bills, empty crisp packets, and worn paperback books. Folders upon folders were stacked in corners of the living room, adorned with scratchy handwriting, collating evidence from a medical malpractice trial from almost seven years ago.

When Kate passed away—due to a catastrophic error during a routine operation—Marty's world had imploded. His career as a journalist continued for a few months, but drowning in depression with nowhere to turn, Marty just stopped turning up at the office. When he finally gathered the strength to fight in court, he was thrust into a battle that lasted the best part of a year, and then destroyed by an army of ruthless government suits.

He was confident the stress from that period had caused his current ailments, but he wouldn't give the medical services the satisfaction of caring for him, looking down in pity as if he were an injured animal. He'd keep going until his body had enough, and then expire on his own terms.

A faded picture of Kate sat atop the paperwork, snapped on a journey the pair took to Paris shortly after buying the house. They both glistened with youthful vigour, completely and utterly in love, living life at a hundred miles-an-hour without any thought of the future. Marty smiled at the bittersweet memory, before setting the photograph back atop the teetering tower of folders.

In the kitchen, he loaded up a heavy handful of spinach, a tablespoon of chia seeds and a selection of superfoods into an old food processor. He hit the pulse button, and the blades span with a defective whirr. The unit was a gift from Kate's mum, and Marty had never had the heart to throw it away, even when it made weird sounds or started smoking after a particularly strenuous task. If it wasn't broke, it wasn't worth fixing—that was his motto.

A thick juice formed, coating the sides of the container with a green residue. He poured the mixture into a small glass and took a large gulp.

As he swallowed, the drink regurgitated back up his gullet and through his teeth, and caused him to cough and sputter most of it back over the processor. His body felt weak and, after swiping his mouth with a tea towel, Marty climbed over his vintage coffee table and collapsed onto the sofa, clumsily spilling more of the juice onto the floor as he sank into the threadbare cushions.

Green liquid sloshed in the cloudy glass, tiny dregs of pulverised greens drifting through the juice. With an agape mouth, Marty tipped the remaining drink into his throat. It sat there for a moment, stagnantly slopping against his cheeks, before a bodily contraction caused it to all splash back out. Marty was perplexed, but his mind was elsewhere.

The jelly cube. The ravenous sensation that overcame his entire being as he experienced the exquisite delicacy. Bursts of flavour mingling in his mouth, the sugar-rush bounding through his veins, diluting the torturous pain that burned through his body twenty-four hours a day.

He needed to experience it again.

Marty fell asleep dreaming of the machine, ready to experience the sensation as soon as possible.

* * *

The air outside was particularly humid that morning. Marty sauntered towards the shopping arcade, a certain pep in his step, eagerly anticipating the experience ahead. Sweat coated his armpits and back, soaking through his shirt. He hadn't had a chance to shower, and smelled like death, but none of that mattered to him right now.

As he approached the entrance of the building, a young man spilled out onto the footpath. Catching his balance just in time, the young man mumbled a quick apology, before scuttling off into the sunshine. The teen left a thick trail of blood on the concrete behind him, though Marty couldn't see any obvious injuries.

Cautiously, Marty peered through the glass door. The building seemed isolated, silent… just as it had been the day before. He shot a quick glance over his shoulder, but the man was gone. Slowly, he shook off the unusual feeling that'd washed over him, and continued into the complex.

Marty hadn't noticed how quiet the building was on his last visit. Aside from the fountain and the static hum from the fluorescent lighting fixtures, the space was pin-drop silent.

The vending machine was freshly stocked with new cubes, each row stacked in an obsessively neat manner. Marty could hardly contain his excitement, and eagerly hovered his hand over the metal front plate. Curiously, the button from the day before had vanished, leaving a deep, cylindrical hole in its place. The LCD screen above the cavity flickered for a few moments, and then loaded a pixellated avatar, similar to a rudimentary chalk outline you'd find at a crime-scene.

Though most of the digital drawing was featureless and simplistic in nature, one of the fingers on the right hand was filled with a flashing red block colour. Marty studied the screen, switching his view between the diagram and the tunnel cavity. The inside of the cylinder was completely pitch black. Marty couldn't see any mechanism or device inside, but he wouldn't know until he placed his finger into the abyss.

Moist cotton wrapped his body like a blanket, and he slowly tugged at his shirt, peeling it away from his skin. Marty's head was cloudy and dazed; he had spent most of the night vomiting in and around his toilet bowl, and the rest of it cleaning up the remnants. He hadn't been able to eat or drink anything since the cube, but couldn't be sure if that was because of the illness or a weird reaction to the jelly.

All he knew was that he needed the energy boost that he felt the day before. He'd give anything for that sensation again. Marty touched the aluminium around the hole, checking for any unusual moving parts he should be aware of, before the craving became too much to handle.

With a slow, dubious movement, Marty slid his finger inside, centimetre by centimetre, the cold chrome surface slithering against the contours of his skin. As he pushed deeper, he began to feel pressure. The metal contracted towards the end of the cavity, taking a conical form, and at three-quarters of the way in, the chamber became too narrow. A patterned ridge was carved into the circumference of the interior, and as Marty tried to withdraw his finger, tiny flaps of his flesh became stuck in the gaps.

No matter how hard he pulled, the flesh was trapped. The skin tugged and tightened, pinching against the metal, grating the upper layer of his flesh away.

"Fuck!"

He slammed against the panel with his free hand, searching for some kind of emergency stop or alarm. The digit wouldn't budge, even though it was moist with sweat and grease. Marty took a desperate look at the cubes inside the glass, just inches away from his face, torturously close to being in his mouth.

He gripped his wrist with his other hand, and tried to manipulate the bone of the finger, twisting it gently in its place. Waves of excruciating pain pulsated through his hand and arm, but the futile attempt made no difference. The middle joint cracked, the bones in the finger grinding against each other as they contorted in opposing directions.

A metallic whirring noise started up inside of the machine, and Marty froze in his place. With a swift, ruthless swipe, a blade jolted within the void, and dismembered the entirety of his finger, leaving a bleeding, confused stump of flesh squirting crimson across the glass display.

Marty screamed, a desperate, childlike screech, whilst the blood continued to jet out, like a mini version of the fountain just feet away from him. His severed appendage tumbled down into the container, whilst the LCD screen ignited with a colourful animation.

"Fuck!"

Vomit rose to the top of his throat, and Marty did everything in his power to stop it firing out of his gullet. He yanked open the chrome flap, as a cacophony of bells, whistles, and unintelligible fairground-style music started to emanate from the box. His finger laid outstretched on the cold metal, a skinny, warped digit with unclean nails and yellowed skin. Marty looked right past the lost flesh, however, when he saw the two jelly cubes sat waiting to be devoured.

Plump and delicious, he shredded the packages apart with his teeth, demolishing both sweets with fury. The effects were almost instant.

Bright lights coruscated in his eyes as the environment around him seemed to melt gently, like an ice cream on a sunny day. The dizzying euphoria enveloped Marty, making him feel invincible, and he immediately felt his parched mouth soak with liquid. Every ailment and hint of discomfort slipped away, and a genuine feeling of belonging vibrated in his bones. He was in harmony with the universe, with society, with himself.

The disfigured stump on his hand continued to spurt out warm blood, coating his limb in sticky crimson. It was kind of twisted, but the only thought running through Marty's head was that it was worth it. A physical offering, a sacrifice, of sorts. The feeling was priceless, and there was very little he wouldn't do to feel like it every second of every day he had left on this Earth. He didn't know why he did it, but he shoved the pumping stump into his mouth, sucking on the stream of blood ejecting into his throat. In the warm heat of his trip, the sensation felt beautiful. He didn't bother picking up the stump.

* * *

The journey home was a blur. Marty had spent several hours walking around the city in circles, feeling like he could bound from building to building like a superhero—luckily, the thought remained a thought, and he didn't try to put it into action.

It was early evening now, and he was finally coming down from the rush. Marty shivered as he walked towards his apartment building, jostling for the keys in his pocket with his good hand. His injured hand was wrapped in a towel he had found in the shopping centre toilets, tied to act as a makeshift tourniquet. The pain had dulled since eating the cube, but it was slowly starting to throb in agony again.

With his head angled at the floor as he shuffled ahead, he almost missed the spectacle unfolding in front of his eyes.

Several fire trucks were pulled up at the entrance of his building, and a small crowd were contained in a makeshift barricade. The last remnants of smoke were pluming from the burnt-out middle floors of the structure, having been extinguished just moments before.

Marty stared at the scene, awestruck, before picking up his pace. He coughed hard as he raced towards the front door, hacking up a glob of dark-yellow phlegm. With a gargled exhale, he spat it out onto the floor.

"You can't go in there, Sir—"

Marty tried to sidestep the fireman at the door, but he didn't have the strength nor the energy to attempt such a move.

"All of my stuff is there, you don't understand." Marty pleaded, trying his best to push through.

"I'm very sorry, Sir, arrangements will be made for a hotel—"

The fireman stopped as he noticed Marty's hand.

"Your hand…? I'll get a paramedic over here."

He turned to wave down a medical worker, but Marty raised his voice.

"No! I don't need an ambulance or anything else. I just need you to move so I can get into my house."

"There's nothing on those floors. It's all ash. Please, Sir. If you're on the floors above or below, you'll get in in due course. It's not safe right now."

"Can you at least tell me what caused it?" Marty pleaded.

The fireman looked around, as if he wasn't meant to divulge.

"It was an old kitchen appliance we think. Some kind of old microwave or blender."

Marty took one last scornful look at the man and retreated away from the building. As his terrible luck would have it, it was his floor that had burnt away, and most likely his ancient food processor that had ignited the fire. He had nowhere to go, no friends or family to call, and all of his possessions were gone.

Life had been hard up until that point—really fucking hard—but Marty was finally ready to call it a day. He was tired of being at war with the world, with himself, with his memories and the torturous idea that he had wasted his entire life doing absolutely nothing of note.

He watched as the black smoke faded into the atmosphere, carrying with it the embers of his possessions. As he turned to walk away, a woman in a hi-vis vest handed him a bottle of water with a worried glance and half smile.

"Thank you."

He twisted the cap from the plastic and took a huge gulp of water, but it still wouldn't stay down. Marty choked it all back up and frustratedly launched the bottle towards the crowd.

* * *

After circling the streets for another hour or so, Marty found himself back at the shopping arcade. He had considered throwing himself in front of traffic and killing himself quickly, but it didn't feel like the right way to go. There was also the option to jump from a building, but heights scared him far too much, even as a way to off himself.

Besides, if it was going to be his last night on Earth, he thought he deserved some peace, at the very least. In a hospice, he would be loaded up on morphine or some shit, so why shouldn't he be allowed to take his final breaths high as Hell?

Though he had expected the front doors of the arcade to be locked, the building was still open, with all of the lights on, and the fountain water cycling through its decorative pool. He pushed on the glass door, and relished in the tranquility of the space.

Marty ambled towards the machine, his skin pale and clammy, his sickly body struggling to stay upright. Step by step, he closed in on the unit, the freshly-polished metal reflecting his own distorted image back to him. As he scanned the front-plate, a sickly chuckle emerged from his lips.

The finger-shaped hole had been replaced with a larger aperture, and the LCD screen revealed the secret to acquiring more of the confectionery. On the body diagram, the entire right arm of the avatar was flashing red. As he stared at the screen, his body shuddered with a quaking cough. He spewed out several pieces of fleshy matter, intermingled with a yellow-red vomit.

Marty was getting close to the end, he could feel it. He didn't have anything to live for any more, the only decisions he had to make were which sacrifices would have the best return, in terms of making him feel better.

Marty wiped the discharge on his t-shirt, and after a moment of consideration, rolled up his right sleeve to his shoulder.

Even though he knew exactly what to expect, he was still

hesitant as he slipped his arm into the void. The cold metal tickled the skin around his bicep as he pushed deeper into the crevice. Like before, the hole narrowed towards the bottom, and the ridged pattern gripped onto his flesh. Marty held his breath, focusing all of his concentration on the treats, and the wonderful daze he would enter when he had one in his mouth. The machine didn't do anything for a few moments, forcing Marty to wait in an anticipatory limbo.

He couldn't take it.

"Please do it now!"

And with that, a rotating blade whirred to life, slicing every tendon and ligament in his shoulder, hacking at the bone which connected the limb to his body. Painful screams echoed across the complex, whilst Marty was tossed around violently.

Moments later, the arm was disconnected, torn from its socket. Marty collapsed onto the marble floor beneath him, flailing convulsively. A torrent of fresh blood spurted across the sanitised environment as he struggled to catch his crackling breath. The funfair-style music erupted once more in unison with the flickering LCD animation.

A metal ring crashed through the hole in the machine, sealing the void. It immediately started to turn brown, then crimson, then bright red. Smoke was rising from its surface, and the beeping soon turned into an emergency alarm. Marty slowly propped himself onto his knees and crawled forwards until he was just inches away from the device. He could feel the blistering heat emanating from the metal pad, and he swallowed hard in anticipation.

He turned his head to look at his thrashing stump, and knew exactly what he had to do.

Lining up the laceration with the hotplate, Marty counted down from three, and flopped onto the scorching surface.

The wound sizzled, the pink meat blackening on impact,

filling the air with a pork spit-roast odour. Charcoal embers danced from the amalgamation of flesh and metal, and the newly cauterised wound sealed like a steak in a hot skillet. The sinew melted and stuck like string cheese, long globs pouring from the amputation.

The pain was harrowing, like a million knives stabbing and slicing, the blades twisting against the bone. Marty's eyes rolled back into his head, his throat too dry to scream. Instead, thick saliva and bloody phlegm gushed from his throat, and with a final burst of energy, he yanked himself away from the hotplate, crumpling to the floor in a thrashing mess.

He convulsed, his body sweating, skin going grey. It took everything he had left in him to stay conscious, but he had to. Marty had done his part now. Now he got to enjoy the reward.

Marty's vision was waning, fading in and out of focus as fresh waves of torment erupted within his body. His heart raced, beating at a million miles-an-hour, and his stomach was in knots. Still, he managed to force himself to his knees, carefully keeping balance with his left arm. He stared at the machine, waiting, anticipating...

The treats would tumble out any minute now...

This whole situation would be worth it for one taste of the jellied delights...

The coils span, the machine whirred, but that time didn't come. Instead, the LCD screen flickered to display an error message. The device was broken and needed a routine repair.

"No!"

Marty slumped against the machine, smashing his head against it with all of his force. He tried to put out his right arm to support himself, forgetting the amputation. With a large thud, he crashed to the floor face-first and shattered one of his teeth on impact. He spat out fragments of enamel, and violently tossed himself back onto his knees, smashing the left side of his body against the glass.

"YOU FUCKING PIECE OF SHIT!"

Marty battered the glass with his left elbow, causing a few cracks to form at the very edge of the window. He continued to pummel it with all of his body weight, shattering the first layer of the safety glass.

His anger erupted into salty tears, as he fought with his whole life.

SMASH...

SMASH...

SMASH...

CLICK.

Marty couldn't believe his eyes.

The entire front of the machine seemed to detach with a deep, otherworldly rumble. Moments later, the thick frontage swung open on titanium hinges, revealing a tiny, bunker-style room.

The space was slightly taller and wider than the unit, and about fifteen metres deep. A bright white glow shone from inside the chamber, and Marty slid into a crawl, dragging himself into the space with bony, torn-up fingers.

* * *

Inside the room, the air was crisp and bitter, and Marty could already see his breath when exhaling. He checked back over his shoulder to see if anyone was coming, but he was alone.

He heaved himself to his feet, crouching to accommodate the low ceiling. Several coloured light filters painted the room an icy blue, whilst a selection of computers ran complex software on parallel sides of the space.

"Hello?"

There was no answer. On the screens, a jumble of code and abstract images were intermingling, with no discernible pattern or information available to interpret. Marty dragged his broken body through the space, applying pressure to the surfaces to keep him upright and stable. His torso shivered, a mix of pain and cold, whilst his vision continued to blur and clear intermittently.

Finally, something a little more simplistic came onto one of the screens. A detailed biography of a man, with what looked to be a profile of his DNA.

"What is this?"

"Welcome to Unit 534t-B."

The voice spat out of a handful of tiny speakers in the ceiling, with a gravelly, glitchy texture.

"What is this?" Marty repeated, clocking the different speakers.

"Thank you for your service," the voice beamed confidently.

Marty studied the information on-screen, but didn't have all of the information he needed to work out this puzzle. As he paced back towards the door, it slid shut with a heavy thud.

"What service? Where are my sweets?"

Marty was going to keep talking, but got side-tracked by the logo he spotted on the wall.

LL Healthcare Solutions.

A new rage burned inside of him, and he was ready to get to the bottom of this right now.

"Who are you? Who do you work for?"

"Thank you for inputting your DNA into our brand-new artificial intelligence vehicle, Unit 534t-B. By donating your data, you are helping us make a better tomorrow, today."

"WHAT THE FUCK IS THIS?" Marty screamed, pounding against the metallic tables that ran the length of the room. He had been fucked over by the healthcare industry so many times in the last few years. This was a cruel, twisted turn of events, and he would not take any further part in it.

"Are you making money from me? From my body parts?"

The voice croaked back onto the speakers, confident and informative, like a well-trained robot.

"LL Healthcare Solutions are a for-profit venture, whose only goal is to make a better tomorrow, today."

Marty span around the room, looking for another exit in the enclosed environment, but the place was sealed.

"I do NOT give permission for you to use my data, or any of my DNA."

"Your donation will help many people, as we strive to explore new ways of helping improve the human race, through medicines, experimental procedures, and cross-organism evolution. As we transition to a new era of the human race, your donation will be the building block of our new foundation."

Marty tried to run at the door, but his body wouldn't move.

"I'm going to expose you. Expose this whole thing! You think I can't do it? I've fought bigger fucks than you before! I will stay alive just to take you *all* down, you crooked fucks! YOU CAN'T DO THIS TO PEOPLE!"

Marty grabbed a monitor and ripped it from its socket, violently tossing it against the door. It didn't move an inch. He continued to pummel the door from the inside, clawing at it with a primal rage.

"In accordance with Section 243-a of the LL Healthcare Solutions Medical Best Practice guidebook, all *spent* organic matter is to be disposed of to avoid any contamination to the outside environment."

Marty stopped in his tracks, ready to unleash Hell.

Suddenly, two plexiglass screens fell in parallel, covering the workstations and all of the devices they were connected to. An emergency light blasted the entire room with a burning red glow, and caused Marty to drop to the ground.

With an overwhelming feeling of disbelief, Marty started to cry and laugh in unison.

On the floor, just a metre out of reach, there was a jelly cube, sat pristine in its package.

"Incineration commence."

With the very last remnants of energy he could muster, he reached out and grabbed the clear package. He ripped it open passionately with his teeth, and swallowed the candy whole.

The effects kicked in straight away, relaxing his body and washing away every ache, every pain.

Sizzling flames erupted from vents in the floor and ceiling, and coated Marty's entire body. His clothes caught alight, and quickly melted, fusing with his skin. His flesh melted away like a pale pink candle, dripping from his skeleton in deformed blobs. His exposed organs bubbled and overflowed from his carcass, as he laughed away the pain.

He could only feel the warmth as his body started to shut down segment by segment. His brain replayed images of the cube on repeat, and even as the fire burnt away his sight and taste, he continued to shake with laughter.

Eventually, with white, jellied eyes and blackened flesh, his brain melted away too, and the fragments of his skeleton were all that remained in the machine.

DROPOFF

It felt as if I had the sunset all to myself.

In the middle of a brand new allotment plot, I had just finished an eight-hour landscaping session. The land boasted a selection of freshly-planted crops, manicured grass, and a range of colourful flowers. I was pretty damn proud of what I had accomplished in just a few days.

That said, nothing could compare to the beauty of the sky in that moment.

Streaks of burnt orange and pastel pink interwove in mesmerising patterns, gradually ushering the sun to its resting place. When nature wanted to put on a show, it really could, and I felt like my job was to take inspiration from what I saw up there and reflect it in my work on the ground.

I had never been particularly green-fingered growing up, but when everyone was leaving school, getting ready for university or starting their careers, I was stuck in a loop. I wanted to do something important, something helpful, but I got far too distracted—and too high every day—to get good grades. So I fell into odd jobs, and used gardening as a way to keep me sane in my free time.

A half-smoked joint was stuffed into my pocket, and it seemed like the perfect time to spark it. None of the security cameras worked in the allotment, and I didn't want to get caught with it whilst driving, so I slipped the butt between my lips, lit the end until it crackled, and inhaled deeply. The burnt, wooden taste of the relit joint was comforting and familiar, a well-earned reward.

In the not-so-far distance, a small plane was gliding in my direction. It seemed to bob up and down slightly, struggling to keep altitude, but I shrugged it off as an optical illusion. The rumble of the engine grew louder, approaching at a steady rate—and that's when I first saw it.

Something was hanging out of the side of the aircraft. No, not something.... *Someone.* They were flailing, thrashing, doing their best to escape. The plane was barely a hundred metres away, and I unconsciously took another huge drag of my joint.

And then came the screaming; a panicked cry, warped in the desolate skies, amplifying at an alarming rate.

With a violent slam, and the crunch of a hundred broken bones, a limp mass smashed onto the floor only a few feet away from me, a torrent of warm blood gushing onto my sunburnt skin. My mind slowly caught up with my vision as I stared at the putrid pile of pulp and tissue, dropping my still-lit cigarette to the ground.

Twisted gore splayed out across the grass, the majority of an upper torso next to a severed head and several dismembered limbs. On closer inspection, the skull had cracked open like a walnut, revealing slimy matter slumped between bruised flesh mounds. The upper body and neck were twitching, the corrupted vessel flailing uselessly. To my surprise, a deep growling emanated from the de-gloved face —or what was left of it at least.

The smell hit me next. As I paced towards the mangled jelly in front of me, a whiff of sickly-sweet egg rippled into my nasal cavity. It hit the back of my throat, and I tried my best not to gag.

The vibrating mound suddenly emanated a weird, low rumble, before it caught me off-guard with words… Human words…

"Fucking shit fuck!"

I slowly circled around the body, my footsteps pointing outwards like a crab, like one of those cheesy cop show reveals. I wished I hadn't...

The gooey pile was distorted in the worst way, a fleshy jumble, one eyeball ripped out of its socket and the other milky and bloodshot. The (half) working eyeball span to look at me with an expression of absolute horror.

"Help me."

I stopped and froze in my place.

"What?" I said, through half-pursed lips.

"Fucking help me... Please."

For a delayed moment, I just stared right at the scene, not responding. Like a crashed computer, all of my brain processes were competing for my undivided attention, and I just wanted to *force quit* the fuck out of my head.

But that wasn't an option. I needed to think.

"How are you alive? How are you *talking?"*

"There's no time, listen—" he started.

"I, uh. I'm gonna call for help. Let me get my phone." I fumbled listlessly through the many pockets of my cargo pants, finding half-eaten snacks, tiny screws, and different varieties of seeds, but the phone wasn't there.

"I don't need you to call anyone, just move me, please!"

I took no notice, already retracing my steps. The grass was freshly mown and treated, so it wouldn't take long for me to locate the device. I scanned the area, my eyes darting from spot to spot, whilst the fleshy nightmare behind me struggled to breathe.

As I continued the search, I started to mutter unintelligible words, my confused disposition manifesting as some kind of jumbled nonsense. The guy must have picked up on this, as he took a deep, crackled breath and began to talk again.

"I will explain everything, I promise. Please just move me."

I couldn't help it; I let a huge chuckle escape my lips. A sick chuckle for a sick nightmare of a situation.

"You WHAT? Dude, how would I pick you up? With a fucking straw? A bucket?"

"Alright smart-ass, what about that wheelbarrow over there?"

My eyes tracked over to an adjacent plot. A wheelbarrow full of soil was sat half-lodged in the dirt, waiting to be of use.

"*If* I get you out of here, I'm taking you to a hospital... Right?"

The sludge man sighed deeply, and I couldn't help but feel slighted by his attitude.

"You can't let them find me. *Really,* I will let you know *everything.* I promise."

I shook my head, losing my patience and my mind at the same time.

"If we're doing this, at least tell me your name."

"I'm Brock."

* * *

The former contents of the wheelbarrow were now scattered, hidden by wooden pallets and various tools that had been left out over the weekend. Using a spade from my neighbour's plot, I hurriedly slopped as much of Brock into the wheelbarrow as I could, mixing his guts into the cake-like layer of dirt and debris that clung to the tool.

The jellied slop was warming up with the movement, and the scent was noxious. I tried my best to hold back, but I couldn't help it. I started to gag, my stomach contents threatening to expel at any moment.

"Oh come on, I don't smell that bad," Brock protested.

"I'm sorry mate... It's worse than you think," I replied.

Brock snorted.

"I appreciate this, but just pick me the fuck up."

"Sorry, sorry."

As I dug into the squelchy heap, I noticed strings of sinew and mangled tissue were somehow reconnecting, reforming like strands of wet gluten. When the larger pieces of gelatinous muscle were contained in the metal receptacle, I started to claw at the last fragments of bone and skin.

"That's about all I can get," I announced, laying down the spade and peeling my sweat-drenched shirt away from my chest, still holding the vomit in the back of my throat. The sky had turned a volcanic orange now, with the final streams of light scattering across the horizon. The journey back to my van was easily a ten minute walk, so I gripped the handles and awkwardly span the wheelbarrow on its axis, trying my best not to let the putrefied slop overflow.

"Let's go," Brock growled.

The uneven terrain was a challenge to traverse, especially with equipment that had seen better days. It occurred to me that I was probably tearing up some of my fellow gardeners' best work, with remnants of grass and flora getting choked up in the wheel, but I tried not to focus on that too much; I would repair it in due course. Repairing Brock, however, was going to be much more of a feat.

At the van, I quickly opened the boot and flicked on a small torch, illuminating the dark space. I grabbed the handles of the wheelbarrow, and then paused for a couple of moments...

"Fuck!"

I hadn't thought this through. I was nowhere near strong enough to hoist the whole contraption into the van, and even if I was, it would topple at the first sign of a road bump. As I stood pondering the situation—and the steps that had led me to this particular conundrum—a plane roared overhead, shaking the foundations of the surrounding structures, flying far too low to be safe.

"Fuck, it's them!" Brock cried, the slush gyrating in the wheelbarrow. I grabbed a large flexi-tub from the back of my van, set it down on the ground and started to scoop with two cupped hands, launching the fluid and rotting remains into the bucket with careless abandon. After a few minutes, I slid my hand around to feel for any last pieces I may have missed, discarded the wheelbarrow on the side of the road, and heaved the tub into the front passenger seat. The slimy residue on my hands felt sticky and sweaty, and without hesitation, I wiped it all over the front of my trousers.

Inside the van, I grabbed the seatbelt and looped it through the handles, before securing it with a satisfactory click. With a booming rumble, the engine stuttered to life, and I backed the vehicle out of the entrance. As soon as the wheels hit the tarmac, I turned to Brock inquisitively.

"I need to know everything, right now."

Under the dim glow of refracted street lights, I stared at the leftover mangle that was Brock's face. It was puffy, bloated and grotesque. His solitary eye spun in its socket, his lips chomping together whenever he tried to speak. Something was keeping this pile of disconnected parts alive, and I felt like I was owed an explanation at the very least.

"I'll tell you everything. Just as it happened," Brock muttered.

As I drove towards the city centre, I quickly wound down the window, hoping Brock wouldn't notice. It was all going so well, until I launched into an unexpected coughing fit, hitting the break and spilling some of the bucket contents onto the floor.

"You wanna be fucking careful mate?" Brock screamed.

I tried to keep my mouth shut in between conversation; I couldn't stand inhaling any more of that ghastly scent.

"Let me start with the plane..." Brock said.

* * *

The inside of the aircraft was freezing cold, and the deafening roar of the engine flooded the enclosed fuselage.

Brock's entire body shook intermittently, the raw lacerations on his upper arms emanating a painful heat, despite the plummeting temperature.

Since being kidnapped three weeks prior, he had been kept at a clandestine facility in the mountains, and subjected to a sick array of experiments. His money, clothes, and identification documents had been seized. He'd been pumped full of a prototype drug and beaten to the point of death again and again. But nothing seemed to push him over the finish line.

A blindfold restricted his vision, but he knew that at least two others were with him. He didn't know where they were headed, but rumours had surfaced about a new facility in the countryside, so that was his best guess.

Brock missed his wife, Kirsten, and his dumb yet adorable kid, Bobby. He missed his home and routine, his friends and relatives. Before all of this, he had been planning his escape, leaving behind his monotonous corporate job and aspirational lifestyle for a more family-friendly existence. He dreamt of living out an early retirement in the countryside, surrounded by nature and community, having the freedom in his late forties that most wouldn't have for another two decades.

But that had been stripped away. Brock couldn't—and daren't—think about the future. These people were animals, predators who had ripped his life away and were intent on keeping him as a human guinea pig until his final breath.

If he stepped foot into this new facility—which was no doubt even more remote and secretive—there would be no chance of escape. Which is why he had to act. Now or never.

Brock was handcuffed, both hands resting on his lap. He had followed every order up until that point, had gained his handlers' trust and ensured them he was at peace with the arrangement, so there had been no need to restrain him. That was their first mistake.

Brock launched to his feet, blindly chose a direction and threw himself forwards. To his amazement, he struck one of the handlers, who grabbed at Brock's face and inadvertently tore off his blindfold. A pair of hands grabbed him from behind, but Brock had enough leverage to sneak from his grip, and pull hard on the emergency exit sign. The heavy metal door decompressed and swung open, sucking all of the air from the cabin and hurtling the passengers onto the floor, dragging them towards the open sky.

Both handlers braced and grabbed a handle on the wall, their bodies flailing in the powerful wind tunnel, anchored only by their loosening grip. Brock tumbled across the floor and was swallowed into the air, caught at the last second by one of the other passengers. He dug at their wrist, clawing into the skin of their hand until they finally let go, releasing him into the atmosphere outside.

Brock's chubby body flung against the side of the aircraft, lightly imprinting the aluminium with his form. He lost all sense of direction, the skin of his face flapping and gyrating with every movement. Brock's heart thumped hard, sending blood circulating around his outstretched mass. With every second, he was descending at a horrifying rate, and could already make out the finer details of the allotment below him. His mouth tore open, expelling a petrified scream as the last few seconds of his flight came to an end.

He braced, just in time for his face to hit the ground. His neck snapped, skin detached, head ripped from his hurtling body. His stomach detonated, flooding the area with undigested food and acid-burnt remains.

Brock had been ready to die, and entirely confused when it didn't happen.

* * *

My van was hidden from view, parked up in the shadows just outside a small shopping complex. It was totally dark out now, and the black bodywork blended into the unlit threshold of the car park. The lights were all turned off, and I was staring at the barely visible outline of the flexi-tub. Brock's story was horrifying, but it was nice to have at least some semblance of a backstory to go on.

"I don't know what to say. It's.... well. It's a lot. Who are these people?"

"*Lifelong Corp.* The dickheads have their logo plastered everywhere... Must think they're untouchable," Brock said.

"And what is your next move?" I questioned.

The slush in the bucket moved, the rotten body parts expelling air as they floated around and change direction.

"I just wanna see my family. Explain things, say I'm sorry. Make sure they're safe."

"And how do you think they'll react? To you, in... well, *this* form?"

"Jesus, you don't mince your words mate," Brock said.

"It's just... well... they won't have seen you. Like this."

"I know, I know. I'll explain everything, like I did to you. I know it's not gonna be the same, but I have to make sure they know I didn't just abandon them."

The glow of a neon sign flickered gently in the distance, signposting the city's single, twenty-four hour petrol station.

"I gotta get some supplies. Do you need anything?"

It was a weird question. God only knew if this man could eat or drink or perform even the most basic of bodily functions. He was a bucket of meat that somehow had sentience, but it didn't feel that way. It was the polite thing to ask, anyway.

"Can I get some wine gums?"

My neck almost cracked with the speed my eyes darted towards the bucket.

"You're kidding, right?"

"No. I like the red ones, they've always been a favourite."

I shook my head in disbelief.

"Uh, okay. I'll be back in a minute."

"You better. Don't even think about leaving me... If they get me and kill me, I'm coming back to haunt your ass."

I chuckled.

"A promise is a promise."

With that, I slipped out of the vehicle and slammed the door, ensuring no-one was around to watch.

* * *

Aside from the cashier and an old woman who couldn't decide between two stale sandwiches, the building was empty.

I jumped into the front seat and immediately pulled out a can of deodorant. I depressed the trigger and shot a huge jet of spray around the car, aiming directly at the contents of the bucket.

Brock startled awake, his torn-off face thrashing in protest.

"What the fuck is this?"

"I'm sorry, mate, I just felt really woozy with this smell. It's getting worse."

"A little warning would have been nice!"

"I'm sorry... But I got Jungle Fresh Cool, it's a really nice scent," I said.

The sound of traffic started to get louder, suggesting more and more cars would be coming past soon. I twisted the key and revved the engine, ready to get out of there.

"What about my wine gums?"

Unbelievable.

With a sigh, I reached into the blue plastic carrier bag, and withdrew a sharing-size pack of the gums. I took a handful and sprinkled them on the surface of the putrid water, as if feeding flakes to a goldfish. Brock's nightmarish face rose to the top, and started to suck up the gums, chowing down with rotten teeth and sloppy lips.

* * *

The main road in and out of the city was a nondescript blur of grey, intermittently peppered with a small off-road café or shop. After almost three hours of driving, the sun had started to peek up from the horizon, painting the sky with a golden glow.

"So tell me about you," Brock inquired.

Sweat was pouring through my vest top and sweater, and my pits and groin felt grimy. My body was a deluge of body odour, but it didn't compare to Brock's distinguished scent.

"Not much to say. I'm just working out my next moves and all that. You fell whilst I was tending to my allotment."

"Jesus, are you fifty years old?" Brock chuckled. He took my silence as a suggestion to keep talking.

"You got a girlfriend?"

"Nope, not right now."

"But there's a girl in your life, right?"

"I mean… There was. Kara. Really great gal. But we had a falling out".

"Ah."

"Yeah."

"It will work out mate, it always does," Brock said. "Give it time, if it's meant to be, it will be, you know."

"Sure," I said, wanting to move on from the conversation. I didn't speak to my own friends about my personal life, let alone strangers, so it felt as if I was in danger of giving a little bit too much of myself up.

"I remember the first girl I fucked," Brock exclaimed. "She was drop…dead…fuckable"

I wasn't expecting the conversation to take such a twist. I half-wondered if a hard-on would appear in amongst the slimy waste.

"We did it *everywhere.* In the halls, her car, my car, her bed, my bed, her parent's bed. She was a perpetual gusher."

"Wow." That was a phrase I could have happily gone my whole life without hearing.

"Just promise me, once you've helped me out, that you'll go and live like a normal young guy. You seem cool, but a bit uptight."

"Thanks for the examination, doc," I joked.

"Pinky promise?" Brock asked, chuckling to himself.

I looked down to see what was so funny, and saw his literal pinky finger floating on the surface, right near his mouth. He poked out his tongue to lick his digit.

I couldn't handle that, at all. I started to gag again, and couldn't hold on to my stomach contents. I spewed a little, all over the steering wheel, trying my best to keep the car on the road between heaves. Slivers of my vomit fell into the bucket, causing Brock to wretch.

Not wanting to linger on my embarrassing expulsion, I decided to update Brock on the journey, intermittently explaining what I could see, or which road we were heading down. We'd traversed a variety of terrains, from forest to dirt tracks to industrial estates, and were now on a narrow back-road with concrete pathways and overgrown plants. We were still safe from public view… as much as we could hope for, for now.

Brock's face slowly drifted around the bucket, chunks of

vomit creeping up on him. His disfigured lips were squeezed tight to avoid any remnants slipping in his mouth.

* * *

I parked up outside Brock's family home, a spacious semi-detached building in the middle of suburbia.

"Is this the right place?" I asked.

After a few moments of pause—with absolutely no feed-back—I asked again.

"Oh, sorry. I thought I was nodding. My face must have just been bobbing," Brock said.

Frustrated, I unclipped my seatbelt and stepped out of the van. I circled around and opened the passenger side door, released Brock's belt, and heaved the bucket out of the vehicle.

"You need a hand with that, mate?"

The voice echoed from across the street, where a young, spotty teen was stood squinting under the sunlight. He was built like a twig, but at least his heart was in the right place.

"No thanks!" Brock and I shouted, almost completely in unison.

The teen shrugged and popped his headphones in, continuing his walk down the road.

After another painful sequence of tugging and shoving, the bucket was outside of the house, and I was frozen at the door with an outstretched hand, thinking about how to deliver this awkward news.

There was no point in overthinking it. The situation was so absurd, so bizarre, I couldn't possibly hope to preempt his family's reaction. I slammed my knuckles against the hard-wood door in a practiced pattern, and was treated to a slew of swearing and shouting from inside the house.

"Wait a fucking minute will you! You better not be fucking Jehovah's!" a woman's voice screeched.

I turned to look at Brock with wide eyes.

"That her?"

"That's my Kirsten." He laughed.

The door swung open with a forceful tug. The woman slouched against the frame, dressed in a purple dressing gown and matching fluffy slippers. Her eye sockets were dark and baggy, encrusted with sleep dust.

"What the fuck do you want at this time in the morning, huh?"

I swallowed hard, before blurting it right out.

"I'm here to talk to you about Brock."

The woman took a deep breath, but hadn't noticed the bucket yet. Brock was letting me get the hard part out of the way—I didn't blame him. Kirsten's face transformed instantly from apathetic to curious, with a hint of desperation. She wanted answers, and hopefully this bizarre adventure could help give her the closure she needed.

"There was an accident and—"

The door opened even more. A young child propped his head around the corner. This must have been Bobby.

"I, uh—"

The woman shook her head, and gestured, indicating I should carry on.

"There was an accident, and, uh… I didn't know Brock well."

"Please. Just tell me what happened to my Brocky".

Before I could piece together the right sentence and emotion, Brock spoke.

"Hey honey."

I couldn't do anything more. I took a step to the side, revealing my dirty little secret.

Kirsten's eyes bulged out of their sockets. She glanced from me to Brock, repeating the movement.

"What sort of sick joke is this? What did you do to my Brocky?".

"Wait, I—"

"Bobby, go back inside!" Kirsten snapped.

"Look. Look at this". I encouraged her to really take a look, but she was having none of it.

"Baby, I need to tell you something important. I really miss you." Brock started.

Kirsten started to break down, disappearing behind the door for a moment. A loud whirring filled the air behind me, and I took a quick glance at the action.

Oh fuck.

A white van, plastered with a huge *Lifelong Corp* logo, had just pulled up. They really were as cocky as Brock suggested. Before the van had even come to a stop, a woman in a white lab coat was readying herself to jump out. I turned back to Kirsten, who had a double-barrel shotgun positioned right between my eyes.

"Wait!" I exclaimed, just as Brock stated the same.

"You need to believe me!" I said.

"Put the gun down!" The woman from the van screamed.

"Baby, it's me!" Brock begged.

Bobby started to scream and cry. I turned to face the mayhem.

"Go back inside, Bobby!" Kirsten screeched.

The boy didn't listen. He ran right up to the bucket, and started to claw through the mush, sliding his hands through Brock's rotten innards, bringing them up to his face as he let out a confused cry. With heavy handfuls of putrid remains, he tried to reform the gloop as if it were a melting snowman.

"Get back here!" she ordered, and little Bobby did what he was told, scuttling back behind her in the doorway.

"Baby," Brock started.

He didn't get a chance to say much more. Overwhelmed by the cacophony of noise and tension, Kirsten squeezed the trigger, sending a jet of sharp bullets into the flesh mounds, splattering them across a well-kept flowerbed, a small decorative wall, various statuettes and the front of my top.

"Nooooo!" I didn't know if it was me or the *LIFELONG CORP* people screaming the word, but I immediately raised my hands above my head.

"You killed my Brocky!" Kirsten spat.

"You hurt my Daddy, you monster!".

"No, please." I pleaded. "I'm just helping."

"Fuck you, you cunt!"

"Mummy noooo!"

"You have to listen to me! Fuck! These people—"

The shotgun jolted upwards, and a burst of hot lava ripped into my chest. My lungs popped on impact, my knees immediately gave way, and rich strands of fresh blood spurted free from my torn skin.

I felt the wind whistle through the parallel holes in my torso, and my vision started to turn black. Someone stood above me, trying their best to resuscitate me, but it was no good, I was fading away.

The last thing I felt was a prickly poke in the face, and another directly into my skull.

* * *

I didn't expect to wake back up.

The inside of the aircraft was freezing cold, and the deafening roar of the engine flooded the enclosed fuselage. My eyes were blurry, abstract shapes dancing in my field of vision as I slowly adjusted to the light. A large oil drum sat in front of me, filled with some kind of viscous liquid.

My chest felt alien, as if it it didn't belong to me—as if it wasn't part of my body anymore. I reached to touch it with outstretched fingertips, and heard the *Lifelong Corp* woman from before pipe up.

"I wouldn't do that if I were you. It's still a very experimental procedure. Serendipitous that all the ingredients for the experiment were right in front of us, actually."

When my eyes fully focused on the scene, I looked down towards my torso, and noticed off-coloured lumps of jellied flesh stitched into my chest. The wound was open, blood seeping from small slivers between the jelly and my original flesh.

"What is this?" I asked quietly, trying to find the energy to stay conscious. My eyes were drooping, it felt like I was running a marathon just to stay awake.

"Brock was a brilliant subject. The serum really connected with his body, his blood fused with it in a way we just didn't expect. And now, his flesh is rejuvenating you. He's keeping you alive."

I looked back at the viscous liquid in the oil drum, my heart slowly sinking into my stomach. It was Brock, his pulverised remains strained and contained in the receptacle. In a separate, smaller drum to my side, his fleshy pulp had been cut up into small chunks, ready to stuff into wounds just like the one in my body.

"Get this out of me," I ordered.

"That will kill you... We're not going to do that."

The woman crouched down to my level, her bulldog grin revealing an overly large tooth-to-gum ratio, her pearly whites gleaming in the fluorescent glow of the overhead lights.

"And we have far too much planned to lose you this soon."

A mess of thoughts raced through my head. All I wanted was to get out. I stumbled to my feet, swaying with every step, and the woman simply giggled, stepping out of my way.

The plane bobbed up and down, causing the floor underneath me to bounce and bend. I slammed into the wall, and reached for the emergency exit handle, curiously checking to see why no-one was trying to stop me. My hand slid onto the cold red handle, gripping it with all my might, and I tugged hard.

Nothing happened. A dampened click rang from the internal mechanism, but even when I pulled it again and again, the door stayed locked.

"Fuck!"

I was trapped. In a massive panic, I started towards the woman, holding my hand above my head as if I really thought I could muster the courage to slap her. She smiled again, that big toothy grin, and simply pushed me back onto the bench.

In my head, I imagined Brock's family waiting down on the ground, haunted by the events that happened right on their doorstep. I imagined my family, desperately wondering what had happened to me and why I hadn't called in so long.

I really hoped I'd have the chance to see them again. And I wanted them to see me. All of me. Not my jellied remains or mangled guinea pig version of myself. I needed to find a way out…

I couldn't let them take me to the facility.

FUSED

Campbell didn't remember what home felt like anymore.

He used to think it was a physical space—the house he spent his entire eighteen years living in, where all of his best memories resided. That concept was uprooted when his dad walked out without warning, leaving Campbell and his mum to fend for themselves, away from the comfort of the family unit and his well-paying government job. They lost their whole lifestyle: their house, routine, and happiness, snuffed out in mere moments.

Perhaps home was more of an abstract concept? Maybe it existed in the relationships you had with friends and family, in the moments shared with your closest loved ones. That sense of comfort had also been torn away when his mum sank into a deep depression right before they were due to move.

With a pile of resumés in one hand and a flask of coffee in the other, Campbell was ready to dive into a day of job hunting. Dressed in a smart shirt and jeans, he locked his front door and paced down the balcony past a dozen doors to a narrow staircase, where he descended five stories to the entrance.

His new home was one of hundreds, each identically shaped and sized, lacking any distinctive character at all. Faded pebbledash facades crumbled to the concrete below, revealing a water-stained structure that had probably never seen a good day, let alone better days. A sense of rot and decay permeated the estate, eroding any attempt at improvement. The space was devoid of personality yet bustling with residents, who scuttled around like insects, living moment to moment without the hope of something better.

The first stop on Campbell's journey was a cramped coffee shop *Lucy's*. A rather apathetic sign loomed above the door, with the name written in a vintage cursive font. The yellow and green colour scheme was both dated and unappealing, but a steady stream of customers visited the establishment, so it couldn't have been that bad.

Campbell wandered into the café, his new shoes squeaking against the textured floor tiles. A haggard old woman grunted in acknowledgement, and ambled over to the till, cleaning grease from her hands with a dirty washcloth.

"Yep?" she croaked.

"I, uh, I'm handing out CVs. Are you hiring at the moment?"

The woman cackled, shaking her head.

"I make enough to cover my own expenses… just about. If I need help, I call family. I haven't hired no help for years. Good luck."

"Okay, well. Just a coffee then please."

He laid out a bundle of coins, and she nodded to a cup sitting on the countertop.

"Take that one. Eddie didn't drink it."

He didn't know who Eddie was, and didn't much fancy drinking his coffee, but he took it anyway.

With that, the woman turned and crawled to the coffee machine, wiping it down with the same washcloth she had just stained with bacon grease. Campbell reshuffled his paperwork, hiding his embarrassment under a fake smile as his feet squeaked towards the exit.

Back in the harsh summer daylight, he took a big gulp of the lukewarm coffee and turned back to look at the café. In the front window, a huge blue sign was taped to the glass with a rough scribble written in permanent marker.

"Staff needed. Apply within."

Campbell snorted in disbelief—he had missed that on the way in. Clutching hard onto his papers, he stormed back towards the entrance, feeling insulted and humiliated in equal measure. He was ready to burst in and demand that he be interviewed for the position, and did not plan on leaving until he had an answer as to why he was unsuitable.

"I wouldn't if I were you."

The voice came from just behind Campbell. Nestled behind a short brick wall, a group of three residents around his age sat slumped on a set of stairs, smoking a huge joint.

Campbell froze, waiting for the scene to play out. In his head, he was already estimating how fast he would have to run to escape, and any potential routes out of the complex. He had been cornered by a group like this before, back in his old town, and it was only his quick thinking that had secured his escape from something potentially dangerous. His gears turned at a million miles an hour, and his heart felt like it needed to escape. But he didn't let the anxiety show on his face, he just gritted his teeth and stayed silent.

"You're not from here, are you?" the leader of the group questioned.

After a slight pause, Campbell shook his head.

"No. I'm not."

This caused the teen to clamber to his feet, slightly hazy from the weed. At this moment, Campbell felt pressure in his back pocket: the extra item he'd packed for his job hunt today—a small pocket knife.

Having been beaten to a pulp by bullies on more than one occasion, and without anyone to look after him at the new place, he'd decided to swipe the weapon from his old house before his dad collected his things. Campbell's memories of the past month or so were patchy at best—probably from the stress of the breakup and the move and his mum's decision to stay at his aunt's for the foreseeable future—but he didn't forget to arm himself. Every day, the knife sat in his back pocket, waiting for a reason to be drawn, for the silky metal to be exposed to the sunlight.

Campbell traced the outline of the weapon in his pocket, ready to end this situation before it even began. His palms were sweaty, but he was hyper-focused on these kids.

"Where are you from?"

Campbell swallowed hard, clearing his throat.

"Like twenty minutes away. Not far."

The teen paced closer towards him, reaching back towards the other two kids with an expressionless face. Campbell's hand twitched, ready to pull out the metal and slice this boy, his fingers gauging how far the knife was embedded under his wallet.

The teen swung his arm forwards, and just as Campbell touched the cold metal grip of the knife, he noticed something in his hand. It was the joint, still burning with a heavy smell of weed. None of the residents in the café were paying the group any mind, just mindlessly tucking into greasy fry-ups and watching videos on their phones.

Campbell looked at the other kids, and then back to the teen. He accepted the joint, slipped it between his lips and took a huge puff. The smoke lingered in his throat, tickling the membrane inside, causing him to sputter out a huge cough. The kids laughed, and Campbell joined them on the steps. He set down his papers, and took another huge puff, slyly slipping the knife to a more comfortable position as he sat down.

Looking forwards, he noticed the brickwork on *Lucy's* had changed. It was buzzing, almost, a blur of textures that couldn't decide where to settle. The weed must have hit him quick, he thought to himself.

* * *

The traffic from the motorway sounded really loud. Like, incredibly loud, for something that was almost half a mile away.

Campbell's senses were hyper-focused, and he felt as if he was a guest in his own body. Every movement, every reaction felt as if it needed to be rehearsed in his head before he played it out physically. The group were talking shit about a film or something. Campbell was tuning in and out, but did notice that the brickwork on the shop was back to normal again.

He hadn't smoked in a year or so, and his tolerance had definitely faded since his last smoke. It was with a girl, Jessie Chapman, at his old school. He had liked her for a long time, but fell at the last hurdle when they were just about to make out. Campbell had loaded up the paper with far too much weed, and a few puffs made them both collapse into a ball, staring at the sky for the rest of the day, before heading home completely exhausted. That memory seemed so distant, as if he had seen it on a film or read it in a story.

He didn't want to get to that level this time, especially in front of new people, so he was taking it easy. Campbell had learned the names of the kids in front of him. The one that had done all the talking was Spence, who was at least six foot tall and built like a bodybuilder. There was also Kit, who was chubby and laidback, and Weasel, who was a ball of frenetic energy, and talked like he had a word count he had to hit every minute.

As he tuned back into the conversation, he heard a weird metallic pattern emanate from below. Rhythmic, but distant.

"Do you guys hear that?"

He looked around by his feet, and the other teens did the same, before Weasel started to howl with laughter.

"Look in your hand man! Jesus!"

Campbell stared down at his clenched fist, and noticed his phone tucked beneath his thumb. It was ringing at full volume, and he quickly swiped it to answer. He clambered to his feet, and the world span in a momentary hazy blur, before settling back to its static position.

"Hello?"

"Hello darling, it's Aunty Ruth. How are you settling in?"

"Aunty Ruth, hey. Err, yeah... I'm just out now, outside, handing out CVs. It's going good. How's Mum?

"Yeah, she's holding up okay. She's sleeping now but I'll get her to call later. Or tomorrow. See how she's doing."

Campbell smiled, trying to focus on the conversation, and not the hundreds of other sounds that were competing for his attention.

"Okay. Yeah tomorrow is perfect, actually. I'm going to a party tonight, so we can talk then. Give her some rest too."

"A party, already? Looks like you're settling in perfectly! I'll tell your Mum you said hi. Be safe, talk soon."

Campbell hung up the phone, and turned around to face the group. Spence was already on his feet, and wrapped his arm around Campbell's shoulder, leading him to a darker space behind some bins.

"Mate, I didn't realise you were packing."

He nodded down at Campbell's pockets, causing him to feel a rush of anxiety.

"I wasn't going to—"

"No mate. It's cool. You just gotta hide that shit better, okay? People will talk, and you don't wanna get caught with it on you. But I get it, we gotta stay protected yeah?"

Campbell nodded, overcome with relief. He was already tired of being high, and the constant rollercoaster of emotions that swam through his body.

"Whose turn is it to roll?" Spence questioned, and the group all turned to stare at Campbell.

* * *

Mixing weed and vodka was always going to be a terrible idea. But that didn't stop Campbell and his new mates downing shot after shot at the house party.

The apartment belonged to Jessie, Spence's on-off girlfriend, and she'd been kind (or stupid) enough to invite everyone their age in the immediate vicinity, which covered both their estate and two more that laid adjacent to it.

The heaving mass of teens created a sweaty, intimate atmosphere, and now he was about ten shots and four joints deep, all Campbell wanted to do was escape for some fresh air. He stumbled out of the door, pressed past a group and slinked down to the ground level.

He inhaled a huge gulp of air, like a diver who had just surfaced from deep water, and pressed his head into his hands.

"Fuuuuuck."

Campbell took another mouthful of air, and looked around at the buildings that surrounded him, trying to decipher the blurry outlines of objects that populated the area. Just behind the bin shed, a flailing shadow was creeping left and right, before disappearing back behind the metal canisters.

"Hello?"

Campbell tried to find his bearings, spinning from side to side. The party upstairs was in full swing, with crowds of screaming teens and loud music echoing into the night. Through squinting eyes, Campbell paced slowly towards the bins, checking his surroundings as he did so, ready to run if anything threatened to transpire. He wasn't completely in sync with his body right now, and he cursed himself for being so vulnerable out in the open, with no-one to help him.

Claaaaang.

The industrial-sized bins clattered together, and one of the lids rolled up on its hinges. Campbell instinctively reached into his jeans, and armed himself with the pocket knife. Its textured grip felt sturdy in his hands, and whilst a sober version of Campbell would leave it folded until the last moment, the drunk version decided to spread the blade to full length, its sharp metal pointed out in front of him.

Claaaash.

The blade led the way, spinning to a three o'clock position. Campbell's arms were shaking, but the weapon gave him comfort. He was confident that with this blade, he'd be able to protect himself, and give any potential bully the fright of their life.

A wisp of air behind him... Then in front of him... He could feel someone was nearby.

He turned on his heels, spinning frenetically to face this antagonist.

Left... Right...

Forwards.

Campbell couldn't take it any more. He jolted his arm forwards, and penetrated a fleshy target.

Under the dim yellow streetlights, he could see a crooked outline of a man... Or perhaps someone his age, it was hard to tell. They were gasping for air, clutching at their stomach with clawed fingers, trying to back up off the blade.

Completely frozen, Campbell stood still for a few seconds, the weapon still inside of the man's streaming wound. It wasn't long until the guy collapsed to the floor, his face illuminated by hazy halogen street-lamps.

Oh fuck no. Fuck, fuck, fuck.

It was Weasel. He had just fucking stabbed him.

Instinctively, Campbell folded the blade shut, wiping the blood on his sleeve, before preparing to slip it back in his jeans.

No. They'll find me with it. It will be my fault.

His brain rushed through a tapestry of scenarios, trying to calculate the best decision in the moment.

What if they find me. What if Spence sees me?

It wasn't worth thinking about. Snapping back into his own body, Campbell launched the knife into the bin, and shut the lid. Without precise direction, he sprinted into the dark, confident in his ability to eventually stumble back to his new house.

He wanted to call his Mum. He wanted to explain everything, talk it out, happen upon a plan like they used to. But she wasn't answering her phone. Neither was Aunty Ruth. He was fucking stuck, all alone in a new place with no family or friends, and a potential murder looming over him.

And it was only day one.

* * *

There was blood all over the chopping board. His Mum's favourite chopping board.

Campbell had thrown together a sandwich of sorts, sliced turkey ham slapped between two slices of stale bread. But when he tried to cut it with a knife, it gave way to a torrent of warm crimson.

He held his hands out in front of his face. The red liquid engulfed his hands with a shimmery glow, highlighted by the red and blue lights that erupted across the estate from below. The music had stopped, but crowds of voices could still be heard outside.

Campbell shook his head, trying to force his eyes to adjust, but the stains on his hands wouldn't disappear. He left the hacked up sandwich on the board and retreated to his bedroom, switched off the light, and buried his head in his pillow. Haunting screams and intermittent cries echoed around the concrete estate, and it was all Campbell's doing.

What if they know it's me?

What if there is CCTV footage?

What if they're on their way up now to arrest me?

What will Mum think?

All questions that weren't worth considering that late at night. He'd deal with this in the morning.

Campbell squeezed his eyes shut, and tried his best to erase the day's memories

The awkward moment in the coffee shop.

Smoking weed with strangers.

The wild blur of the party.

Weasel's panicked expression, his eyes wet with fear.

Campbell tossed and turned for a good few hours before finally slipping into a world of numb darkness.

* * *

Daylight burned through the curtains, exposing every imperfection on the magnolia bedroom walls. Small cracks, uneven layers of plaster, holes from picture frames hung and taken down generations before Campbell lived there.

Campbell's eyes broke through the crusty debris of the night before, and for just a moment, it was like none of it had ever happened. A smile almost dared to appear on his face, before reality came crashing down on him.

His whole body ached, and he had sweated right through his sheets, the thin cotton material plastered onto his moist skin. He really needed to piss, he knew that much, but he couldn't bear to stand yet.

Campbell's head was pounding, tense and fragile in equal measure. He slowly lifted his arms, positioning them in front of his face, ready to decode whether the stains were real or imaginary.

His left hand was clean, with no trace of blood or any type of dirt. His right one was a different story entirely.

Jolting into a seated position, Campbell rubbed his eyes, trying to ascertain the reality of what he was looking at.

The pocket knife was back, outstretched in his hand, buried under layer upon layer of hardened skin. Wrapped like a puff pastry, each layer entombed the weapon into his clenched fist, so only the block colour and shape were visible beneath the flesh.

Like a new, manmade appendage, the knife was fused to him, an extension of his limb. With his left hand, he attempted to claw at the new flesh wrap, but it was thick and crusty, like a geriatric person's toenails. There was sensation in the flesh, sure, but it was impenetrable.

With clawed fingers, he scratched and scratched, but the layers wouldn't disintegrate.

He threw the knife in the bin—he *knew* it. So what was happening?

Campbell sprinted into the kitchen, and grabbed the knife he had used to cut the sandwich the night prior. He unconsciously noted that all of the blood had disappeared from the board—had it even been there in the first place?

With only a momentary hesitation, he placed the blade against the husk, and ran it gently in a vertical sweeping motion. He gradually added pressure, but the skin didn't even peel.

"FUCK!"

He slammed the knife onto the counter, and span in a semicircle, looking for the next best option to try. Before he had a chance to grab something, the doorbell rang.

No. Oh fuck no.

The curtains were still ajar from the day before, and whoever was at the door would probably try peeking through the window as their next move. Campbell plummeted to the kitchen floor, slinking behind a cabinet to try and hide his frame.

With a growing impatience, he began to bite at the flesh, his teeth met with a nondescript rubber taste. When that didn't work, he dragged the husk against the sharp side of the kitchen unit, hoping to create a crack or wound of some kind, which could be used to manipulate the weapon from his fingers. But that didn't work either.

The doorbell rang again, this time with an elongated tone.

"Mr Ashby? It's the police, we know you're in there, please come to the door."

Fuck. This is it. You stupid prick, what's Mum going to think? She will top herself, this will push her over the edge, you IDIOT. She hasn't even moved in yet and you've fucked up.

Nothing was going to work. Campbell rose to his feet, and snatched a tea-towel from one of the moving boxes on the side. He wrapped the appendage in the material, and bent his arm behind his back.

Clutching the lock, he took a deep breath, before twisting the mechanism. The door propped open, and he was met by a friendly looking woman and a slightly rougher older guy.

"Hello, Mr Ashby. I'm DI Taylor, this is DI Clark."

Campbell swallowed, imagining himself in the near future, being handcuffed whilst his rights were read out to him under the nosy gaze of the entire floor of flats.

"We're going door to door to get information about an assault last night. Can I ask where you were between approximately 9:00pm and 1:00am?"

Campbell shook his head.

"Last night? Uh, well… I was at a party, on the floor below me. I left around 10:00pm, I guess? Honestly, the move tired me out, so I called it a day quite early."

"You're new right? Who did you go to the party with?"

"Oh, erm. Some kids around my age. Spence, and uh…

Kit. And Weasel. Those three."

DI Taylor nodded.

"How long have you known them?" she questioned.

"We met just yesterday. When I was handing out CVs. They seemed cool, and I'm here on my own, so I thought it would be good to socialise."

The two DI's nodded.

"And were you aware of the assault? Around midnight?"

Campbell shook his head. He wasn't sure if it was on cue or too early... Would they suspect something was up?

"No. I was fast asleep. Sorry. Is everyone okay?"

"There was an incident. Your friend, Weasel? He was attacked. So you're *sure* you didn't know anything about it?"

Campbell swallowed hard, before telling another lie.

"No. I'm sorry."

They both looked at each other, holding their gaze for a painstaking beat, before agreeing on a nod.

"One more question. What's wrong with your hand?"

Campbell grinned, confused, before shaking his head again.

"My hand? Uh, nothing, why do you ask?"

"Because it's behind your back. Can we see?"

FUCK. This is it. I'm totally fucked.

Campbell grinned nervously, sweat beginning to drip from his forehead.

"Oh, this? It's nothing, honestly."

She didn't ask again, instead instructing with a single nod.

Apprehensively, Campbell bent his arm back around his body, removed the tea towel and showed them his outstretched hand. Their eyes bounced between his hand and his face, before they both nodded in agreement again.

"If you hear anything, let us know."

They handed over a business card and left. Campbell

couldn't believe his eyes.

The whole appendage had disappeared. The knife, the flesh, the crusty husk, all gone. It was all his imagination.

How he wished that the stabbing had been in his imagination too…

He could call his Mum and explain it all away, explain that everything was just fine at the new house and he was getting it prepared for their new lives together, a fresh start after all of the trauma and sadness of the last six months.

* * *

Weasel's face was plastered over the local news channel, complemented by a running commentary of police findings and a rather apathetic newsreader reeling off details like they were reading the menu at a restaurant.

They weren't revealing what condition the teen was in, but Campbell had already decided in his head that he was a murderer. He was starting to imagine what his cell would look like, and getting his story straight for the judge, jury, and his Mum. In his head, he was jumped by the teen, and happened upon a knife whilst they fought on the floor. In a final act of survival, he grabbed the knife—unwillingly, of course—and stabbed the boy once to get away from him, all in the name of self-defence.

The TV seemed to emanate a weird light. The textures didn't seem right again, just like the brickwork at *Lucy's* the day before. Campbell stared until it settled once again, and for just a moment, he couldn't place where he was or what was happening. Was he disassociating? It definitely wasn't the weed any more, maybe it was the stress?

Then he got to thinking about Weasel again… and the overwhelming fear in his eyes….

The images in his head ran on a loop, and after hours of

building the narrative in his head, he was almost starting to believe his own lies. With the TV continuing to run in the background, Campbell sauntered over to the kitchen, disposed of the stale, mouldy sandwich, and removed a pizza from the freezer. He whacked it onto a baking tray and slammed it into the oven. On his phone, he set a timer for thirty minutes before scrolling through his notifications.

In a neat list, he could see that his mum had tried to call five times whilst he was watching TV.

Fuck it.

He immediately redialed the number and waited with bated breath for her to answer.

"Hello?"

"Mum. It's so good to hear your voice!" Campbell said.

"I've only been gone a few days. Bless you. How's the house?"

"It's, uh. It's nice! I've started unpacking. Already met some friends..."

"Oh, that's good," she said ,apathetically.

"Yeah… It's good. How are you?"

There was a moment of pause.

"Heard from your Dad?"

"Uh, no. I wouldn't talk to him even if he did reach out. Why do you ask?"

"The bastard is trying to deny me any maintenance. I need you to call him and make sure he gives us the whole amount."

"I don't know if I can do that. Don't we need to wait for court?"

"I'm in no position to go to court! I'm signed off with depression, you know that, and I need you to help right now. Otherwise we'll have no money and you'll need three jobs to pay the rent."

Campbell shook his head.

"I'll try and call him, Mum, if it will help."

A loud knock against the front door.

"I have to go. I'll talk to you tomorrow."

"Once you've called your Dad?"

"Yes. Okay. Bye."

For just a moment, Campbell froze in position, standing perplexed as he looked around at the room. Something wasn't right.

Echoes of his mother's voice rang from different angles, hidden behind walls and floorboards and the plaster on the ceiling. He lifted the device and checked if he had hung up —he had.

His skin felt strange, as if it didn't belong to him. All of his senses were dulled, as if suddenly switched off in his brain. His mother's tone evaporated, and just as fast as the surreal moment had started it came to an end.

The door shook again with an impatient knock.

"Coming!"

Campbell ran over and placed his eye over the peephole. It was Spence, looking shifty and anxious. Cautiously, he opened the door and invited him inside.

"I've been looking everywhere for you. We never exchanged numbers or addresses."

Campbell nodded.

"I know. I only heard today, I'm pretty shook up by what happened. Being new here and that..."

Spence stared at Campbell, as if trying to weigh up what he was saying with his obviously manic aura.

"I'm gonna be straight with you, man. You seem cool, but we don't know you. You're new here, and that makes you suspect number one. And we know you have a knife."

Campbell felt a lump grow in his throat. His next movements would be crucial. One decision out of place could get him jailed, or worse.

"I know. But it wasn't me. I'd never actually use it."

Spence stared at him, evaluating his posture, reading his eyes, searching for a crack in his armour.

"This whole situation is so fucked," Campbell offered, breaking the icy tension between them.

Spence stared a moment longer, before relaxing back into himself.

"Yeah. It's fucked up. I'm here for two reasons. Firstly, to see if you saw anything. Secondly, you need to get rid of your knife. The police are gonna be hot on everyone's heels, and you can't give them room to set you up."

Campbell heard the words, but took a moment to react. He felt as if he was high again, trying to interpret the best movements and replies to keep the spotlight firmly away from him.

"Okay. I will. Where should I get rid of it?"

"I'll take it for you. Go get it, quick."

Fuck.

Campbell froze. He had no idea what to say or do, and could already imagine the beating he was going to get when Spence found out.

"Sure. Okay. One second."

He sidestepped into the hallway and backtracked to his room. Just as he passed under the doorframe, he hear a loud siren bleep outside the entrance to the estate.

"Fuck!" Spence shouted.

Campbell headed back out to him.

"Plan B, meet me tomorrow, I can't take it now with the pigs out there. Lay low and don't say anything to them if they ask, okay?"

He fist-bumped Campbell—who awkwardly tried to go in for a handshake at first—and went on his way. Campbell slammed the door behind him, and finally exhaled the oxygen he had kept locked in his lungs.

That was enough drama for one day. Campbell spent the rest of the afternoon glued to the TV, watching re-runs of vintage soaps, mindlessly moping the day away. He used his CVs as a placemat for his coffee, which he refilled several times before passing out on the couch.

* * *

Campbell was halfway on the sofa and halfway on the floor. Caught in some kind of gravitational glitch, he awoke to the strange phenomenon of being in stasis, floating above the ground. His right arm itched like a motherfucker, and with a lazy stretch, he led his fingers to his arm and began to scratch.

The feeling of rubber dug under his fingernails. He tried to snatch his wrist back towards his body, but it wouldn't move.

The world was beginning to sharpen, the hazy shapes clarifying in real time. Campbell tried to snatch his hand back again, but all he could feel was a sloshy, warm sensation. He opened his eyes wide—and was face to face with Weasel's lifeless body. His bloated face was grey and scaly, his lips a pale blue. Campbell tried to pull back, but noticed his hand was embedded within the fleshy knife mass again, which in turn was penetrating directly into Weasel's torso.

Like a moment froze in time, Campbell was stabbing Weasel, unable to release his hand, entombed in his stomach cavity by a wrap of flesh and sinew. Each jolt of his wrist removed and punctured the lesion, with lashings of bile and stomach acid coating Campbell's wrist and forearm.

Campbell launched himself to the floor, in turn pulling Weasel's body from the couch directly on top of him. In the intimate, face-to-face position, Campbell writhed and tried to pull himself free with his unoccupied hand, but it was no use.

Weasel's dead lip's slipped open, releasing a torrent of undigested food and blood onto Campbell's exposed face. The smell was inhumane, the rotting liquid dripping onto his forehead and nose, remnants dripping into his open mouth.

With a panicked heave, Campbell managed to rotate Weasel's body off of his, his arm twisting to stay enveloped in his gut. The knife continued to enter and exit the laceration, slipping back and forth through the same few inches, like a virgin trying to pleasure his girlfriend.

Campbell wanted nothing more than to call for help, but doing so would get him a one-way trip to prison. He didn't know how this was happening, but he knew damn sure that he couldn't get caught like it.

Sliding Weasel onto his back, Campbell climbed onto the corpse, and tried to rise from a squat, pulling his arm upwards with a fleshy extension. The body was sprawled in a heap, but the wound wouldn't let up. Campbell jerked and yanked the corpse across the floor, directing it towards the kitchen until he could reach the knife block.

He grabbed the large knife from atop the chopping board and tried to manoeuvre it between the wound and his wrist, but every laceration he made seemed to heal itself with fresh tendons and flesh.

"FUCK!"

What do I do now? FUCK ME.

Running out of options, Campbell tried to think. None of this made any sense, but the next option that came to his mind was to heat the other knife, and try and melt the flesh.

He snapped the ignition on the gas hob, and turned the largest ring onto the highest heat.

Moments later, he was hovering the blade over the flame. After the metal began to glow with an orange heat, he quickly swung the weapon down to the flesh mound, and placed the scorching edge onto the skin. A pork-like smell emanated from the sizzling flesh, and though it looked as if it was finally making a mark, the burned laceration amalgamated into a new, seamless join as soon as the heat was removed.

"FUCK! FUCK! FUCK!"

Campbell threw the knife to the side and jostled with the blade that was already embedded in Weasel. Every movement made the wound deeper and wider, but it didn't let up. Weasel's empty white eyes rattled in their open sockets as Campbell's limb twisted in its socket, sending shooting pains from his wrist to his neck.

In the heat of the moment, he didn't notice the tea-towel on the cutting board, which flopped onto the open flame. The hob ring singed the towel on impact, causing a black scorch mark to develop, giving way to a smaller flame that grew from the darkness.

Campbell looked around, and noticed the fire build from the hob to the closest wall. It spread in mere seconds, engulfing the entire wall and a small patch of the ceiling.

Orange flames danced across the kitchen surface and sent a plume of black smoke hurtling towards the smoke alarm. It took a few moments to take effect, before ringing out the most intense siren imaginable.

"FUCK! HELP ME!"

Campbell slipped on the tiled surface, and fell on top of the body, pushing the knife right through the laceration and cracking a fragment of the spine away. Campbell began to cry, tears of frustration welling between his eyelids and cascading down his face. He tried to crawl away, but the body was too heavy.

Outspread on the floor, he was moments away from giving up. Embers crackled from the ceiling above, and dropped onto Weasel's stale clothing. Small flames bred on the material, growing into a fiery mass of charred skin and blackened cotton. The body was slowly inundated with white hot flames, and Campbell could feel the heat on his mangled hand. The heat was starting to melt the fusion of skin, but it wasn't separating quickly enough.

His mother's voice echoed around the house again, vibrating behind hidden corners, out of reach yet intimately close. A thick fog of smoke plumed from the oven, causing Campbell's eyes to itch ferociously. The words were muddled, as if another language entirely.

"MUM? IS THAT YOU?"

He knew it wasn't. The auditory hallucination was skittish and ethereal, neither here nor there, existing in a space that wasn't real but not quite fiction. The heat smothered his exposed body, his clothes crisping up in the torrid air. This was the end, and he couldn't quite grasp his emotions.

In a split-second decision, Campbell stretched his fingers out and retrieved the kitchen knife from the floor. He allowed the blade to heat up in the flames, and began to saw at his own wrist, just above the newly fused flesh. Blood spurted from each laceration, and Campbell immediately felt light-headed and sick, letting out a constant scream as he did it.

The pain was indescribable, but the smoke had already filled his lungs, and this was a last-ditch attempt to save his life. The entire room was alight, eighteen years worth of memories set ablaze, but Campbell wasn't ready to give up. His mum needed him, he knew that deep inside, and he wasn't going to allow her to experience any more trauma if he could help it.

His wrist was a disfigured mangle of flesh, blood and bone now, already flopping like a spiral of pasta. Without warning, he switched his grip up on the knife, and started to hammer down on the bone with the blunt edge of the knife, obliterating the last remaining tangles of sinew that connected his limb to his digits.

Moments later, he was free. Blood gushed from the fresh stump, coating the flames in a red haze. He crawled to the front door slowly, whilst the smoke alarm rang out at full pitch. When he finally cracked the door open and slumped his body halfway out of the threshold, he looked back to the remains of Weasel's body—only to notice it wasn't there. He chuckled maniacally, just in time for the flames to reach the gas pipe and detonate the entire floor of flats.

His body was tossed into the open air like a rag doll, straight over the balcony, sending him careering to the concrete slabs underneath. He felt his body mash against the pavement, before everything went black.

* * *

Was this real? Or was this fiction?

Campbell slid his neck from side to side, the bone crunching with every rotation. His body wasn't working right, nothing underneath his shoulders had any sensation whatsoever.

He didn't know where he was. This wasn't home, not as he knew it. Not the old house or the new house, or anywhere that bared any resemblance to his memories.

His memories... They were blurry now, like when you woke up from a vivid dream. Everything is so real and life-like in dreams, entire universes and timelines created, with relationships, friendships, hobbies, aspirations, fears, likes, dislikes, all entangled into one truth. But he felt none of that.

The light outside his window was too bright. The bird-song was too sharp.

Campbell was strapped into a wheelchair, his left arm

lying motionless on the armrest, and his right arm flopped on his lap.

He was missing his right hand... Cut off at the wrist, with surgical skill, it seemed. Not hacked or torn away.

The skin that wasn't hidden by loose leisurewear was all burned, a mesh of featureless flesh in violent swirled patterns.

In front of him, a pen knife and half-smoked joint were on the table, alongside a tray with a vast array of coloured pills and containers. Some tablets were crushed, others were whole, a rainbow of colours arranged into neat rows.

By each row, a number was etched onto a small post-it note, as if they were being administered one by one.

His mother's voice rose up from the background. But this time, she was there. He could feel it.

Campbell would have called her, if his voice worked. He could hear the muttering clearly, but had to really tune in to understand it.

Why had she left him in there alone? What had happened to him?

As he rotated his head further left, a board full of actors headshots came into view. It didn't take a genius to contrast actor's headshots to those taken for passports or fun, they had a distinct look to them... Shallow depth of field, blurred background, precise framing. The photos were printed on glossy paper, pinned to the giant board with brass tacks, with notes scribbled onto each individual face.

His mother's voice was becoming clearer. Campbell could just about make out the conversation, though he would need more than three guesses to speculate who was on the receiving end of the conversation.

"The drugs aren't working. We've tried twenty-four combinations. Twenty-four cocktails of these tablets, and he still wakes up fresh. Why won't they stick?"

A woman's voice, mature but nervous, answered back gently.

"This is going to cause some real damage. I haven't perfected this trial yet."

"I don't care," his mum fired back. "He can't have *any* memory of what really happened. Whatever he is dreaming in these sessions is better than the truth. If he found out what really caused those burns, the *monster* that really took his hand, well... I couldn't live with myself."

There was a short pause, before the mature woman came up with an answer.

"We have no way of knowing what hallucinations this is causing. He could be building a whole life whilst he's under, and to keep snapping him back and forth to new realities is going to completely mess up his brain."

"Then that's what we do. We mix it up, slush it around until he's so confused there's no way he can remember. Nothing of what he has experienced is real, but we have to convince him it is. To avoid the real truth."

Campbell could feel his heart beating fast—not in his chest, but from the palpitations that were pumping through the veins in his neck. He wished he could look around the room, see what was in the rest of the space, try to ascertain where he was. In front of him, he could only see a desk and a window, with bright sunlight streaming through the glass panels. But the world outside didn't look right. The birds moved in glitchy patterns, the colour of the light seemed artificial. He was almost certain it was a fake environment, being played out on a digital screen.

The feeling of artifice encouraged him to take another look at the actor's headshots. He scanned through the faces, imagining who these people were in real life, where the photos were taken, who they wanted to be.

And then he stopped.

Oh God no.

Spence. Weasel. Lucy from the café. They were all there, with the same nondescript, expressionless face. They were all actors, imprinted into his brain by unconscious exposure to their headshots.

But even worse, the final picture his eyes happened upon…

His mother. The woman he was closest with... was just an actor's headshot.

He knew the voice was his mother… he had no doubt in his mind. It's the only thing that was real in this world.

But everything else was a complete mystery. He tuned back into the conversation.

"Listen to me. Not many people know what I do, and if *this* came out, if the public caught onto this? It will ruin years of work. Absolute decades. So I am asking you, as a friend, as a colleague, *please* find a way to erase those memories, and get his brain to make up something else. Just something simple that covers my ass. There's a hundred ways he could have gotten these injuries… We just need one."

The mature woman groaned, before finally giving in.

"We have another few options. A few more drugs."

"Then let's get to it," Campbell's mum concluded, before the sound of high heels clacking against hard vinyl emanated from behind him.

Campbell wished he could feel his legs.

He wished he could run away and get real help.

Most of all, he wished he knew what caused these injuries, and could finally know some truth about his life. Everything he had dreamed was a lie… There was no Spence, no Weasel, no *Lucy's*. And if that wasn't real, what else had people lied to him about? What had really happened to his body?

He made it his one and only mission to find out.

NEOTON

ELIJAH

Elijah was building the world as he wanted to see it.

A world without pain, disease, breakups or depression. A world where every client would be the main character in their own story.

If you could recreate the world as an ideal environment without any of these negative aspects, what would it look like?

For Elijah, it was a bright summer's day every single day, in a fictitious city called Neoton. This world was bustling with people of all backgrounds, races, sexualities, and creed, co-existing in the most pure, harmless manner.

The environment was built from the ground up, starting as a blank landscape with only the bare essentials—terrain, water, and empty buildings—and slowly adorned with people, vehicles, plants, weather systems, and everything that made reality realistic.

Various schematics and drawings papered his walls, with designs of everything from the terrain through to interior architecture and décor. The entire project made use of his considerable IT skills, mixed with a passion for virtual reality and a niche interest in cybernetic organisms. Elijah thrived on the boundary of humanity and technology, and his latest invention, Bioland, was about to shake up the entire tech industry... he was sure of it.

Bioland was a system that linked the human body to a virtual processor through a connection in the side of the head. Elijah had hardwired a connection slot manually, directly into his left temple, but he was still exploring options that were slightly less invasive. Still, it would be well worth it, and if he could prove the limitless possibilities of this project to the general public, a small procedure was a trifling price to pay for transcendent experience.

Elijah was on the cusp of something huge, and he couldn't wait to see how it played out.

TARA

Tara sat at the kitchen table, head in hands, trying her best to stay awake. Elijah worked in the spare room adjoining the kitchen, making a racket. She was straight off a late shift at A+E, and could barely touch her microwave meal. The carrots were soggy. The chicken was off, in an indescribable way. And don't get her started on the "mashed potatoes".

Just once, she'd love to come in to a home-cooked meal. Was that so much to fucking ask? Instead, she would have to eat dinner, go for a shower, and get ready for tomorrow, all in a half-hour timeframe, to be afforded a four hour sleep. Something had to give.

"You gonna come join me for a bit?" she asked, uttering the words in Elijah's general direction. He didn't answer, of course. He was too caught up in his dreamworld. The house was a museum of unfinished promises—a half-built cot sat in the spare room, yellowed adoption papers lay piled under tech magazines, and Tara's online university application had been abandoned somewhere in there too.

For all of the ambition and initial attraction, their partnership was slowly decaying—Elijah chased the shadow of a dream that didn't even make sense to her. Tara had put all of her ambitions on hold… when would it be her turn to be selfish?

She was letting her head run wild again, and she hadn't even finished the carrots. Now she'd have to get all this done in twenty three minutes. And Elijah was still fucking around with computer parts in the next room, ignorant to the fact she was even in the house.

Tara was tired. And she wasn't sure how long she could go on like this for.

ELIJAH

After a brief sleep, and seeing Tara off to work, Elijah was ready to get stuck in and start troubleshooting Neoton. Two years of hard work had built to this moment, and if he could just get the next few weeks to work in his favour, he would have a product that would change the landscape of this type of technology. And then he could give some more time to Tara and their shared goals, as he knew he'd been a little selfish with his time in recent years.

A team would have made this a hundred times easier, of course, but it was in his contract that he work alone, and keep all information hidden under an impenetrable non-disclosure agreement. The company bankrolling the project would provide everything he needed in terms of resources to build the project, and on completion, he would have a 50% stake in the most groundbreaking project of this century.

Elijah grabbed the end of a thick red wire, which he had named the "starter cable" in the first draft of his instruction booklet. He grabbed the metal input, and slipped it between flexible flaps of flesh, which parted ways as he applied some pressure to the area. He felt a satisfactory click as the connections linked, and a small electrical wave started to pulsate through his skull.

On the other end of the starter cable was a small, flesh-coloured device, shrouded in a gelatinous wrap, which simply had an ON/OFF toggle and a small LCD screen. Eventually, Elijah would build a more contemporary device, but this would get him past the first finish line. The future was bright with new ideas and updates, and he could hardly wait to see how advanced the technology would become in a year or two.

There was one hard and fast rule with prototyping this tech—always build in a failsafe. The device had an inner mechanism that would trigger a "hard departure" after thirty minutes, which would bring him back to the real world. The whole project was new territory for Elijah, and the last thing he wanted was to cause some serious damage.

After a few moments, he felt another, larger jolt of electricity through his skull, and he closed his eyes. He transitioned to a view of the sky, big fluffy clouds against a blue background, and though he knew this was only an image imprinted onto his brain, it felt as if he was hovering right there in the atmosphere.

Moments later, he dropped into a completely different world. This was Neoton, a luscious amalgamation of nature and architecture. The environment was spotlessly clean, and had the basics one would need for their day to day life. A mall, a school, a hundred two-bedroom houses spotted around, as well as a couple of leisure venues. Right now, all of these structures were built on a grid-like system, but Elijah would eventually add a touch of spontaneity to reflect the rather messy geography of real-life towns and cities.

His plan was to cover the space row by row, starting with the shopping mall, leading onto the swimming pool next door, and the twenty or so houses that completed the horizontal assignment of buildings. Then, tomorrow, he would move up a row, and continue until he had scoped out the whole space, troubleshooting for any bugs or unusual features.

Elijah stepped forward from his spawning position, feeling the lifelike textures of the concrete terrain beneath his feet. In the real world, he was completely still as he lived out this experience, which was mind-blowing enough to him. But the added subtleties of each of his senses really made the adventure that much sweeter.

He could smell a nondescript candy flavour, which he'd decided to code in as a placeholder but actually proved rather effective. The scent was equally dispersed around the environment, so that each step would receive the same whiff. He could hear a joyous soundscape of kids laughing and birds chirping, even though neither of these existed in the world yet.

With a slight hesitation, he ambled towards the shopping mall doors, and was met with a sliding mechanism that invited him straight in. He was greeted by a bustling centre with people shopping, going about their days in a joyful manner, each looking ecstatic to live in the city.

Elijah stopped one of the characters, a woman of about twenty years of age.

"Hey, could you tell me where the best place to shop is?"

The woman stared at him for a few moments with a large smile, shuffling through a few of her pre-programmed statements, before chuckling and answering him.

"You gotta hit The Zone, it's packed with cool outfits for every occasion!"

With that said, she nodded and wandered back off into her simulated existence. Elijah noted that it would be a good idea to get some product placement to open up a new revenue stream—he could get the characters to recommend certain businesses, for example, or play out certain adverts on the mall intercoms. The possibilities were endless.

He continued into the shopping area, and right into The Zone. Once inside, he felt the textures of the fabrics, each amazingly lifelike, and took a few moments to congratulate himself on generating such an immersive experience. He spent the rest of the afternoon browsing the mall, taking in the sensation of each and every event.

TARA

Tara slumped through the front door, absolutely depleted.

"I'm home," she muttered routinely, not expecting an answer. Which was lucky, as one didn't come.

She stepped into the kitchen, and then through to the spare room.

A long desk had been plonked in the middle of the space, with various monitors and devices resting on top of it. The slick technology contrasted with the décor, which was painted a pastel blue with a few scratched-up decals of bears and smiley faces. The room was decorated as a child's bedroom, but had yet to live up to its purpose.

Instead, Elijah sank back in his tatty leather chair, a wire protruding from his skull, his eyeballs rolled back in his head. He jittered, looking around from left to right, before jolting back to a resting position. It was fucking creepy, and she had no time for it.

She barged into the room, and started to shake him.

"Hey! You even gonna say hello?"

There was absolutely no response.

Tara flew out of the room and straight to the kitchen cupboard. She grabbed a large tumbler and sloshed a triple measure of vodka into it, downing the sour liquid before she'd even replaced the bottle cap. Unsatisfied, she glugged another two, before stuffing the bottle back in its place.

As she turned towards the sink, she accidentally nudged the glass from off the side counter, and it shattered into several pieces. Instinctively, Tara leaned over to pick up the pieces, but sliced herself on a large segment. The laceration started to bleed profusely.

"Fuck!"

She grabbed a large handful of kitchen towels and held them tight to the wound.

"Isaac, can you help me quick?"

Silence. Frustrated, she tried to open another cupboard with her elbow, before giving up and using her hand, smearing blood over everything that sat in front of the bandages.

Hand eventually wrapped up, she stormed back through to the room, straight up to Isaac's face.

She looked at the plug in his head, and followed the wire to the mini, flesh-coloured device. She tried to touch the screen, to perform a function, but the old technology didn't compute. Instead, she found the ON/OFF toggle.

"Hey! Answer me or I'll turn this off."

She nudged him again, to no avail.

"You're not even here to help in an emergency. What the fuck?"

The device jiggled in her hand as she shook from the pain —and the alcohol in her system.

"Fine."

With a simple click, she toggled the device to an off position, and clunked it back on the table. When she realised that wouldn't make him respond either, she tore the device from the wire connection, and threw it at the wall in a fit of rage. The starter wire dangled out of Elijah's skin jack, with nothing to connect it to. No hardware. No failsafe.

ELIJAH

From a vantage point on the third floor, Elijah was overlooking his creation. He had built each personality, each stock character profile of the hundred or so people traversing the mall below, and the complexity of it baffled even him.

He stared right up until the last moment, when suddenly, the whole world changed.

The lights flickered, and without warning, the whole population of the mall disappeared without a trace. The emergency lights flickered on and off, before the main lights returned at a dimmed level. The sound and smells from before ceased, instead replaced by a damp, inexplicable scent and a loud whirring, interspersed with glitchy soundbites of the real world.

Fuck. What went wrong.

By Elijah's calculations, he had been in the world for twenty-seven minutes, so it would only be three minutes until he was thrown out of Neoton. In the janitor's closet, he had built in a control panel which would help him troubleshoot the situation, and plan how to avoid it happening next time around. There were hundreds of these toolboxes built into the world, and it was lucky he had been so forward-thinking. This world was haunting when it was stripped back to its bare shell, and Elijah didn't like it one bit.

TARA

Tara stared at the remnants of the device on the floor. She couldn't quite quantify what she was seeing.

She expected the inside of the device to be all plastic and metal, like motherboards and shit. But it was nothing of the sort.

Through cracked plastic and torn, latex-like material, she could see what looked like a miniature organ squirming within the casing. Whatever was in this thing was alive and unnatural, and she really started to doubt Elijah and her taste in men entirely. What the fuck was he doing? Was this some kind of experimentation? Had she married a psycho?

She tried to piece the five or so fragments of the device together—without touching the weird beating organ, of course—but they would not connect. The LCD screen had died too, cracked in half by the collision. The only thing she could read on the casing was a small etching: *Fleshkey Tech - Lifelong Corp.*

ELIJAH

No. This couldn't be happening. It had to be a glitch.

Connection Severed.

This was insane. Had Tara come home from work early? Had someone broken in and disconnected him from the device? Elijah had no idea what had happened, but it was bad. There were other failsafes built in to the project, but they weren't tested as thoroughly as he'd have liked.

Elijah started to panic, pulling levers and hitting switches on the console. As his emotions seared to a boiling point, a realisation came over him—if he really was stuck, he'd die in this game. What a horrifically ironic way to go, given that this was meant to be the sweet escape.

No. He couldn't consider that. It was time to think.

After pushing more buttons and whacking the console a few times for good measure, Elijah gave up. It was time for Plan B.

He descended a large, ornate block of stairs onto the main floor of the mall. In every direction, a haunting silence clouded the scene, with only a subtle whirring of electrical circuits breaking the quiet. From memory, each direction looped back to the exterior front of the building, so he would be safe to take any exit.

Raaaaaaaacchhhhh.

Elijah jumped back, shocked by the woman whom he'd asked about shopping. Her face was glitchy, her eyes and mouth distorted as if they were melting. The woman didn't speak, she just stood facing him, her shoulders snapped back and neck extended forward, still as a photograph.

Elijah took a step to the side, and with an unwavering stiffness, she mirrored the step.

"Excuse me, I need to go," Jared said, his voice breaking slightly.

The woman moved forwards, closing the gap. Her curiously abstract face was almost touching his—but he didn't feel flesh. He just felt coldness and artificial textures.

Without wasting another second, he sidestepped her in the opposite direction and jogged down the hall. To his utter surprise, she just fell forwards, smashing into the ground face-first, the rest of her body collapsing in on itself, until she was a crumpled merge of textures and colours.

He jogged forwards, right past a row of opposing shopfronts, each fitted with LED fixtures and dressing ready for clients. The place was spotlessly clean, and nearly every sign of humanity had been wiped with the glitch. The bins were suddenly empty, there were no scuffs on the white tiled floor, and the plants had returned to their initial, less developed size.

The only other inhabitants were a spontaneous handful of these human-like sprites, empty shells of the characters he had breathed life into, peppered in random spots. They were completely out of place, glitching and walking into walls, stuck in doorways.

The air in the mall felt heavy, as if he wasn't meant to be breathing it. Each breath was a conscious movement, and a strain to complete. He kept on thrashing forwards, eventually reaching the fire exit, and pushed his way to the outdoor world.

The sky above was a bright, seamless blue colour, devoid of any clouds or atmosphere of any kind. There was no wind. No precipitation. No sound. It was completely surreal.

To the side of the mall, there was a leisure complex with a swimming pool and gym. Adjacent to this structure, the unoccupied houses stood in a grid formation, each a carbon copy of the other. The final failsafe he had created involved a triple lock mechanism, hidden behind three boiler panels in the hundred or so houses. That's where he was headed right now.

TARA

Elijah still wasn't moving. His chest raised and lowered in a rhythmic pattern, so he wasn't dead.

Congrats, can see why you're a nurse.

He inner dialogue taunted her, but she wasn't in the mood. This was a huge fuckup, and she'd have to call for help if he didn't wake up soon. And what in the living fuck was that weird fleshy thing in that device? It still made her skin crawl.

She stepped over to Elijah and shook him a few more times, increasing the intensity with each movement. After the futile attempt at waking him physically, she started to tear through his notes, looking for a hint of some kind that would help her get him back to normal. Scratched onto various sheets of A4 was weird jargon and patterns, different drawings that made no sense at all to her. It was all gobbledygook; it might as well have been a different language.

Tara let out a huge groan, and then reached for her mobile phone.

ELIJAH

The first house was on the second row of the grid, three from the left.

Each building was fitted out the exact same way. A white PVC door guided guests into a modest hallway, painted a light grey colour. To the immediate left, a carpeted staircase led to the upstairs, whilst to the right, the living room entrance opened up onto a cosy room, with a brick fireplace and a single, grey sofa. The end of the hallway led to a simple, stock bathroom on the right and the kitchen straight through.

The kitchen also looked ripped straight from a catalogue, because quite frankly, it was. Elijah hadn't been so excited about the intricacies of interior design as he was in creating a functional world, so there had been a lot of shortcuts. Still, it was clean and tidy, and most importantly suited to its purpose.

The black and white tiled walls gave way to some cupboard space, and a small cream-coloured boiler in the corner, with copper pipes cascading behind the kitchen counter.

Elijah stepped up to the boiler, worked out how to remove the front plate, and set it aside. Behind a circuit of pipes, he saw a small green button, which he quickly depressed. A small LCD touchscreen, nestled within an embossed rectangle at the top of the boiler, sparked to life.

Elijah started to quickly tap the screen in different quadrants, loading up a minuscule keyboard. With a pointed finger, he inputted the password from memory. This process gave way to a small lever, which sprouted from underneath the boiler.

He hadn't realised how thirsty he had become from all of this running around. To be quite honest, he wasn't sure why he was thirsty at all; his basic needs should have been met in this world; the food and drink experiences were complementary, not required. As he twisted the tap to quench his thirst, not a drop of water fell from the pipe. It was bone dry.

"Fuck."

With a flick of his wrist, he gripped the lever and twisted it to the left. That was one of three, and that movement started off an invisible timer. Elijah had fifteen minutes to complete the process, or he'd be back at square one.

On his way back through the hallway, he tripped and fell hard onto the carpeted floor. As he looked back to see what caused him to tumble, he was met with a far more disconcerting sight. His foot had disappeared. Not in an invisible, ghost kind of way, but it had properly vanished, without any kind of wound or dismemberment.

The area at his ankle seamlessly wrapped in on itself, a smooth blend of skin where his shin should have met his foot. He even started to stroke and caress the area, completely dumbfounded as to why there was no pain or blood. This world didn't have phones. It didn't have medicine, and it most certainly didn't have the emergency services.

The road ahead was looking dire, and he needed to get out by any means possible.

TARA

Tara couldn't help but gag. She had no idea how she didn't see this before, but the pure sight and smell was enough to knock her back, causing her to cover her mouth with her arm.

Elijah's right foot had started to rot, the wet flesh bleeding out pus, which oozed through the delicate knitwork of his sports sock. His shoe had slid off from the moist stream of putrid bodily fluid, and she had been curious enough to tear the wet sock from his skin. She immediately regretted that decision.

The emergency services were already on their way; she had called them as soon as she noticed the injury. The skin on his foot was a sickly yellow, bloated and fetid in equal measure.

Tara knocked his shoulder with a hard fist, but he still wouldn't wake up. The plug in his head was starting to ooze the same viscous discharge.

"Come on. Wake up, Elijah."

ELIJAH

Elijah stumbled into house two of three, and studied the identical layout of the building, before lumbering through the hall and into the kitchen. The very same boiler waited in the corner, and hobbling on one foot, he snatched the front cover from the device, hit the button, and started to tap the password onto the painfully small LCD screen.

The screen glitched. The electricity seemed to cut out intermittently, resetting the hardware and restarting the process. In his head, he was trying to count down the minutes from the first house, but he didn't know if he was anywhere near the real number.

After finally getting through the process, the keypad made a dissatisfied beep, and illuminated red.

He was in the wrong house.

With sweaty palms and an awkward limp, he quickly rushed out of the doorway, and hopped out of the door, taking two immediate left turns, right through to the next building.

He dove through the hallway, careening across the carpeted floor.

Jared tore off the boiler front plate, and followed the complex set of motions to enter the passcode.

Nothing in this one either.

"Fuck! Fuck this!"

As he strode back through the hallway, he took a quick detour into the living room and pushed the sofa up against the wall, before pulling it onto its back surface. He left it in this messy state, so at least it could have a semblance of a personality of its own.

Left.

Left.

Through the PVC door. He let it swing back to its widest point, the handle chipping the paintwork of the wall behind.

The same layout. The same furnishings. The ambient daylight fell in the exact same pattern through the window blinds.

Fifteen steps from the front door to the kitchen threshold. Three steps from that point to the boiler. Three seconds from removing the plate to setting it on the counter. Fifteen seconds from hitting the button to revealing the code.

Nothing.

How could he have been so careless? In his haze of endless design work, he had misremembered the pattern of the houses, and was wasting time checking the wrong buildings. He needed to stop and think, try and remember the exact location of the failsafe switches, but he didn't have time.

Back he went.

His mind was overcome with the most torturous sense of boredom imaginable. Nothing in this environment had changed for what seemed like years, it was excruciating.

Next house.

He went to push the door, and kind of fell in on himself.

His hand. Oh fuck no.

His entire left hand had disappeared. No blood. No sensation. Once again, the skin just wrapped around his wrist, as though the limb had never existed.

"HELP MEEEEE!" Elijah screamed into the ether.

No use.

TARA

Two paramedics carried Elijah out on a stretcher, and it hit Tara just how serious this could be. The anger she felt towards him had dissipated, and she was instead overcome by a sense of shock and panic. How had this happened? Did she do something when she severed the connection?

She went to hold his hand, gesturing a final goodbye, but was instead met by a red raw fist, skin flaking off in large chunks of soggy discharge. She couldn't help but scream, and as soon as Elijah was secured in the vehicle, one of the paramedics had to return to help her out to the ambulance for the ride along, guiding her as she started to disconnect from her reality.

"Look at me and keep breathing. What has he taken?" one of the paramedics asked.

"What do you mean?"

"Has he taken any drugs? Or been near any chemicals?"

Tara shook her head, and it felt as if her whole world was burning and imploding and disintegrating at the same time.

He's not gonna make it.

No. Fuck. She wasn't going to entertain that thought. She hated her mind sometimes, especially at moments like this.

He's slipping away right in front of your eyes. You said you didn't love him last week.

No. Stop.

She was getting through this.

They both were.

ELIJAH

Think Elijah. Think.

Elijah hadn't entered the house yet. He had his back turned, and body perched up against the door, balanced against the plastic entrance on his remaining leg, whilst the opposing hand rubbed against his face in an unsettled panic.

In the dreamlike moment, he took a look around at the environment. Aside from the relatively small area of constructed buildings, the rest of the identifiable universe was a trimmed grass terrain, with hills in the far distance and an even, ambient light from an unidentifiable source beyond the blue sky. Like the sandbox mode at the start of a computer simulation, Elijah was deep in the uncanny valley in a parallel world that was stripped bare of any personality.

Several sprites were glitching across the landscape, torsos melting into building textures, their deformed mouths clutching onto melted tongues. The pixellated characters moved in circles, tripping and falling, hurtling themselves into thin air.

The silence was resounding. His ears were starting to hurt from the absence of sound. He begged for the chirping of birds, or the distant hum of traffic, or even Tara's nagging. God, he missed Tara. She was a total nightmare to be around sometimes, but he wished he had her company right now.

TARA

"I don't understand. Please tell me what's happening!"

Tara begged the paramedic for clarity, but he was too busy checking Elijah's vitals, studying the growing decay of his body and ordering the driver to go as fast as he could.

"Come on baby. It's not your time yet. Hold out for just a little while. I know you can do it."

ELIJAH

What was that sound?

Tara? Did she find a way through?

Elijah hobbled towards the sound, trying his best to determine where it was coming from.

"Hold out for just a little while. I know you can do it."

He lumbered down the road, glancing over several houses before stopping right outside the nineteenth house in the row.

The sound was emanating from a mailbox right outside the house. A red, cylindrical unit, erected on a metal pole, much like the post boxes in the US. He grasped the little flap with his right hand, and pulled down on its hinge.

"Hello?"

There was no answer at the end of his sentence. But he had a eureka moment just as he looked up to the house.

This is where the second lever was.

Instantaneously, he bounded into the house, hopping and trying to keep his balance, hyper-aware of his missing features. Elijah slid into the kitchen, tapped in the passcode and twisted the lever.

Two of three. One more to go.

He didn't know how long he had left, but he had to try. His body was slowing, grinding to a halt, but the next house was just one row up. Step by step, he pushed on, his brow moist with sweat, body completely shattered. He thought of Tara, of his real life, and of their future child.

TARA

The paramedics heaved the bed from the back of the ambulance, and quickly ejected the trolley and wheels. They took off ahead, rolling him straight into the emergency department. Tara sprinted in behind them.

"Wait!"

A doctor tried to catch her, attempting to direct her to a waiting room, but she was having none of it. She caught the door just before it closed, and followed them right through the hospital.

The paramedics were ushered straight into surgery, and this time, Tara did have to wait outside. She could see what was going on through a small window to the side, and she didn't let herself look away from any of it.

ELIJAH

After a drawn out, agonising walk up to the next house, Elijah reached the kitchen. The boiler frontage had been removed, and he had hit the green button. He had his finger propped ready to tap the LCD screen, excited to finally get out of this nightmare.

He fantasised about seeing Tara and explaining what had happened, before discarding this entire project and finding a normal job of some kind that could use his IT skills. This was far too much of a nightmare to risk releasing to the public, and he had a feeling that no amount of troubleshooting in the world could rescue this reality. It was missing too many things that made it safe, that made it lifelike. He had greatly underestimated the work it would take to recreate day-to-day life and was paying a huge price for his ignorance.

On the outside world, things would be fine, he knew it. This would be a funny story to tell his kids one day, that's all.

He began to tap the first few keys of the passcode before the input stopped. It took him a few moments to realise what was happening, and as soon as he did, he wailed in fear.

Elijah's other hand had disappeared, covered in a seamless flesh wrap, a clean stump resting on the end of his arm.

"No, no, no, no, fuuuuuck!"

He tried to use both stumps to retrieve a pen from his pocket, but he couldn't gather the friction.

TARA

What the fuck is happening in there?

Several doctors were sprinting around the room, completely flustered. They looked as if they had discovered an extraterrestrial, and for all of the panic that had ensued, they weren't doing anything to help. They were staring like dumbfounded kids who had seen their first dead bird.

She struck the window twice, and aside from a momentary glance, they paid her no mind. She tried to rip open the door by its handle, screaming incessantly, but it was no use. They were far too preoccupied with what was on their table, a slowly decomposing thirty-something male, with no obvious cause for his illness. It's the kind of thing that would make anyone's head spin.

ELIJAH

Through his screams and a cascade of salty tears, Elijah noticed that both of his arms had become shorter, cut off right under the shoulder.

He flailed against the boiler, trying to touch the LCD screen with any part of his body that would reach. Every touch was too clumsy to compute, he needed a fine point to register with the sensors he had created, and after a few minutes of restless attempts, his remaining leg started to give way, with his foot disappearing, leaving him balancing on an unsteady stump.

With every last bit of energy he could muster, he hopped, shuffled and slid across the wall to get through the hallway, and outside onto the grass. He flipped himself onto his back just in time for the rest of his leg to vanish, and the lower part of his body to follow suit.

TARA

"LET ME THE FUCK IN!"

With a final burst of energy, Tara smashed through the door, the lock splintering the wooden doorframe. She launched one of the doctors out of the way, her eyes shuffling back and forth to see Elijah. When she finally reached the side of the bed, her stomach dropped, and an acidic tidal-wave rose to the top of her throat.

On the bright white sheets, a swamp of mucus and disintegrated bones lay in a putrid mess, with only Elijah's face and neck intact. His organs had fully rotted, with fleshy shells spread across the festering pile of gore.

Tara screamed at the top of her lungs and passed out before she hit the floor.

ELIJAH

The still silence was just as haunting as before. He thought he would find some peace in seeing out his final moments under the light, but it didn't have the same effect he thought it would. It was no match for the sun in the real world, it provided no warmth or comfort. It was like a large light panel, exposing his world but playing no part in it. There were no insects to feel crawling on him, no birds to sit next to him as he drew his final breaths, no bystanders to call for an ambulance or give him some encouraging words as he slipped away. As hard as he tried, he couldn't even imagine these things, as his mind trembled with panic.

The last time he was able to look, the only parts of him that remained were his head and chest. He said goodbye under his breath, first to Earth, and then to Neoton. He hoped that no-one ever discovered this God-forsaken hellscape.

ROE

Maggie was so incredibly close to the life she yearned for.

A life of peace and quiet. A life away from distractions, responsibility, or service.

Maggie wanted to live out her days walking in nature, catching and eating her own food, singing old songs to herself, and she'd never been closer to that dream than she was today.

Born in the late sixties, Maggie had lived a full life—marriage, divorce, career—but had dropped all of that for the peace and quiet of the Scottish wilderness, living off the land and a sense of adventure. In Maggie's eyes, she was living the dream. Well, something very, very close to it.

There was only one thing that shattered the reality she yearned for so deeply...

A harrowing, torturous, incessant screeching.

Wherever she went. Whatever she did. The screech remained. It undulated in pitch and cadence, of course, but she hadn't been able to get away from it, nowhere near.

Instead, she tried to track it down. Every day, she walked four or five miles in different directions, setting up camp as she went. She followed the sound, momentarily celebrating when the volume increased, because it meant she was that much closer to stopping it.

Whatever *it* was.

Well, today was the day she was going to have a breakthrough.

Maggie had reached one of the main rivers in the area, a luscious treasure of the highlands. She'd followed the screaming, the unrelenting howl of an unidentified being, which was as cartoonish as it was bothersome.

And she couldn't quite believe her eyes when she tracked down the culprit...

A half-beached salmon, located on the side of the river, coated in water but by no means submerged. There was nothing special about it at all, aside from its powerful set of vocal cords and complete disrespect for others around it.

Maggie had thought about stomping the fish to death, but decided to try and save it by throwing it back into the deep current. To her dismay, however, it floundered right back, floated onto the rocky bank, and started to screech again. The whole scenario was completely insane.

She would do whatever she needed to to absolve the salmon of its anguish and get some peace.

* * *

Maggie slid the final cotton band over the tent pole, and secured it with a metal stake. Her trusty collapsible tent was erected neatly by the river bank, just a hundred metres or so away from the salmon. She'd been considering the best course of action to take, and killing it was the only obvious answer. That didn't make her feel any better about the fact, however.

It was always difficult to bring an end to an animal's life; it was something she'd reflected on a lot since being out in the wilderness. Although a life of solitude was her ultimate goal, she'd be lying if she said she didn't miss just an inkling of the human experience, of living around others with their own goals and destinies and personalities. This thing had a personality, and stood out from the other animals she had hunted to survive. But she couldn't deal with this for the rest of her days.

Maggie laid down her hammer, and decided to go and see it. A final offering of peace.

"Hey. You gotta zip it."

Maggie knew she was talking to a salmon. But in her

head, it seemed like the polite thing to do, before potentially mauling it to death with blunt force. Barely seconds after her sentence ended, the salmon screeched at a higher pitch, its tiny mouth vibrating with the sound, its rigid goggly eyes stagnant and unmoving.

The sound tore through Maggie's head, scraping her brain with its wailing waveforms.

"Shut up!"

The fish did as it was told. It seemed to stare at her with unwavering attitude. Maggie had never studied a fish up-close, she usually went straight from gutting to the grill, but it was a sight to behold. Its weird, slimy coating glistened in the sun, just wet enough to keep the thing alive, though she questioned if it was some kind of mutant fish, for the fact it could stay halfway out of the water this long.

She was taken aback by its gall.

"Really! Fuck you!" she complained.

The fish paused long enough for her to scold it, and then continued its cacophonous song.

Maggie turned on her heel, completely exasperated. She charged over towards her tent, leaned over to grab the hammer, and stormed all the way back.

"Final fucking chance fish. Shut the fuck up."

The fish froze.

Maggie spent a few seconds thinking that maybe, just maybe, her threat had worked.

She even thought about turning around to finally go and rest in her tent, symbiotically existing with the scorned salmon.

But no.

Oh no, no, no.

It couldn't be that easy, could it?

A shrill warbling erupted from its mouth, at an even more ungodly volume and pitch.

SMAAAASH.

Maggie thumped the hammer down onto its face, tearing apart its scaly membrane, nearly decapitating it with just one hit.

And then, there was silence.

Sweet, sweet silence.

* * *

The only sound Maggie could hear was the gentle rippling of the river, and the crackling coals underneath a makeshift barbecue.

Did she have reservations about eating the fish? Yes.

Did she have to eat the fish to survive? No.

Was she going to eat it anyway?…

Yes.

She had gutted and deboned the salmon, and was grilling it over a fire she had slightly dampened with wet leaves. The fish had some eggs sitting in its stomach, which she had removed and kept safe in a small container by her side.

Any guilt she had about killing the fish melted away with the serene ecstasy of the moment. Pure, blissful silence. There was nothing like it.

* * *

It tasted good. Really fucking good.

Maggie savoured every fleshy bite, the lightly burned skin providing a gentle crunch with every mouthful.

When she finished the main course, she decided to give the eggs a try. She had tried roe before, but only from a supermarket, where it was no doubt pumped with preservatives and other nasty chemicals. This was the real thing, straight from the source, so she could hardly wait.

In her new life, Maggie rarely came across fresh experiences, so this was a real high for her, and a complete contrast to her former life as a high-flying accountant. She'd had everything she thought she wanted: money, status, a rich husband, three cars, but none of it had made her happy. *This life* made her happy.

The eggs had a slightly clammy, viscous feel in the mouth, but the salty bubbles were incredibly satisfying. The tangy pops of flavour captivated her taste buds, and she quickly devoured the whole lot.

After finishing her meal, Maggie headed to her tent, where she had already laid out a thick blanket from edge to edge. She slumped onto her back, and closed her eyes softly. Her whole body loosened, and slackened into a deep slumber.

* * *

She awoke to an intense itching. Maggie thought that she was most likely reacting to some bug bites, but when she looked at her exposed skin under the pink haze of the sunset outside, she noticed something much more distressing.

The membranes of her arms had started to peel in scabrous flakes—if she ran her fingernail down any part of her skin, she would descale her own flesh much like that of the fish.

The fucking fish.

Maggie wrapped her jacket back around her body and stepped outside. She basked in the glow of the glorious sunset, enjoying the chirping of the crickets and the distant birdsong. The itching was intensely uncomfortable, but she had learned to disassociate from her body with a type of meditation—unlikely, yes, but it was the only book she had found so far on her travels—so she leaned into a calming, relaxed pattern of breathing, and took it from there.

It helped for a little while, but she was eventually overcome by the prickly, taunting sensation.

Just one scratch wouldn't hurt, would it?

Defeated, she rolled up her left sleeve, and scratched hard with several long strokes. To her absolute disgust, flakes of crusty skin grated off of her, revealing the pink flesh of her muscle underneath. It didn't hurt, as far as she could tell, but the itching was only relieved for a moment. She wanted to claw down into her flesh, tear at it with jagged fingernails and scratch the dry bone underneath... But those were the thoughts of an insane person. And Maggie wasn't insane.

She tuned back into the birdsong, and relaxed into her breathing patterns again.

* * *

Maggie crawled on her hands and knees, dipping her extremities into the water. The cool waves soothed the scratchy feeling, but she knew it was only temporary.

She swished about for a few minutes, before the most violent palpitations started to bombard her stomach. The blasts of pain were enough to collapse her onto her front, half-submerged by the water.

Maggie thrashed about in a violent struggle, before doubling over and fumbling for the soil beneath her. She dug into it with pained claws, pulling back her fingernails with the force. One snapped away from her finger, exposing the tender, bloodied skin behind it.

She needed to take her jeans off. The constriction was too much, she could feel her bloated midsection battling the waistband.

With shaky digits, she fumbled for her button, and

quickly undid it. The zip was next, ripped down with impatient force.

Maggie's head was soaked with sweat, and she could feel herself almost ready to throw up into the river. She peeled her jeans down to her ankles, and savoured the momentary relief she felt.

The palpitations in her stomach started to bubble, as if her organs had turned to jelly and were ready to make a swift exit. The fizzy acids in her gut caused her to belch violently, with a slight reflux on every hit.

"AAAAAAH!"

Maggie screamed and bent in half, ready to explode. She had never felt so sick.

After struggling for several minutes, a wave of relief washed over her—followed by a torrent of gelatinous orange beads that flowed freely from her vagina. The viscous mass bypassed her underwear, leaking from slight gaps between skin and material, forcefully erupting in a volcanic deluge.

She screamed on release, relief equally matched by the complete absurdity of the situation.

The eggs floated atop the water, staining the river a soft red.

* * *

Maggie wasn't sure how long she had been lying half-submerged in the water. She felt no need to eat or drink, and she had counted several sunrises and sunsets. She took comfort in the little things, the warm glow of the light behind the trees. The ticklish sea plants that caressed her slowly rotting feet.

Her dream had been achieved, though she wasn't quite sure at what cost.

Maybe this is what life would look like now. She would

be plonked down like a rock, unable to move but pretty much content. The sights and sounds would keep her company, a truly natural gift.

Well.

That dream was totally shattered within minutes, when she heard it…

A piercing.

Cacophonous.

Grating.

Torturous.

SCREECH.

Maggie's lips turned in on themselves.

And then there was another screech.

And another.

A whole chorus of fucking screeching fish.

She had the motion to gently rock her head to the side, only to discover that the gelatinous bulbs from inside her had all grown into mutated, freaky fish. Their eyes were weirdly human, having the same colour pupils as Maggie. Their skin was pale white, and their scales seemed almost like flaky human flesh, which didn't glisten like the salmon, but just soaked up the sunlight.

Were they slightly sunburned, too? Was Maggie dreaming all of this?

The screaming increased in volume, up and up and up and up.

In the end, there was nothing left for her to do.

Maggie inhaled deeply, and let out the most thunderous, high-pitched squeal imaginable.

There was a slight pause, whilst the fish computed what was happening, and then they returned one of their warbling wails.

Maggie was so incredibly close to the life she yearned for.

A life of peace and quiet. A life away from distractions, responsibility or service.

But in the end, Maggie got something entirely different, but strangely comforting.

A feeling of community and purpose.

She was a God amongst her screaming fish children.

SMOTHERED

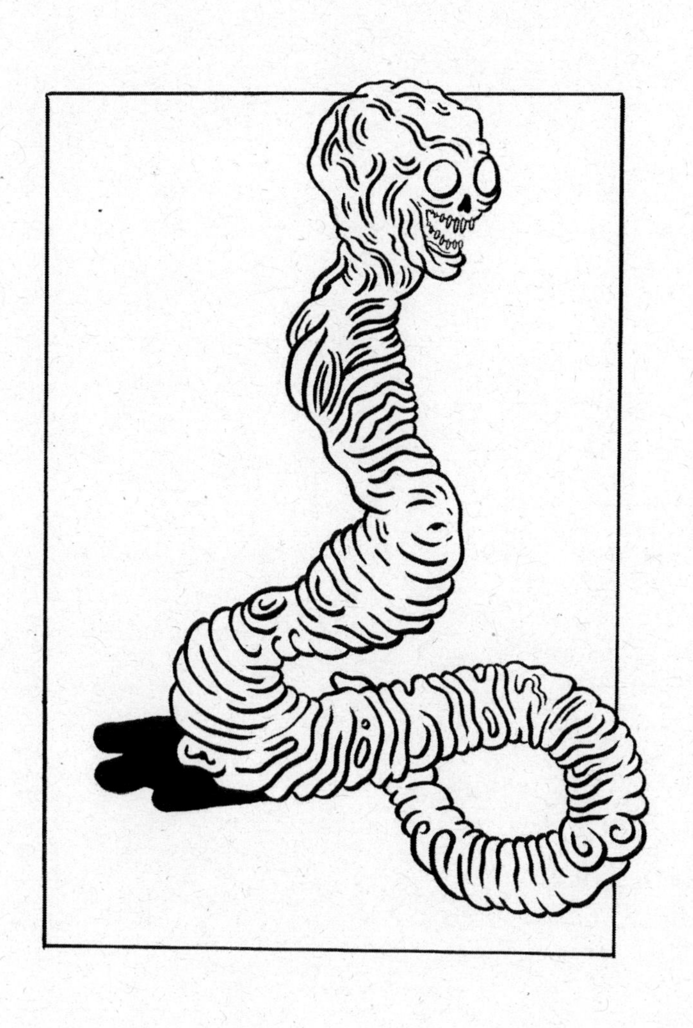

Is this what life was meant to be? A cycle of moderate highs and pitiful lows, interspersed with moments of complete dread and boredom?

A collection of Katie's stuff was spread across the bed in Jared's nondescript spare room. Since their divorce three months ago, he had been piling up any small memory of her, half-promising himself to send it to her new address, but never quite getting around to it.

The pale pink bedspread complemented the magnolia walls—in a dreary, tasteless way. When Katie and Jared moved in five years back, they had completely skipped any decoration in that particular room, planning to come back and put some real effort in when she got pregnant. But that day never came, not for lack of trying, but simply another cruel twist in the life story of Jared.

Jared had split Katie's items into three scruffily arranged moving boxes, ready to send off to her new home with her new beau. He hoped that seeing the contents would give her a pang of guilt, but deep down he knew she'd probably roll her eyes and discard it all.

The room looked particularly sparse, and the horrendous décor wasn't doing much to liven it up. 70s colour palettes amalgamated with Swedish DIY furniture, and a heavy handful of bargain-bin accessories. It's a room he wouldn't offer to anyone ordinarily, but it now had a purpose—a space for his ailing mother to recover whilst she battled an unusual infection she'd picked up on her latest holiday to Tenerife. That, however, was a whole different story.

* * *

Maude stumbled through the door, slowly placing one foot in front of the other, making a whole play of her dramatic entrance. In a loose-fitting metallic top and baggy chinos—

and faded, fluffy pink boots, of course—she looked the very picture of middle class casual-wear. With each step came a forced groan and a woe-is-me glance, but Jared wasn't going to help her any more than he had to. He had offered up his house to the old bat, free of charge, so he couldn't care less for this display. She was a bit ill, that was all, and he wasn't going to drop everything in his life just to take care of hers.

Upstairs, he had made an effort to clean the bedsheets and duvet covers, and even placed a table by the side, for easy access to medicine and drinks. There was a selection of snacks at her disposal, and napkins and wipes just underneath the table, within easy reach. Jared didn't care too much about hospitality, he just wanted to make this whole thing run as smoothly as it could, and that meant as few trips and as little interaction as possible.

"You wouldn't believe the 72 hours I've had, Jared," Maude moaned. In actual fact, Jared could believe it, because he had been given every tidbit of information from his sister, Mel, in advance. She was conveniently jet-setting around the world on her honeymoon, so couldn't offer up her own home.

"There I was, taking my first steps onto the beach and into the sea, same place as every year, and the lifeguard says… my God, what's that there?"

Jared nodded, hoping to hurry this whole thing along.

"And I turned around, and no word of a lie, this… thing! My God, it was the size of a snake, flat and white. My mind couldn't quite comprehend the fact it was there, and it slithered right into my bikini, and whoosh… it was gone. *Inside* of me… The doctors tried their best to get it out, but they think dissolving it is the best course of action."

Jared nodded again, trying not to imagine anything to do with his mother's insides.

"Can you believe that? A mutant tapeworm, inside of my body? I mean, who knows what it could be doing right now?"

Jared nodded for a final time, and encouraged Maude into bed. She let out a huge sigh as she sank into the mattress, flinching before she had a chance to lie down.

Bending her brittle arm behind her back, she pulled out a small bracelet, which Jared had missed when packing earlier. She held onto it wistfully for a moment, before reaching out and giving it back to him.

She sighed again.

"You know, I don't know why you and her couldn't work it out."

Jared shook his head, holding his tongue and trying to keep the peace. She'd only been there five minutes, after all. He had to schedule his outbursts wisely, for his own sanity.

"Well, she had different plans, didn't she?"

"But what about what you want? What I want? You'd be a great dad."

Jared placed the bracelet on a side table at the other end of the room, and headed for the exit.

"You know where everything is. I'll bring dinner up in a couple of hours."

"Oh don't be like that. I mean well."

Jared faked a smile, and walked out, relieved to be away from her needy grasp.

* * *

"Yeah. She's settled in fine. All the usual," Jared said, talking into his mobile phone.

He was speaking to his sister, Mel, sharing some of the discomfort of the situation with her.

"Let's play mum bingo," Mel said through the phone.

Jared chuckled—it was a game from childhood, poking

fun at anyone who came with their own unintentional catchphrases or repetitive stories.

"Talked about dad?"

"Yep. Cross it off."

"Fred?"

"Yep."

"Her achey hip?"

"Haha, yep."

"Hmmm, I must be missing one..." Mel teased. "Oh. Of course. How hard done by she is now she's alone?"

"Bingo!"

They both laughed into the phone.

"Well, hopefully it won't be for long," Mel started. "I must admit that I'm happy it's you dealing with her butt worm and not me."

"Ew. Don't say that... Ew."

"Right I gotta head off, dinner in a mo," Mel said.

"That's one that I can cross off your bingo card. Always so predictable when you're bored of talking," Jared said.

"And that's one I can cross off for you, moaning and complaining again."

They said their goodbyes and Jared walked over to his laptop smiling.

The internet didn't have much information on Tenerife tapeworms. Or water snakes. Or anything that corresponded with her story. If it wasn't for the prescription from the doctors, he would have assumed that this was her latest ploy to crawl back into his life. But he'd give it a week. Two at the most. And then he'd either shift her back to her own home, or to some kind of nursing home. She was old enough and ugly enough to look after herself.

There was a little commotion upstairs, in the form of sliding and bashing, but Jared presumed that Maude was just getting to grips with the en-suite bathroom. At the very worst, she had tripped and fallen over a stool, but she'd be fine getting back up. Nothing to concern himself with.

Scrolling through a series of results online, Jared studied a few pictures of potential tapeworms and other creatures that could fit the description his Mum gave him of the snake-like creature that slithered up her behind. The thought made him gag.

* * *

Dinner was served. Chicken breast with various vegetables and a cooked-from-frozen Yorkshire pudding, because he was feeling generous.

He slid the plate onto Maude's lap, and was immediately met with a look of disgust.

"Where's the gravy?" she asked rudely.

"What do you mean? It's right there, it's the wet stuff on top of everything."

"Don't be snide with me, son. I didn't teach you to make thin gravy like this, it's like water on top of my food."

"You didn't teach me at all, actually. And just see it as a way to make it nice and sloppy so it doesn't take so much effort to chew, you ungrateful woman."

Jared stormed out of the room, and slammed the door, muttering profanities to himself the whole way downstairs.

He collected his dinner from the kitchen counter, and sat on the sofa in the living room, treating his last few brain cells to some mindless TV. He finished his food and slowly slipped into his regular evening nap.

* * *

Jared awoke to the sound of a hacking cough, simultaneously wet and aggressive. Though not out of place for someone feeling under the weather, it did sound pretty grim and disgusting. He half-debated going to check on her, but decided against it. He was too comfortable where he was.

Rolling his eyes apathetically, Jared started to slip into the limbo between wakefulness and sleep, recalling memories of his step-dad Fred, and the absolute shitstorm he had caused the family. He had repressed so many of these thoughts over the years; it was easy to put things to one side and forget when he didn't interact with his mother. But now she was back and dragging up the past, the memories felt more vivid, more alive.

Maude's first falling out…

Her first bruised eye…

The family's first Christmas without her, because she "wasn't feeling up to it" (this coming from the woman who kept a full-size backup tree in the attic in case of an emergency.)

Like a poison slowly eroding someone from the inside, Fred had eaten away the membrane that held together his family, and in Jared's eyes, it was pretty much irreparable.

The cough echoed through the landing and down the stairs, followed by a strained gargle and gasp for air.

Sighing deeply, he decided to get up and check, ambling up the stairs, acutely aware he was moaning about his aching body under his breath, just like his mother did. He reached the landing and turned towards the guest bedroom.

The door creaked open slowly, letting only a minuscule sliver of light into the room. Maude lay stretched out on the bed, duvet slung over her body carelessly, gently jolting about in some kind of dream.

As Jared stepped back out onto the landing, he felt a small damp patch underfoot, which was slightly sticky and gave off a bittersweet scent. He crouched down to take a closer look.

The patch seemed to start and end around the doorframe,

in a roughly semi-circular pattern. He looked up at the door for a few moments, trying to ascertain a potential cause. But nothing seemed out of place, and he'd already checked inside the room.

Stumbling back up to his feet, Jared turned to walk away, just as a deep thud echoed across the hall. The bedroom door shook from the impact, and before he knew it, a second hit thundered against the frame.

Jared froze for a couple of moments, and swung the door open. Maude was still in bed. Everything seemed normal.

He crept down the stairs, feeling watched by an unknown presence. The house seemed eerily quiet and calm, as if the smallest movement would shatter the dense atmosphere. Without taking a moment too long, he poured a drink, shut off the lights and headed back upstairs.

Jared slipped into bed a little quicker than usual, and tucked the sheets around him on both sides. He felt paranoid and uncomfortable, and just needed to sleep the whole day off. Squeezing his eyes shut, he discarded any thoughts of family or his issues, and tried to think of something more positive.

* * *

"I couldn't find many, I think you had them all."

Jared stumbled into the spare bedroom, where Maude was sat up excitedly, pinching her hands together, as if to say *"gimme"*.

Cupped to his chest with interlinked fingers, he held a box full of old developed photos, dating back to when he was a kid. The second the box made contact with the bedding, Maude was already sifting through a chunky handful of pictures, smiling at each snapshot.

"Oh remember this one? You looked so cute here!"

Maude presented the photo, and Jared noted that he did not look cute by any stretch of the imagination. Stuffed into a cowboy outfit several sizes too small for him and sulking about the hot weather, it was definitely not his best look.

"I think there's a few of you and Dad in there too," Jared said.

Maude forced a smile, a look that fell somewhere between happiness and guilt.

Jared's dad had died when he was a teenager, and it had completely devastated the family. Before the tragedy, they had been a picture-perfect group, complete with days out at the beach, daily dinnertimes, and plenty of hugs and affection. Jared and Mel were there for Maud when it happened, but she quickly found Fred—out of desperation and fear of loneliness—and clutched onto him, even as he made her life Hell.

Rifling through the second half of the photos, she stopped and stared for a few moments. Awkwardly, she started to flick through faster, avoiding eye contact with Jared.

"What was that one?" he asked.

"Oh never mind, just misplaced that's all!"

"No, let me see."

Jared snatched the box and thumbed back a few photos, falling upon the one she had tried to hide.

It was a selfie of him and Katie, beaming after one of their very best dates. It was near the start of their relationship, before they gave up trying to have a kid, before she ran away with the man across the road. Just seeing the snap broke his heart.

He replaced the photo and handed the box back to Maude. She looked up at him and back at the collection a few times, unsure of how to break the silence.

"That was a lovely shirt you wore in that picture. Whatever happened to it?"

Jared laughed, shaking his head.

"What?" Maude asked.

"Never mind."

"No tell me."

"It got covered in your blood after Fred hit you. When you said you'd finally leave, and then stayed, remember? Made me look a fool."

Maude shook her head.

"I don't think that happened. It must have got lost in the wash."

Jared snatched the photos back.

"Yep, that's what it must have been. The mythical, clothes-eating monster under my bed, not the real one *you* shared a bed with."

"Don't be like that Jared."

"We're done here. I hope you enjoyed these little memories, because that's all they are. Memories."

He slammed the door without letting her get a word in. After stewing in his own heat for a moment, he kicked it back open.

"And another thing. I'm glad he's dead and rotting! Most peaceful two years I've ever had!"

Jared stormed back out, leaving Maude with the repercussions of his anger.

Laid on top of the pile of photos, the happy snapshot of him and Katie taunted him, their wide grins almost intermingling.

"Fuck you," he said to the picture, before flipping it upside down.

* * *

Jared spent the rest of the day sulking, quite possibly recreating the facial expression from the picture of him as an overgrown cowboy.

He watered his plants.

Did the laundry.

Gave Maude her pills (without a single word or any eye contact.)

Played some video games.

Did some work.

Prepared a meal.

Gave Maude some dinner (a smaller portion than he had, because she had fucked him off.)

At the table, whilst he tucked into a meat pie and chips, he started to hear a raucous stirring upstairs.

"Jared? Jared? I drank all my water. I need some more!"

He couldn't believe what he was hearing. He'd loaded up around twelve bottles of water in her room that very morning, there was no chance she could have drank it all. She was obviously just looking for attention, and Jared was far too tired to get up and play good little son. She could wait until later, or indeed just drink from one of the many bottles in her room.

She piped up again for a minute or two, but then surrendered to silence. Jared stuffed a mouthful of his dinner into his face, and chewed loudly, drowning out his own thoughts and the dramatic huffing that would no doubt ensue in a few moments.

* * *

Just before bed, Jared filled up a glass with tap water, and pressed out two tablets from the nondescript blister packaging. The tablets seemed generic enough, but had a weird symbol of sorts imprinted onto them. It wasn't one Jared was familiar with—he only took sleeping pills—and they had a smooth surface, without any detail.

When he entered Maude's room, she was already sat up, staring at him right in the eyes. She near-flailed to get the water, snatching it from his hands and gulping it down in one like a dehydrated dog.

"I have your tablets," Jared muttered. "But I'll have to get more water now."

Maude didn't answer initially; she seemed suspended in a daydream. Eventually, she shook her head and came to.

"Don't worry about that. We need to speak," Maude uttered.

"About what?"

"About Fred. About what he did to you. What he did to us."

Jared recoiled.

"I'll make this clear right now, Mum, we won't be talking about Fred under my roof any more. Not a word. Now take your pills."

"But—"

"Not a word. Look, we can make nice, I'll look after you because you're my flesh and blood. But don't pretend like we're here for therapy or to hash out old frustrations."

"You never talk to me anymore. I don't know anything about your life!"

"You made that choice. By ignoring me. By falling back into his arms over and over again," Jared snapped.

"I just want to talk. I want to say sorry. I want to explain. Please just hear me."

Jared slammed the tablets onto the side table and left.

* * *

That night, the rain gently pattered on the conservatory outside, creating a relaxing pattern of soft sound. In the distance, the gentle hum of motorway traffic undulated peacefully.

The only light in Jared's room was from a small lamp on his side-table, which glowed in a warm orange hue. Since Katie had left, his nightmares were getting more and more intense, and the light helped to ground him in some kind of reality. He didn't sleep as deeply as he used to, but he managed to get through the night without any big panic attacks, so that was a plus.

The peace and quiet lasted another few minutes, until a squishy, slithering sound rose from the silence—like peeling flesh. The sound was otherworldly, emanating from every angle around him.

The light in the room started to flicker, gently at first, but then more violently. Jared snapped his eyes open frustratedly. He looked around at the room… Nothing.

As he finally started to doze off again, he noticed a strange shadow forming, lost in the refraction of raindrops on the wall. His freshly conscious vision couldn't quite make out the shapes in the room, but he started to sit up, ready to turn on the light.

Without warning, his glass started to lift from his side table, wrapped in some kind of fleshy appendage. Panicked, he grabbed at it, certain he was hallucinating, but it flew out of his grip.

The glass fell and shattered into several serrated shards, the contents splashing up the wall and against the mattress. A slimy, inhuman tentacle retracted from the space, and slapped against the wall as it snuck back out. Jared immediately bounded to his feet, flicking the covers off of his body, and chased the appendage out of the room. As soon as he had time to fumble for the light switch, it had vanished.

He shook his head, attempting to make sense of the situation. He burst through the door to Maude's room, and stared at the darkness for what seemed like a lifetime. Nothing was moving, aside from the gentle motion of her chest, rising and falling in natural rhythm.

* * *

Jared was losing it… he was sure.

He didn't sleep. His sleep medication didn't work, and he couldn't help but replay the absurd scene in his head. Whatever really happened had been masked by his tired, fed-up brain, and he really just needed some fresh air.

So, that morning, he walked over to his local corner shop, taking the scenic route to get as much time outside of the house as possible.

The store was a modest square box, built inside an old detached building on the edge of town. As he entered, a friendly older woman behind the counter was helping a young boy decide on his purchase. The boy's small hands were overflowing with bubblegum packets in every colour, and he was desperately attempting to choose which he'd go home with.

The tired displays and faded décor contrasted again the polychromatic selection of foodstuffs on offer. For such a small space, the owners kept a wonderful variety of stock, boasting everything from locally grown fruit and veg through to national chain savoury snacks and frozen dinners. Maude used to bring Jared to the shop when he was very young, and it had remained his local ever since. He half-guessed the owners had probably remained the same too; it was a nice anchor in an ocean of uncertainty.

After paying for a few essentials and exchanging pleasantries, he headed outside and lit up a cigarette. The time outside had offered a new perspective on his situation, a reminder that the whole setup was temporary and there was probably some kind of lesson to be learned from the ordeal. He took a drag, enjoying each mouthful of smoke before blowing it out between pursed lips. When the stick grew too short to smoke, he let it fall to the concrete, and stomped it out before sliding his key into the front door.

Jared closed the door gently, conscious that Maude might be asleep. He set aside the plastic bag of shopping, and started to pace towards the kitchen.

In the corner of his eye, he saw a long, distorted shadow right by the stairs. It didn't even register in his mind, until he got closer… and then stopped dead in his tracks.

Maude's head was upside down, exhaling deeply, her eyes buried deep in yellowed sockets. A grotesque growl spat from her lips, as her skull twisted three hundred and sixty degrees.

Jared stood frozen in fear. Maude's neck had extended over the landing balcony, stretched like warm plasticine, dragging her flailing body to the top of the stairs. Before he could mutter a word, her head retracted like a measuring tape, coiling back in on itself, snapping back to her body. She scuttled to the room and slammed the door. The sound of wet flesh and crackling bones penetrated deep inside his head, looping through his damaged mind.

Jared dropped to the floor in the same spot, completely overwhelmed by what he had seen. Half of him thought it best to just run and never look back, taking his essentials and starting a new life someplace. The more realistic half of him took a couple of moments to catch his breath, and get back up on his feet.

* * *

Maude was fine. Well, she wasn't, but there was no obvious evidence of what had transpired. She was asleep, flopped across the bed in a comfortable position.

Jared was about to leave when Maude spoke up.

"My bones... They feel like jelly..." she creaked.

"I'll call the doctor," Jared asserted, already reaching for his mobile phone.

"I don't need them, Jared. It's too late."

"What do you mean it's too late? You're just tired, I'll call—"

"NO!" she ordered.

Jared sighed. He was quite possibly hallucinating all of this nonsense, and his role as caregiver was nosediving. But however much he hadn't cared initially, he didn't want to lose her.

"You never let me help. What the fuck am I supposed to do? You guilt me into feeling sorry for you, even though it should be the other way round, and then refuse to do anything about it... What do you want?" Jared pleaded.

"I tried to leave. I really did. He had this control..."

"Not this again... He's DEAD mum. Dad's dead... Fred's dead. There are no men in your life left to blame."

Jared turned around, twisting the doorknob, ready to leave—but a hand slammed against the wood, just inches away from his head. He didn't dare turn around, instead remaining frozen against the frame, suddenly ready to listen.

"I, uh... I need to get your tablets. Let me go and get them," Jared begged.

The hand slid off of the wood, leaving a slimy streak of yellow pus in its wake. He was outside of the room in a split second, already sprinting down the stairs.

* * *

The second cigarette didn't have as strong an effect as the first. Jared was shivering and felt sick to his core. The thing inside that room wasn't his mother. His mother was feisty, a complete wreck, unruly, but *that* was something else entirely.

Her tablets were laid out on the counter, squeezed from their packaging, ready to be administered. Jared didn't know whether to up the dose or toss them in the trash. The doctors weren't answering, and he didn't know what would happen to Maude if he called an ambulance.

From the modest garden at the back of the house, he could hear her heavy breathing, each exhale croaking loudly. He needed a plan, to be able to take control of this situation, but none of it made sense.

"Jared? Where are you?"

He flicked his stub and lit another cigarette, his feet restlessly shifting on the floor as he tried to make a decision.

* * *

Jared collected a few pills and chucked them onto the side counter. With the end of a rolling pin, he ground them into a dust, and sprinkled the residue into a glass of water. He used his finger to stir in the solids until they dissolved, and he started up the stairs.

A thick coating of slime covered the walls of the upstairs landing. Yellow streaks dripped from the ceiling, and the carpet was damp to the touch, exuding a wet cat scent which whipped into his nostrils.

He heard Maude rambling, her voice deeper than before.

"No Fred, please. I need to see my children. I'm sweaty now... I'm so hot. Where are you? Where did you go?"

"Mum? I have your medicine."

Jared slowly stalked towards the room. He could feel the carpet compress with each wet step, but kept his eyes trained on the door, unwilling to dive any deeper into the dark depression he was drowning in.

The room had been trashed. Maude was still in bed, covers draped over her body, but the table had been overturned, spilling leftovers onto the floor. The walls were covered in spots of slime and blood, and the soft furnishings had been ripped to tatters.

"Mum? You need to drink this."

"Go away, Fred."

Jared shook his head.

"It's me, Mum. I'm going to call an ambulance," Jared explained.

"No. Get away from my children. I want to go with them! Let me go with them please."

"Mum? You're scaring me," Jared said.

"I feel sweaty hot. Hot and sweaty, and I need to leave. I need to break out of here, my children *need* me, Fred. Why are you stopping me? Why *me?"*

"Mum, please stop."

She was facing the wall, so Jared couldn't make out her facial expression. Something really wasn't right.

Jared placed the water on the closest surface to him. Carefully watching the back of her head, he slipped his hand into his jeans pocket, fumbling for his mobile phone. Without obviously removing the handset, he tapped the screen three times, hoping to God he was hitting the correct numbers for the emergency services.

As if she could read his mind, her neck cracked backwards towards the door, her eyes leaking a stream of yellow pus. The rest of her body ruptured into a standing position, her disfigured spine pushing against the skin of her back, showing prominently through her thin pyjama shirt. Her limbs bowed, unsupported by her skeleton, which seemed to be disintegrating. He could hear the crumbling, chalky sound of her bones.

She opened her mouth wide, ready to speak, but words were overcome by a rush of viscous black liquid, which spilled from her throat. Unflinching, she casually wiped her lips with her elbow, before starting to shuffle backwards towards Jared.

From his pocket, he could hear a muffled voice. It was the ambulance service, trying their best to get his attention. Jared couldn't risk it any longer. His hand dove into his jeans, and he removed the handset.

"I need—"

A fleshy tendril smashed the phone from his hand, a juicy swipe which splattered foul-smelling liquid across his face and the wall behind him. Jared tumbled to the floor, and quickly squirmed towards the door, twisting the handle and curling around the frame. From the landing, he jolted across the hallway and dove into the opposite room.

He was in his bedroom, sweat pouring from his brow. Frozen in position, he tried to think of his next steps, and was encouraged to do so at a faster pace by Maude's guttural screams.

The world outside was taunting Jared. The sun-kissed town looked particularly beautiful today—uncharacteristically so—but he was trapped. Hands pressed against the window, he knew the two-storey drop would disable him. He needed another way out.

A fat, worm-like limb shattered the door. Maude's frail hand was attached to the end of the brown, viscid tentacle; it was as if her arm had mutated and extended to gross effect. It whipped across the room and shattered a photo frame.

"JAREEEEEED!"

The deformed roar was a horrifying reminder of the monster in the other room. This wasn't his mother anymore. He had to defend himself... or else.

Jared grabbed a shard of the shattered frame's glass, and sliced the appendage, severing a segment of the decaying flesh. He was greeted with a spew of small, thrashing tapeworms, pale and rubbery like calamari.

They slopped to the floor, and began to make tracks towards him. Jared slashed the appendage again, and the entire segment collapsed onto the floor. Black blood squirted from the stump, and covered Jared's face and neck as he sprinted past and out of the door.

He hurtled down the stairs, unable to keep up with the rest of his body, and misplaced his footing around halfway down. He tripped and plummeted to the bottom, his body crumpling on impact with the wall.

Maude cried out in pain, flailing around the room, her withered stump oozing a putrid pus. In a dark, horrifying growl, she started to spew phrases in a frenzy, her humanity being taken over by this disease.

"Jared... Baby. My baby... Hurting. Stop him hurting. *CCRAACCH.* Fred. Fred dead. Jared alive. Jared and Maude..." Tears poured from her eyes, but they quickly turned to torrents of viscous black blood instead.

Whatever was left of Maude was fading away, utterly consumed by this beast.

Jared's head was numb. His vision blurred and flickered, the world around him felt imaginary. He looked up to the landing, and noticed a cascade of mutant tapeworms tumbling towards him, closely followed by the monstrosity his mother had transformed into.

"Fuck."

Jared crawled into the dining room, under the table and into the kitchen. Maude made her way down the stairs—not on her feet, but on surprisingly agile tentacles, which moved and stalked in an alien way. She was hovering, almost, and when she landed on the ground floor, her neck started to protrude. Her head launched off of her body, and her neck became another tendril, a horrific appendage which swirled and contorted to allow her to see wherever she wanted to.

Her body was still frozen in position at the end of the stairs, but her head drifted through the air, scanning the area like a predator.

Eventually, Maude's mangled face happened upon Jared, and her neck stretched to allow her to come face to face with him.

"I… I just want to talk," Maude croaked. Her tongue moved in three segments, each one caressing her black teeth.

"You need a doctor, Mum."

The creature started to cry, a glitchy, distorted sound emanating from its mouth.

"I need to talk, Jared. Please just hear me out. Please help me!"

"I am Mum. I am."

Before she had a chance to reply, Jared slid right under the deformed neck, and bolted for the front door. It was futile, of course. Maude's body launched itself against it, and another tendril started to grow from her chest, splintering through her flesh. This appendage wrapped itself around Jared's neck, and launched him into the sky, tightening its grip around his throat.

The air was leaving his body too fast, and he couldn't inhale. Maude's neck slithered back into his view, her face once again pressed right up to his.

"I've been a bad mother. I know that. I want to say sorry. I'm really sorry."

"Fuck off you freak!" Jared squirmed, before starting to claw at the tentacle.

Frustratedly, Maude released Jared, allowing him to fall to the floor. His arm fractured on collision with the laminate and he let out a small shriek.

Maude's tendrils started to jolt and pulsate, whilst more fleshy lengths started to grow from various orifices. Like an old potato sprouting all over its surface, Maude's body was a breeding ground for these inhuman, worm-like limbs, which flicked around the room frenetically.

Within moments, the walls and floor were covered in perpetually expanding tentacles, a sea of clammy, putrefied flesh, swarming through his home. Her body was overtaken, and the room soon became one surge of slithering meat.

Jared slowly slid himself towards the back of the kitchen, attempting to reach a knife or sharp utensil, but unable to fight through the flesh. The walls were closing in, the free space in the room dwindling, claustrophobic.

He could feel the gelatinous friction of the oscillating tendrils, which seemed to rub up against him and drag across his body, leaving a potent stench in their wake.

"MUM! STOP THIS!" Jared screamed, but it was no use.

As he crawled back into the dining room, he noticed that his mother's face had ruptured into smaller fragments, each birthing a colony of smaller tapeworms. The rancid murmur of this nightmare was ringing in Jared's ears, and he was unable to move any further.

He tried to stand up, but the weight of the flesh was too much for him to fight. A spew of tapeworms slid from one appendage into Jared's agape mouth, landing on his tongue with a salty tang.

He immediately tried to force them out with a cough, but this just lodged them further into his throat. Jared's arms and legs were pinned down by the wall of tendrils, and he was completely overwhelmed. He tried to scream, but no sound could get past the chunks of tapeworm slithering across his tonsils.

Eventually, one rogue tendril flicked into his mouth,

pushing down his throat and cutting up his insides as it forced its way in further.

The windows started to shatter. The roof began to crack. The room had no more space to offer the growing size of this inhuman flesh, and in Jared's dying breath, he noticed his mother's fragmented face saunter through the kitchen, a disfigured mosaic of eyes, nose, and skin, dead but still somehow related to the woman she once was. He could have sworn she smiled on her way through, but maybe it was just his imagination at play.

The room went dark, and all Jared could feel was the pulsating tendril ejaculating tapeworms into his guts.

REPLACEMENT

Introducing FleshKey technology from LifeLong Corp.

The world's best self-care units, delivered direct to your door!

Our FleshKey units are for users with various skin diseases and progressive ailments, and feature the following:

Custom moulded flesh with industry-leading stem cell connecting technology

Advanced pigmentation blending, which can get as close as a 99.99% colour match with your natural skin tone

An easy plug and play process, with subscription options for users with progressive or ongoing issues

Money back guarantee

Early access to other LifeLong Corp products

100% cruelty free and not tested on animals.

Clara awoke to a loud knocking. Weaving through her apartment with dreary eyes, she called out to announce her presence, and unlocked the door. A handsome delivery driver handed her a box, which she placed on the table whilst her sight adjusted to the bright daylight.

She trudged back through the open plan apartment, shuffling things around a bit whilst she woke up. The computer in the corner was still on standby, halfway through Clara's latest clickbait headline for work. It had been left mid-sentence, when she had decided enough was enough and it was time to get some shuteye.

In the bathroom, she pulled up her white vest, revealing a scarred midsection and a medium-sized bandage packing a wound in the centre of her chest. Gripping the vest material between her teeth, she slowly peeled away the bandage, clenching her jaw, letting out a tiny squeal of pain. The bandage detached from the skin, uncovering an apple-sized cavity around four inches thick, with an irregular, jagged border. Dried blood and desiccated flakes of skin clung to the interior meat of the crater as fresh blood started to well.

Clara quickly dropped the used bandage into her bathroom bin, and headed back to the living room.

INSTRUCTIONS FOR USE:

Open box carefully, without using scissors or any other sharp objects

Apply the numbing solution to the interior and exterior of the cavity, and use the included brittle brush to work away any loose skin

Tear open the vacuum-sealed exterior mould, and discard the outer layer

Unwrap the LifeLong Iced Bandage Wrap from around the FleshKey unit, and discard the wrap

Spray the activation liquid (bright blue vial) onto the unit and into the cavity, in a 50/50 ratio

Line up the etchings on the FleshKey with the shape of the cavity. You may need to apply light force to push it into place.

Remove the sticky mesh from its packaging and apply directly over the FleshKey, ensuring it covers both the unit and 1-2 inches of the surrounding skin

Remove the mesh in the shower after 24 hours, and the join should look seamless

Repeat with any other cavities. PLEASE NOTE: The most urgent/ serious cavities should be taken care of first, and only one unit should be inserted per session, to ensure the body doesn't reject the material.

Clara had been using FleshKey technology for most of her adult life. In her early teenage years, she received a diagnosis of *Caro Foramina,* a debilitating condition which caused her flesh to eat itself, leaving painful blisters and craters in her skin.

In the years between her diagnosis and the introduction of the technology, she had almost died three times, sick with sepsis and a bundle of different infections due to the open wounds. FleshKey had saved her life, and the only reason she was still standing at thirty-five years old was due to a regular subscription of the units.

Each pack included a hyper-precise mould of flesh, measured through a 3D-printing mobile app from the user end, and grown in a laboratory from cloned skin cells. The exact technology was top secret, but to say it was a miracle of modern science would be an understatement.

The cavity in her chest was the biggest eruption she had had to date, and the delivery sitting on the table in front of her was an emergency supply, in addition to her regular allocation. Due to the shape of the wound, the flesh was shaped like a slightly flattened potato, which made the whole situation even more absurd - but this technology was a lifesaver.

She'd been through the process a hundred times, so the procedure was second nature now, but she still followed the instructions word by word.

Clara worked her way right through to the insertion stage, and held the fleshy mass up to the crater. Rotating it in the light, she allowed a shadow to fall into the tiny etchings, making a hundred percent sure that it was positioned correctly.

She lined up the rearmost curve and gently slid the mass inwards. The squishy penetration was agonising, and it took everything Clara had to stop herself screaming. This part never got easier, but it was something she had to accept as part of the process. After an extra squeeze through the narrow canal in her flesh, she set the unit neatly into place, and applied the sticky mesh over the procedure site.

But something was wrong…

Usually, that would be the end of it… Insert, apply mesh, done. But this time, the flesh seemed to be wriggling. The mass was vibrating, small lumps protruding from the surface, skimming around the skin facade with a hellish tickle. Clara pushed the front of it deeper into the crevice, checking that she hadn't placed it incorrectly, but it fit like a puzzle piece. The pressure against her inner wound was torturous, rubbing against the raw flesh with burning friction.

It started to push harder, and eventually slipped halfway out of the wound, severing the mesh and the minuscule flesh connections that had already been made. Clara panicked and grabbed the unit, tearing it entirely out of the crater. The pain was excruciating, but as soon as she had it back in her hand, she threw it down onto the table with a frustrated *thud.*

For a few seconds, she simply stared at it, perplexed at the difficulty she was having with such a simple, routine task. The shape was correct, the texture was correct, and the flesh was connecting properly—so what was wrong with this unit?

The wriggling started again, and Clara got a full view of what it looked like when it wasn't in her body. A protruding lump under the skin skimmed across the surface, as if a large finger was trying to burst through the membrane. She leaned in closer, disgusted but curious, and even reached out a hand to touch it—before immediately recoiling.

The membranous shell started to tear, a small oval gradually opening up in the flesh. Underneath, a milky substance pooled in the centre, swirling in an unusual pattern. The texture was jelly-like, a bright white ball forming and rising to the surface, starting to poke out slightly from the plane.

And then it blinked…

Clara took a step back, cocked her head, and then audibly gasped. The mound of skin had an eye. An actual, functioning eyeball, which had just broken out from beneath the membrane.

That *thing* had been inside her moments ago. What the fuck was happening?

The FleshKey started to pulsate, a slow, undulating motion passing through its form. It was subtle, but Clara studied every tiny movement. The eyeball span in its shallow socket, circling the room, studying the environment it found itself in.

Clara couldn't handle how bizarre this whole situation was. She nudged the thing with a careless swipe, and sent it hurtling to the floor. It landed hard on the laminate, before flopping onto its other side, allowing it to see again. The eyeball tracked around the room, and landed upon Clara.

With a creepy, slug-like movement, the flesh potato started to haul itself across the room. Clara's wound had started to bleed out, and stained her white vest in damp drips of yellow-crimson. As it made its getaway, she noticed a tiny trail of putrid slime, discarded through the smallest of holes on its underside.

Glasses and kitchenware took flight as Clara carelessly searched for a big enough receptacle to contain the unit. She had dozens of different takeaway containers and lunchboxes, but she wanted something that would trap it without too much space to spare.

Eventually, she happened upon the perfect size.

* * *

The FleshKey had disappeared.

Clara studied every square inch of the apartment, checking under chairs, the sofa, on top of cupboards and even in drawers... and then she saw it.

The fleshy mass was inching up her bookcase, leaving a trail of slime in its wake, trying hard not to be seen. But it was too late, Clara was already on the other side of the room, trying to trap it beneath a circular lunch container, missing it by mere millimetres with each swipe. Sweat pooled on her brow as she chased this thing, as if it were a naughty puppy or terrifying creepy crawly. Finally, with an exhausting swipe from above, she had it trapped, pinning it down with her foot. Clara felt the sides of the container shudder left and right as the thing tried to break out, but she wasn't in the mood for another game of chase.

Clara had so many questions... *so many.*

But first, she needed to get in touch with the suppliers.

* * *

FleshKey had a 24/7 hotline for all manner of queries and difficulties, and after listening carefully to the offering presented by the robotic operator, option four (to get through to customer services) seemed like the correct choice.

Clara used handfuls of tissues to pack out the wound in the meantime–she daren't leave the thing alone to go and get her bandages—and covered it with masking tape from her DIY drawer. Her head had gone a little light from the blood loss, but she was focused on getting to the bottom of the situation, and getting the flesh ball out of her house.

Her bare foot stepped right into a trail of slime, as the phone connected to the operator. The other foot was still pinning down the container, but she slid it around the laminated floor to get around.

"Fucking shit!"

"I, uh, hello ma'am. I'm Rodney, your FleshKey solution advisor. How can I help?"

"Sorry. I almost slipped over... My name is Clara Shaw, uh... I got my FleshKey unit today, and there's something wrong."

"Wrong? Oh no, we can't have that. Did you already key in Option Three for help and support?"

"No, I'm a regular user, I find it's easier just to come right through to customer services."

"Right," Rodney muttered. "Well, we do have a process for a reason, as well as an extensive FAQ listing on our website, but I have no problem letting it slide this time for a loyal customer."

"Thanks," Clara said.

"So, what is the matter exactly?"

"Well, I—"

The FleshKey squeaked. Clara couldn't believe it.

With a shuddering tremble, it seemed to act up anytime she tried to talk, hurtling its misshapen form against the container.

What the fuck is going on?

"I, uh. My unit. It's alive."

The thing squeaked at a deafening pitch. Clara couldn't do anything but shake her head.

"I'm not sure what you mean, ma'am."

"This flesh is *moving*. I mean squirming across my floor and leaving trails and shit."

There was a heavy breathing at the end of the line, before it disconnected, ringing out with a monotonous dial tone.

"Fucking shit!" she screamed, throwing her mobile phone onto the table.

Without even noticing the container had slipped from under her foot, the unit was pressing against the window, its underside slopped on the glass, hanging on with sticky mucus. Whatever it was, it wanted to escape, and didn't seem to want to go back in her body. She didn't have time for such tomfoolery. Clara left the flesh mass on the window, and went to pick her phone back up.

555-4321-6694

Her boss' direct line. Clara held the phone up to her ear, waiting only a couple of seconds until Darren answered the phone.

"Hey. I got something you're gonna wanna see," Clara said.

* * *

Clara held her phone towards the window, holding still whilst the camera filmed the unusual thing slithering across the previously spotless glass. Darren was on a video call with her, appearing as a small avatar at the top left of her screen. He looked in utter amazement.

"This is from FleshKey?"

"Sure is."

Darren knew about FleshKey from Clara, but also from the menagerie of clickbait articles they had written about Lifelong (their parent company) in the past.

Some of her favourites included:

- You won't believe what this corporation feeds their workers for breakfast

- Fight or flight? The truth behind LifeLong Corp's dodgy dealings with local passenger airlines

- Food or dude? Are these super close-up images of food or the latest skin cell technology.

"That's so fucked up. Why am I not more surprised?" Darren said.

"We gotta tell someone," Clara suggested.

Darren shook his head slowly.

"This isn't enough. We need to go bigger."

"What do you mean? What do you suggest?" Clara questioned.

"We need to get into the factory. Get some proper solid evidence of *everything* going on in there. Prove some of those online rumours true. Could you imagine the traffic we'd get?"

Clara wasn't sure. Darren was always chasing "big" stories, always on the lookout for the big break that would enable him to transform their company into something more professional and worthy, as opposed to a Z-list meme site.

Then again, the journalist in her really did want to know what was going on, and why she had a sentient hunk of flesh crawling around her house. Whilst on the phone, she grabbed a can of cola from the fridge and sat on the edge of her sofa, downing the drink to combat her lightheadedness.

"That's a big risk. What if we get found out?"

Darren screwed up his face, thinking for a second.

"We have to give it a go."

It was a bat-shit crazy plan, full of risk with very little reward. Who would believe a site that relied on clickbait articles?

Clara's thought was interrupted by a wailing siren, getting closer and closer to her house. It didn't take her long to guess who would be in the vehicle careening to her apartment.

Lifelong.

"Shit, they're here."

"Who are?" Darren asked.

"Lifelong. I called them first, they're probably here to investigate."

Clara was panicking, already looking for alternative exits out of the house.

"Don't let them in. If they take that thing away, our biggest story ever goes with it. We need this Clara."

He was right... They did. And it was up to her to formulate a way out.

* * *

"Miss Shaw? We're from LifeLong, here to talk about your FleshKey unit. Can you let us in please?"

Clara's legs trembled as she propped herself on the window sill, straddled between the interior of her bedroom and the exterior wall outside. She was still wearing a vest and pyjama trousers, and had scooped the flesh unit into a small backpack. The air was warm and humid, causing her sticky hands to slip and slide as she tried to manoeuvre herself into a safe position to continue.

She could hear the representative at the front door, patiently knocking and awaiting a reply. He would no doubt call the police for a safety call-in if she didn't answer, to check that she hadn't fallen unconscious trying to secure the unit. That meant she had five minutes, tops.

Clara took a few deep breaths, carefully angling herself out of the window, balancing on a protruding piece of brickwork as she transferred her weight from her arms to her base. As soon as she had safely cleared the window opening, it was time to jump.

She hadn't thought this through at all.

If Clara launched herself from her current position, she'd get a face-full of concrete and quite possibly squash the thing in her backpack. She needed to shimmy to the left, reach the end of the wall and then jump, where a patch of overgrown wildflowers would cushion her fall.

"We're going to need to do a safety check if we don't see you in one minute, Miss Shaw. We're concerned for your welfare. Go ahead and answer the door now."

By the end of his speech, Clara was already sidestepping across the crumbling brickwork, hands extended flat to the wall, giving herself an extra point of balance. The fleshy mass in her backpack was thrashing about wildly, obviously not keen on the experience, but she had to try and maintain her composure.

* * *

By the time a second set of sirens started to echo in the air, Clara had reached the end of the wall. She jumped into the bed of flowers beneath her, causing a shockwave of blunt pain to burst through her body—but she didn't break any bones. That was all she could hope for with such an out-of-character display of gymnastics.

Patting down her chest, she forced the moist tissues back into her wound, gritting her teeth and praying for a better solution to come around soon.

Clara stalked around the back of her house and hurtled into the car park, dodging the handful of vehicles surrounding her home. She reached her car, slid in the key, and watched as the representative entered her building, flanked by two rather angry looking police officers.

FleshKey were trying their best to contain this by the looks of things, which made the anticipation for this story even stronger. Maybe this would be their big break, and she could finally start her career as an investigative journalist, where she could make a difference every day rather than a cheap joke.

* * *

Darren had set up a meeting at his house, about twenty minutes away from Clara's apartment. She had managed to get on the road without any issues, and had parked up around the corner to avoid any suspicion.

She didn't know what to expect from the meeting. Darren mentioned he had a friend who could help (he always did), and that it would be best to all meet together before heading to the factory, especially given the current circumstances.

The inside of Darren's house was chaotic, but in a constrained and liveable manner. The windows were covered in blackout blinds, the shelves were overloaded with different books, gadgets, and vintage accolades.

Clara and Darren sat at a small table in his kitchen, joined by the guest of the day…

Gary.

Gary was an ex-mechanic who had a run of jobs working for LifeLong's engineering division before taking on a janitorial role in his retirement. What many people didn't know about Gary, he explained to them, was that despite his sixty plus years on this planet, he had an undying thirst for knowledge, and had been spending his time at hackathons and learning how to breach security systems in his spare time. This was all above board, but he did have a slightly rebellious streak. In combination with a grudge against LifeLong and their less than fair retirement packages, he was the perfect candidate to help.

He had just one question:

"Why are you going in there?"

Clara and Darren looked at each other, and then back to Gary.

"We think something less than savory is going on," Clara explained.

Gary looked perplexed, until Clara pulled her backpack up off of the ground and let him peek inside. The FleshKey unit was relatively relaxed at the moment, but she still only unzipped the bag partly open… she couldn't risk another escape.

"Jesus," Gary whispered.

"You didn't know about this?" Clara asked.

"God no. Nothing like this."

They all stared down at the bag, until Darren leaned closer to Gary, as if ready to whisper a secret message.

"We need to get in there… Tomorrow afternoon at the latest. Can you bypass their systems? Or do you have an old keycard that still might work?"

Gary got lost in thought for a few uncomfortable seconds, before finally jumping back to reality.

"They update their systems weekly, like clockwork. So a keycard won't work… They do, however, have a failsafe. And there'd be no need to update that, as only engineers know about it."

Clara and Darren smiled in unison.

"That sounds like it could be a perfect plan," Darren gleamed, and the three of them drank tea and shared stories for a few more hours, until Gary got up to leave.

"I'll see you two tomorrow. Oh, and don't forget our agreed fee."

* * *

The FleshKey lab was part of a mega complex owned by LifeLong Corp. Clara had only just begun to peel away the layers of what the corporation did, but she knew that a large part of their work was hidden away to the general public—and anyone without top level security clearance.

Gary met them at the crack of dawn, instructing them to meet outside a staff carpark at the rear of the vicinity. In the back of his vintage car, he had packed a couple of staff uniforms—aka branded lab jackets and trousers—and helped them change into them. Darren handed over a small holdall full of cash (his life savings, in fact, that's how much was on the line with this story) and Gary promised to keep their things safe for when they surfaced.

After drawing a map on a scrap notebook page and handing it to Clara, he got to explaining how they would be getting into the complex.

"The thing you have to remember," he started, "is that they will expect a ruckus. If you blend in, they'll assume you're part of the furniture, and a couple of small mistakes won't raise too much suspicion. There are always new starters at this factory, it's where most people start before they get deeper into the system."

Clara and Darren nodded, following along.

"There is a small service building which houses the electric meter, the water stopcock, boring things like that. Because tradespeople are in and out all of the time, there is only a basic keypad entry. However, there's also a failsafe, because those codes are changed all the time, and the security guards can't be bothered to contact the higher-ups for the latest updates. It's simply a pattern which resets the keypad for a single entry."

"Surely to God they don't let tradespeople anywhere near the main building without an escort though?" Darren quizzed.

Gary shook his head, a smile growing on his face.

"Of course not. But what many people, even the guards,

don't realise, is that there is an old access tunnel that runs under the bathroom and connects directly to a janitor's closet in the main complex. I only found it by mistake when checking a leak once, and I didn't tell anyone. I'm willing to bet all the money you just gave me that they still haven't sealed it up."

It was a thin plan, they had to admit. It had been several years since Gary retired, but it was their only real option if they were going to get results quickly. Journalism involved a leap of faith, sometime a gargantuan leap of faith, and now that her life was on the line too, Clara found it easier to rationalise such a plan.

"Oh. And take this."

Gary handed a spy camera to Clara, a tiny brick shaped more like a pack of chewing gum than a recording device. She slipped it safely into her trousers.

After a handshake and a nod, the pair got to it, ready to embark on an adventure best suited for a spy, not two lowly journalists. But it was worth a try. Worth giving everything they had.

* * *

Up until around halfway through the tunnel, the journey had been a walk in the park. The pattern reset had worked on the keypad, and the access panel in the bathroom floor had been relatively easy to find (after shifting the sink cabinet to the side and squeezing into a less than spacious gap.)

The tunnel, however, was full of old furniture and equipment, so much so that the route had been blocked.

"In the mood for some heavy lifting?" Darren joked.

Clara was in the exact opposite mood. Blood was pouring out of the wound in her chest, along with pus, and the tissues had completely disintegrated. The skin on her neck and face felt clammy, and she knew that she couldn't risk getting an infection—she'd have to find a covering of some type, and some sanitation liquid if she was lucky.

That didn't detract from the fact that they were at an impasse, and would need to heave some of this junk out of the way to continue.

"Let's get this done," she remarked.

* * *

Clara could hear voices behind the door. Two men were having an awkward yet casual conversation at the urinals, and with intermittent splashing sounds and grunts, she counted a further one or two people in the cubicles.

After waiting for what seemed like an hour but was probably only ten minutes, the coast was clear, and Clara slammed her shoulder against the door. It didn't budge. She tried again, but due to the cramped space in the closet, she couldn't get much of a run up.

Eventually, she burst through, spilling onto the floor, Darren right behind her. They immediately scouted the area, checking no workers were caught with their pants down—quite literally.

The bathroom led into a long, narrow corridor, with rooms branching off from each side in equal intervals. The pair unruffled their jackets, attempting to look presentable, and got ready to step out into the hallway—just as Clara's backpack rattled, and the flesh unit made a run for it, darting across the vinyl floor, tucking itself into a nondescript office.

"Fuck!" Clara muttered, before speeding after it, trying her best to look professional and calm.

* * *

It wasn't in the first office they checked. Or the second. Or the third.

On the fourth try, they found an empty meeting room, tucked inside the door, ready to draw up a plan.

"We have to let it go for now. There will be other specimens," Darren said.

"I don't think we really have a choice. We need to find the factory, where they're actually making these things. Get that evidence and get out of here."

Darren nodded in agreement.

"But where—"

Darren was cut off by a man in his mid-40s entering the room, dressed in business attire as opposed to lab uniform.

"I don't believe you've booked out this meeting room," the man said, his voice deep and unnerving.

"I, uh. We're sorry," Clara started.

"We are looking for the... production line," Darren guessed, hoping he hadn't just put his foot in it.

"It's our first day, and these hallways are so confusing!" Clara added in support.

The man stared at them for a few moments, his bushy eyebrows framing curious eyes.

"You're in the wrong place completely. Who is your supervisor, I'll call for an escort."

The pair panicked, unable to think of a solution, before Clara tried one more time.

"We really don't want to get in trouble on our first day. And we'd hate to disrupt the line."

Another few awkward moments, before the man nodded.

"Out of this room, you turn right. Next corridor intersects, you turn left. End of that hallway, production line."

He motioned them out of the room with a nod, and invited his colleagues inside, ready to chair a meeting of some kind.

* * *

The room was a breathtaking sight.

A seemingly boundless white space with jet black conveyor belts starting at a small desk with microscopes and test tubes, running through to a small pressure oven, a disinfectant shower, vacuum sealing, and then packing, ending at quality control and distribution.

It was unfathomably intricate, running like clockwork, with several hundred technicians working in their own mini teams. A large, ominous logo hovered above them, projected from a series of devices scattered across the room. A series of metal walkways ran overhead, presumably for higher level staff to check on the worker bees.

Clara took a step forward, sneakily holding the spy camera just above her pocket, filming everything she was seeing. There was no sign of her FleshKey unit, though it was probably the last place it would return to, if it was indeed scared as Clara imagined. The fact that these things had even a semblance of sentience was worrying enough, but part of her felt like it was her job to protect it. How fucked up was that?

Trying their best to merge into the hustle and bustle, they paced right through the middle of the factory, and turned left into a quieter, albeit similarly vast, space.

What they saw in that room would haunt them for the rest of their lives.

A dozen imposing machines stood in the background, with rotating blades and pins slicing through the air, accepting lumps of meat as they were fed into the opening. Once the blades caught a small piece of flesh, they pulverised it, spitting it back out as smooth goo, ready for its next destination.

A rancid pile of sentient flesh was abandoned in a corner,

occasionally fed to the machines by a young technician, who looked absolutely nonchalant at the fact she was killing sentient beings.

Clara and Darren froze with a shared sense of shock as the technician grabbed mounds of oddly shaped, writhing flesh, battling against its will to live, and chucked it towards the deathly blades. The resulting meat was minced to smithereens, ending its journey by slopping onto the conveyor belt.

Clara held a plume of vomit in the back of her throat, her body shaking with panic. She kept her spy cam trained on the action, knowing that this would be the footage to finally wake people up.

Suddenly, a spray of crimson vomited out of the top of the machine, scattering way beyond its bounds and landing upon Clara and Darren. Writhing in disgust, she let out an audible gag… which gave away their position.

The technician span around, clocked the pair and noticed the tiny camera they were filming with. She raised the alarm, tugging a lever which flooded the factory in a saturated red light. Heart in her throat, Clara launched forward and smacked the worker with her elbow, sending her to the floor like a sack of potatoes.

She landed in the pile, causing the other flesh mounds to scatter across the floor, squirming, slithering and dragging their way to safety.

"Over here!"

Darren was halfway up a service ladder, clambering onto an overhead walkway. Three technicians and a security guard were chasing after him. Before Clara could react, a chubby technician charged her from behind, sending her and the spy camera cascading to the ground.

"Contain this!" one of the head technicians screamed. "By *any* means necessary!"

Clara didn't want to stick around long enough to know what that meant.

The camera had become lodged between two sections of metal, and from her vantage point, she could see Darren fighting with the group above.

The chubby technician on the ground grabbed a fistful of Clara's hair, dragging her towards the side of the room. She put up a fight, trying to claw at his hand, but that ended with her head being slammed into a machine.

Through blurry eyes, she could see the shapes on the walkway above, tossing and turning, grabbing and punching. She tracked down and noticed they were right above the mincing machine, and knew she had to act.

Clara stretched her hands out in front of her, ready to crawl and stand up, trying to break through her hazy disposition.

But it was no use…

The chubby man stepped onto her outstretched fingers, cracking two of her bones, as the room erupted in a cacophony of sirens and red lights. Clara screamed, but the sound was drowned out by the commotion.

"Contain this!" someone shouted again, trying to control the nightmare unfolding in front of them.

Clara was slowly losing consciousness. It was a battle to hold herself up on her feet. Her chest was leaking still, globs of sickly flesh dripping down her stomach. The wound seared with an intense burning, ejecting fluids with nothing to soak up the moisture.

Nothing about the situation felt real.

She looked up at Darren, fighting for his life.

And then to the right, where a large TV was playing a glossy advertisement on a loop. A small child was tucking into chicken nugget shapes, licking her lips as she dipped each one into a variety of sauces, coating the snacks with far too much condiment.

A tagline appeared on screen:

Made fresh at LifeLong Corps' Food Division.

Her eyes darted to the conveyor belt, where mushed up discarded flesh was being spat out into shapes, very similar to the ones the little kid was eating on-screen.

Oh God no. Anything but that.

"Clara!" Darren screamed from above. Her head snapped up to see him, just in time to see a look of complete fear. A mix of acceptance and true horror.

Two of the technicians lifted him from his feet, and launched him over the edge of the walkway.

He fell like a rag-doll tossed from the top of a skyscraper, flailing and bending in unusual shapes, a scream of terror escaping from his mouth.

His arm hit the machine first, snatched in between the metal gears, pulverised to crimson soup in a matter of seconds. His shoulder and chest followed, bones splintered into tiny fragments, grinding against the iron with a deafening screech.

"NOOOOOO!" she screamed, unable to help.

Darren's skin was flayed like the casing from a sausage, whilst his organs popped and spewed out their contents onto the front of the machine. The technician above clapped his hands and cackled like a hyena.

Clara couldn't help but scream her lungs out, but had to pull herself away. She couldn't look anymore.

She had to escape.

Reaching forward once more, she snatched the camera and wiggled it free from the metal, slightly relieved to see it had pointed at the machine the whole time. It was a miracle.

With the painfully haunting sound of the laughing kid

from the advert looping around her head, she got up and jumped onto the chubby technician, biting into his cheek and ripping a mouthful of flesh away from the bone. She spat the chunk back into his face and sidestepped him on her way out.

He was still falling by the time she burst through an access door and slammed it behind her.

The electronic lock blinked as the door closed. Clara grabbed a fire extinguisher from the wall, and hammered it into the mechanism, causing it to spark and glitch. A robotic voice rang out from a tinny speaker overhead.

"Emergency alert. Doors locked as a precautionary measure."

She looked up to check the door was sealed, just in time for the technician she'd mauled to hit the glass window, trying his best to break through and get her.

* * *

Clara burst through a fire exit, clutching her excruciating wound, the camera tucked safe into her vest. She leapt across the landing and turned, completely missing the floor, launching into a free-fall down the stairway. Each step jabbed her skin, tearing open old scars, and she ended her journey with a hard blow against the brick wall.

The world was blurry. An emergency alarm rang out.

She felt wet. Rancid.

Her chest wound had spewed all over her clothes.

The liquid was on the floor too.

The door at the top of the stairway was still shut.

No-one was around...

Where was Darren?

She started to remember.

The camera. Oh fuck the camera.

It was still in her pocket.

Slightly damaged but still intact.

The memory card would still be fine.

She could take it to a professional.

Get up Clara, her brain instructed.

She willed her legs to work.

Nothing wanted to work.

She was tired.

Exhausted.

She slid her fingers across her chest, felt for the crater.

...

...

...

It wasn't there.

The flesh unit had slipped back inside, out of its own free will. It had come back to help her.

What did this mean?

She could feel a slight tickle. Its eyeball fluttered inside her meaty wound.

Get up Clara.

She felt full again. Somehow, the wound didn't hurt as much as before.

Get up Clara.

What would she do with her next wound. There was no chance she could escape this. Would they even provide her with more units? Of course they wouldn't.

Get up Clara.

She was fucked. She was going to die. She might as well die now.

GET THE FUCK UP AND RUN CLARA.

* * *

The door burst open, and two technicians sprinted onto the landing. With a hoarse roar, Clara jumped to her feet, ignoring the burning pain of her legs and back, and hurtled down the stairway.

The corridors flew past in a hypnotic blur, and without any real calculation, she decided to slam through the first door she saw.

She locked herself into the room, and snatched the map from her pocket. Her eyes wouldn't focus. The lines were a blur. Everything was a blur.

COME ON CLARA. FOCUS.

Eventually, she worked out the rough placement of the room, and where it was in relation to the bathroom. It wasn't far, but they were already on her trail. She couldn't possibly make it now, could she?

SLAM.

Someone had found her.

SLAM.

Clara stepped backwards, trying to find a weapon. She imagined the chubby technician coming after her, ready to bite her this time instead, taking his revenge.

SLAM.

The door splintered open, the lock tumbling to the floor.

Clara couldn't quite believe her eyes.

Gary.

"We need to go. Like now."

* * *

"What are you doing here?" Clara screamed, trying to keep pace with the surprisingly agile old man. He turned corners in a confident, practiced way, the directions still very much ingrained in his mind.

"I heard the alarm. Nothing good ever comes after that alarm... Right here."

Clara could hear the brigade of workers chasing them down, their plastic footwear slapping against the vinyl.

"Right here."

They came to a smaller corridor, with a selection of doors at every angle.

"What about the bathroom, it's the other way?" Clara asked.

"Too dangerous. They've seen me, they'll know the way I got you in."

"But I thought no-one knew—"

"Left here."

They entered a dark meeting room, adorned with black metal panelling and LED fixtures, and slammed the door behind them. The room was a complete contrast to the bright white rooms that populated the rest of the building.

The lighting was low, Clara could only just about make out Gary's silhouette.

"What now?" she whispered.

The only answer she got was a resounding, "Sssssh."

Moments turned into minutes, but they seemed to have lost their trail.

"Gary? Gary, are they gone?"

There was no answer.

CLICK.

A door opened and closed in quick succession.

"Gary?"

The overhead lights flickered on, and it took a few seconds for Clara's eyes to adjust.

Gary was gone.

Another man stood in front of her instead.

The man from earlier. The man from the meeting room.

"I'm Walter Johnson. You must be Clara."

* * *

"GARY!" Clara screamed, looking around for him.

"What have you done with Gary you fucker?"

Walter chuckled, his face hauntingly unmoving as he did so.

"Gary. Show your face to let this lady know you're okay."

One of the mirrored walls brightened, exposing a two way mirror. Gary was behind it, looking relaxed and calm, his hand bent into a wave. The wall flickered back to black.

"When Gary mentioned you and your boss wanted a tour of the facility, well, I had to oblige, didn't I?"

His face wrinkled into a disgusting grin, exposing yellowed, tobacco-stained teeth.

"Do you really think that you'd be able to get into this facility if we didn't want you to?"

He laughed, a thunderous bellow that could have shook the ground beneath them.

"I understand you have a problem with your FleshKey unit."

Clara smirked.

"I have a problem with this whole Goddamn company!"

Walter raised his eyebrows.

"It just so happens that I also have a problem with yours. Your articles might seem like a silly joke, but there are people that latch onto these rumours, Miss Shaw. These fictions."

"The reality is much worse than the fiction. And I have the proof!"

Walter nodded his head.

"Let's tackle the first problem, shall we, Miss Shaw?"

He edged closer to her, his giant feet closing the gap with clambering steps.

"You know that our technology has a brilliant support team, ready to help at any time of the day. And failing that…"

Walter was within touching distance now.

"We operate a brilliant returns policy."

At breakneck speed, Walter launched forwards, dug his hand into Clara's chest, and tore out the FleshKey unit, along with a spew of flesh and yellow pus. Clara toppled to the floor, writhing in pain.

The unit dropped to the floor, but before it could escape, Walter brought his foot down, pulverising the flesh.

Clara tried to push away from Walter, sliding across the floor as the contents of her chest erupted outwards.

"Please... Stop..." Clara stuttered.

The camera had fallen from her pocket on impact.

"You won't be needing this either."

Walter brought his foot down onto the camera too, smashing it to smithereens, the plastic casing intermingling with the sinew from the flesh unit.

Clara was fading away, her vision was blurry, and all she could do was scurry to the edge of the room in a panic.

Walter reached into his pocket and retrieved a pocket knife, sliding the blade from the handle.

"Miss Shaw, you are a long-time user of our products. We have helped you live a long, full life so far, no?"

Clara didn't answer. She was in too much pain, shivering in sickness.

"I think as a company, we should also be able to operate our own returns policy, for customers who don't appreciate what they have."

He launched forward again, digging the knife into Clara's back, and sliced out a jagged lump of flesh. Clara screamed, but Walter dove right back in to her shoulder blade, taking another chunk.

Laughing incessantly, he kicked her wrists out from under her, causing her to slam her face on the ground.

"You see your unit over there? That's what we do to the ones who are accidentally born with sentience."

Clara couldn't really see anything right now, but she could make out the splattered remains of the unit.

"You didn't give us a chance to correct our mistake Clara! That's all this would have taken to correct."

She sputtered, blood pouring from her mouth, from her wounds, from her nose.

"I would hazard a guess that your body is probably more *flesh unit* than natural matter now, Miss Shaw," Walter remarked, stepping around to the side of her, his shoes knocking hard against the ground.

"And that, my darling, means you deserve the same treatment as the ones who are accidentally sentient."

"Wait," Clara said.

But he didn't wait.

Her skull shattered on the first impact, his foot plummeting onto the back of her neck. Walter got into a rhythm, slam and lift, slam and lift. Her pulverised brains intermingled with purple flesh and bright red streaks of blood, staining the vinyl floor. Clara's face was disfigured and caved in on itself, half of her head spread out into tiny fragments on the floor.

AFTERWORD

I see,
I hear,
I pull you near,

I watch,
I thrive,
our worlds collide

I tug,
I tear,
we fall to bits,
you're inside out,
we call it quits.

WANT MORE HORROR IN YOUR LIFE?

Sign-up to the ***Deadly Dispatch*** at www.robwriteshorror.com for the latest news, plus discount codes, offers and giveaways on merch and future releases!

ABOUT THE AUTHOR

Rob Ulitski is a director and writer based in Portsmouth, UK. Having grown up on a steady appetite of horror films, books and TV shows, he started making films at age thirteen, and working on various film sets in entry-level roles.

After graduating from the University for the Creative Arts in Farnham in 2013, he has held a variety of roles, including:

- Filmmaker
- DIY store assistant
- Adult (Sex) shop assistant
- Writer for a music video blog
- Film Festival Organiser
- Producer for a Korean TV show startup
- Corporate video editor
- Photographer

Writing has become a main focus over the past few years, so keep an eye out for more books coming soon!

SOCIALS:

@robulitski

@robwriteshorror

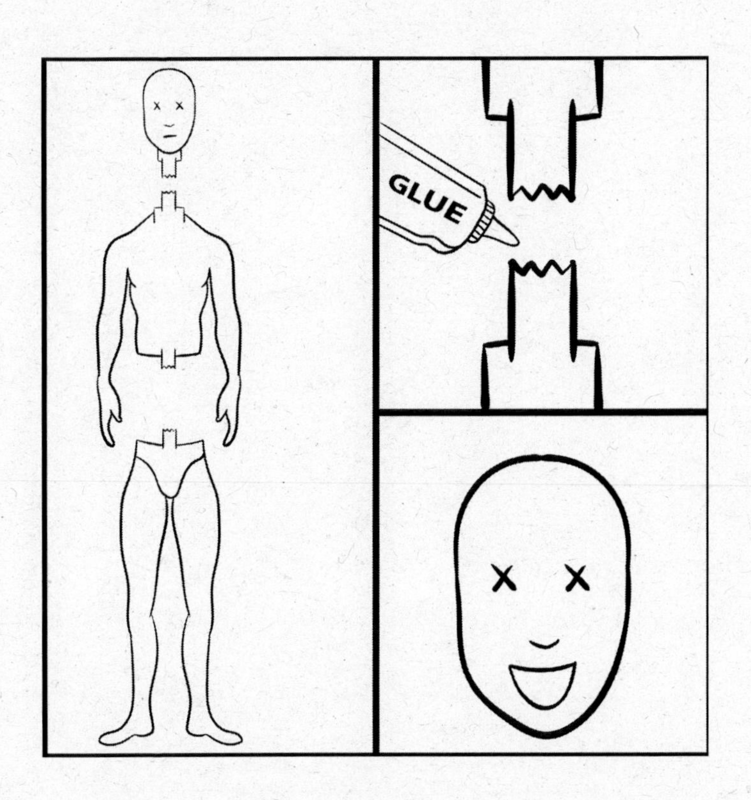
GLUE

Supported using public funding by
ARTS COUNCIL
ENGLAND